Mari

this takes place in the
mantains of East Tennessee
where my parents grew up.
and it's a great location for
a murder mystery.
May God bless you always.

SHADOWS ON IRON MOUNTAIN

What Readers Are Saying About
SHADOWS ON IRON MOUNTAIN

"Chuck Walsh is a master storyteller, a writer of extraordinary sensitivity and craftsmanship. Walsh's fiction shows an uncommon understanding of his characters and their relationships. His writing is both dynamic and economical, with a special energy in dialogue that keeps the reader turning pages."—*Charles Israel, Ph.D., Professor Emeritus of English*

"The writer draws you in quickly with his descriptions of the characters and their surroundings. This book is full of suspense. Intrigue and twist and turns that will keep you turning page after page guessing until the very end."—*Amazon reader review*

"Chuck Walsh is a new kind of disciplined writer who- unlike many of his contemporaries in the e-media age where everyone sees themselves as a writer - serves as a model of the old school where mastery of the art is the only way to earn (and truly own) the title, 'writer.' Walsh is indeed a writer in the purest sense, and a marvelous one at that; his mastery of the craft demonstrated by the ease, deftness, unpretentiousness, and authority with which he tells a story."—*W. Thomas Smith Jr., author, columnist, former adjunct professor of journalism, and a New York Times bestselling military technical advisor and editor*

Don't be surprised if you find yourself looking over your shoulder as you read to make sure no one is watching you. Chuck Walsh's words paint such a vivid picture that you will find yourself totally immersed in the setting and the characters.—*Buckeye Gal, Amazon reader review*

"A great read. Criminal Minds meets Kiss The Girls."—*Jessica Hoffman, reader review*

"Chuck Walsh makes you want to visit Tennessee, but scares you so bad you may never go."—*Jeannie L, reader review*

Jason stirred, awakened by the sound of breaking glass. Lying on his side, facing the wall, he sat up on his elbow and looked about the room. He rubbed his hand through his hair and yawned. "Baby, you rearranging the furniture in there?" he called out.

A faint cry answered him. He hopped from bed and quickly slipped into his jeans before walking down the hall. Once in the kitchen, he noticed shattered glass on the floor. The refrigerator door was open.

"Kara?"

The door to the porch was open and the wind brushed against his exposed chest when he looked through the screen to the backwoods behind the house. "Kara?" He opened the screen door and glanced to the side of the house by the trashcan. He hurried back into the kitchen, and closed the refrigerator door. "Where are you?" he called out as he walked down the hall.

Confused, he went to the front door to see if she was retrieving something from the car. Moving around to the back of the cabin, he stopped in the cold of the room, hearing nothing.

"Hey, this isn't funny." He returned to the kitchen through the porch door. "Baby? Kara!"

The silence of the cabin surrounded him.

He burst through the front door, checking the car again. He looked down the narrow driveway. Nausea rushed through his gut. His body rotated, searching, listening, breath heavy as he panted, small wisps of pale white coming from his mouth. He pushed the thumb of his right hand into the palm of his left, rubbing in a circular motion as though he were trying to remove the skin. He always did that when he was confused; when he was worried.

Circling the cabin, the thick woods unfamiliar. "Kara!"

He sprinted up the driveway and called out again. "Kara" echoed through the trees before dissipating into the air, as was his confidence that he'd spot her walking along Shady Valley. The curves of the mountain highway were tight, bending in either direction, limiting his view.

"She's okay," he said softly. "She's okay. God, let her be okay."

The breeze turned bitter. Clouds gathered, turning the horizon above the towering trees into a hovering, opaque ceiling. Standing in the middle of the slender dirt road, he looked for signs of movement. The rustle of the wind stirred the forest, all about him a dizzying landscape of random movement. The isolated activity surrounding him left him lightheaded. He ran his hand through his sweat-laced hair, and his eyes welled with tears. Should he run? North or south?

He bolted back down the driveway. Ferns pushed against the rugged mountain floor as the wind roared in sporadic waves like an angry sea around him. The treetops rattled above him like the bones in some ancient burial ground.

By the time he made it back into the house his body was shaking, a combination of fear and bitter cold against his bare upper body. Looking once more throughout the cabin, room-by-room, hoping she was playing some sort of evil joke on him.

His phone was on the small nightstand beside the bed and he dialed 9-1-1. "Son of a bitch," he yelled as he noticed it had no signal. He slipped on a sweater and found his sneakers by the rocker. His wallet and keys were on the nightstand as well and in a moment he was out the front door.

The car bumper scratched a knotty maple as he backed the car out of the driveway. Once on Shady Valley, he whipped his head left, and then right. Which way? Where should he go? Pulling onto Highway 47, he turned left, and looked about for something— anything. The trees and mountain laurels formed shapes and figures, making him think he spotted her everywhere. He sped toward Johnson's store half blinded by the vision of her looking into his eyes as she sat on his lap just minutes earlier, her tears after they'd made love a confirmation that she loved him with her entire being.

He smashed the top of the steering wheel with his fist. Why did he not awaken when she did? He should have been by her side, clinging to the soft aroma of her perfume.

He fishtailed into the lot of Johnson's store, jumped out of the car, leaving the door open. Once inside, he found the three men occupying the same positions they'd held earlier.

"My wife's disappeared," he yelled as he ran to the counter.

"What'd you say?" the man asked, sitting as before on his stool.

"My wife. She's gone."

Champagne Books Presents

Shadows On Iron Mountain

By

Chuck Walsh

Champagne Books
www.champagnebooks.com
Copyright 2014 by Chuck Walsh
ISBN 978-1-77155-166-3
September 2014
Cover Art by Christy Carlyle
Produced in Canada

Champagne Book Group
19-3 Avenue SE
High River, AB T1V 1G3
Canada

Dedication

This book is dedicated to my parents, and my relatives who called Johnson County home. You enlightened me to the unique and colorful ways of the Tennessee people, the lure and mystery of Iron Mountain, and an appreciation for the beauty of the surrounding fields and farmland of Doe Valley.

FOREWORD

I have such vivid memories of childhood experiences in those alluring hills of East Tennessee, especially around Iron Mountain. It's where my parents were born. It's my heritage, and I am proud my roots are buried deep in that rocky soil. I'll never forget the first time I heard the rush of the cold waters along Doe Creek, or felt the brush of mountain air against my face, or the sheer beauty of the sun rising above Doe Mountain as I sat on my grandparents' front porch.

As I wrote this book, I drew upon colorful stories of Nick "The Hermit" Grindstaff, moonshiners, and the unique and sometimes quirky people my parents and relatives spoke fondly about on and around Iron Mountain. I also based certain characters on my relatives, people I love and admire dearly. Conversely, I drew upon fear I had when I was a boy as I walked along the property on Iron Mountain with my father, on land that's been in the Walsh family for almost two-hundred years, wondering who might be watching from those deep backwoods. That childhood fear made it easy to create the "bad guys" in my mind and to imagine a tough, spirited mountain people who were fiercely independent and untrusting of the outside world.

In writing this work of fiction, in creating evil doings in those backwoods, I want to make sure folks along Iron Mountain understand that, not only are the ones doing evil derived solely from my mind, but in reality, I love and admire those from that region. I'm extremely proud to be linked via lineage to them. It's because of them I have such a deep affinity for the people, the land, the way of life, and it's why I intend on returning year after year for as long as I live.

I understand why Nick Grindstaff sought that heavenly solitude of Iron Mountain.

FOR YOU

Prologue

It hides in the gentle folds of the mountainside. It slips through the waters of the icy creek. It hangs on the wings of the hawk soaring above the valley. It hides behind the solemn sunrise. To some, it's called fear. To others, it's perhaps the subtle feeling of a constant battle waged between good and evil. And so, the mere snap of a twig, the slightest movement of the leaf when the gentle breeze blows, brings it to life. When the sun casts its warmth across the valley, it's the shadow in the distance that catches man's eye.

So when that twig snaps in the distance, and when that leaf trembles on the limb, confusion clouds the mind. Is it Mother Nature, or perhaps evil, that lurks in the shadows? And if it isn't evil, will it be evil next time?

One

The sun hung above the western skyline of Iron Mountain, shadows stretching long and dark across Doe Valley. The winds were still in that high country and there was no movement on the mountain. Kara removed her sunglasses and placed them in the open crease of the novel laid across her lap. She looked out the passenger window, studying a land that looked as though the world had passed it by.

It had been six years since her last trip to the Appalachians, and time had dulled her memory of those Blue Ridge Mountains. While she stared out her window, Jason drove them along the highway that was a steady mix of rising peaks and sinking valleys, the mountains changing shape and form in front of them as they drove. When they reached Baldwin's Crest, the sun splashed across the car, its hood glowing like some sluggish neon sign.

Black Angus cows bunched together on the hillside, and Kara watched them through Jason's window. She started to point them out but looking at Jason's steady stare, she passed on the notion. Instead, she looked ahead to the small bridges spaced along the highway like concrete mile markers. Doe Creek flipped and weaved along that country road, the bridges serving as reminders the creek was there long before the highway.

They drove on past the tall, crème-colored steeple of the Antioch Baptist Church that rose above a row of locusts and maples on the backside of Doe Creek, two hundred yards from the highway. On both sides of the road, farmhouses dotted the hillsides. A faded red barn near the highway overflowed with fat spindles of hay.

The final traces of day evaporated, and the countryside was swallowed up by the darkness, a fact not lost on Kara. Familiar shapes of trees slipped away into some empty void of a world where form held no meaning. She fidgeted in her seat. *Why couldn't we have gone to the beach?* She whispered it so only she heard.

She played with the radio and found a station. The twangy guitar sounds resonated through her senses, a sullen tune from long ago, sounding an entrance antiphon to a land sundered from all things civilized. She shook her head and searched for another station, and a raspy, aged voice was singing about death's sting, so she pushed the CD button and rock and roll charged through the speakers.

"Going from one music extreme to the other, huh?" Jason asked as the faded lights of a vehicle approached down the highway.

"I don't mind country music, but not when I'm in the middle of it, especially at dusk. It makes me feel so isolated. A thousand miles from nowhere."

"Sounds like a line from a country song right there. Maybe we can find that one on the radio." He smiled and patted her thigh.

"You aren't helping your chances for later, if you get my drift."

"I'm just jerkin' your chain a little. Where'd that sense of humor go?"

"It fell with the sun behind that massive mountain."

He laughed, but he didn't seem to understand. He surely thought thoughts common to men; that the dark was simply nighttime, and more interesting to think of the possibilities that could take place at night between a man and woman than the daylight offered up.

She turned on the vanity light and removed a Map Quest printout from the glove compartment. "In a few miles we should come to Shady Valley Road," she said. "We'll need to make a right."

"Thank God for Map Quest," he said. "These roads don't look like the kind that would show up on your basic road map."

"Well, Map Quest only takes us to the entrance of Shady Valley, so we're going to have to wing it from there."

"How hard can that be?"

How hard indeed?

The car continued on and darkness, in some smug delight, dimmed the fact the rolling valleys and streams had dissipated into tall timber and steep-sloped mountains. As though a veil had been draped to hide the landscape, so that by morning she'd realize the mountain was not some weekend playground.

Along the side of the highway, entwined with ivy, Kara spotted a wooden sign, not much bigger than a breadbox. It was nailed to the side of a walnut tree and read, "Shadee Valley Road," crudely hand-painted in white.

"We are back in the sticks, aren't we?" he asked.

"Sure looks that way."

"Do we know the house number of the cabin?"

"Nope. A handwritten note on the receipt says, 'four miles on left.'"

With no light other than the high beams of the car, he cautiously turned onto the gravelly road. The unpaved street became an immediate track of elbow-shaped turns, with sharp, rising banks on the right and downward slopes on the left that seemed to fall into nothingness. The car lights split the darkness in two, illuminating gray hardwoods close to the road. If nothing else, the trees provided a sharp contrast to the massive depth of shadows behind them. The sound of the tires rolling over the bumpy road echoed into the mountain.

Kara lowered the passenger window to get an unobstructed glance into the night. "I don't think there's anybody within a hundred miles. Kinda wish the cabin was in Doe Valley." She searched for something other than the cold emptiness. "This place is creepy. Maybe this isn't the place to celebrate our two-year anniversary."

"It's just the darkness. This place will be great, and we can do whatever we want, whenever we want."

"I guess. I just hope we get there soon."

As they snaked their way up the winding mountain, they came upon a dilapidated barn located a few feet from the road. The headlights turned the rotted hay hanging from its open loft gray. On the opposite side sat an abandoned shack, its porch hidden by rampant weeds. A bony possum darted uncaringly across the hard, earthen road a few car lengths ahead.

As the car crawled along fog encased it. The dense, smoky air began to reflect the beam of lights against the underside of mountain laurels on the high banks, giving the appearance of faces peering from the dark. Strangers come to a desolate world.

Finally, he pointed at a small post protruding from the ground with a reflective metal plate along a weed-laced dirt path.

"I think this is it," he said.

"Thank God."

Limbs of white pines hung thick and low above the narrow

driveway. The vehicle's lights struggled to cut through the ground-hugging fog, limiting visibility in front of the car to ten feet. Finally, a dim reflection from the handle of the cabin's front door came into view. Jason eased the car up to the small, two-step porch. The smothering fog and darkness gave the exterior walls a shadowy tint. A pale, tin crossbar split two dark windows, the only distinguishing difference between the cabin and a shack.

Kara exited the car. The chill of the night air was a hollow welcome to Appalachia. She stepped onto the creaky porch, removed a key taped to the underside of a burnt-out porch light, and used the smoky beams of the car lights to help her find the keyhole of the front door. Her right hand maneuvered the key into the rusty lock while her left hand clutched a paper bag of food and drinks.

Once inside, she wiped her right hand along the wall in search of a light switch. No luck. A string from above tickled her ear when she walked in the room. She pulled on the string, and a dim, yellow bulb came on.

"We have light," she said as if to ease her own worries.

An owl screeched in the distance, echoing through the still, April night. Jason killed the engine after she turned on the light, and the darkness returned. He became a silhouette as he made his way to the trunk. She stood at the door until he walked in with the two matching pieces of luggage.

She stood in silence looking about the room. A brown, denim couch with well-worn arms sat along a wall, a barren oak coffee table in front. Above the couch was a wood-framed picture of a black bear and her two cubs alongside a rock-laced stream. Into the kitchen she moved, Jason next to her as she walked. A wall light switch was flipped, the room containing a rectangular, green Formica table with two wooden straight-back chairs. They walked down a narrow hallway that led to two tiny bedrooms and a bathroom with a sink, commode, and shower stall.

"This place looks comfortable enough," he said as he turned on the bathroom light and twisted a dusty spigot. "Water works."

Back in the kitchen she placed a bottle of wine in the rust-laced door of a beige General Electric refrigerator. "The fridge works too. It's not big on amenities, but I guess it will do."

After peering out a small kitchen window that looked out onto a porch enclosed by a dust-covered screen, she turned and crossed the room to a dingy picture window. A faint light flickered through the treetops, fading in and out of the fog. Jason's footsteps were a welcome sound.

"Is that a plane?" she said as she leaned closer to the windowpane.

Jason stood beside her. "It's not moving. I think it's a light from a tower."

"Good Lord. Seems this mountain stretches to the moon's doorstep." He moved behind her and she nestled her back into his chest. He surrounded her with his arms. As she turned toward him, she kissed him gently. "Let's make this a weekend we'll never forget," she said.

Jason removed two mason jars from the pine cupboard while Kara opened a bottle of Chardonnay with a corkscrew she'd brought from home.

"Come on," he said in a mock country accent. "Let's sit on this here porch and drink from these fancy wine glasses."

He opened the windowless wooden door to the narrow porch. To the left, in the corner, a rickety screen door. Jason grabbed a folding chair lying against the wall. As he sat, he motioned for Kara to sit on his lap. He glanced over her shoulders as lightning bugs ascended from the rugged mountain floor, intermittently interrupting the darkness.

"Well, I think we're about as alone as we can possibly be," Kara said.

She took a sip, lightly moistening her upper lip. Leaning slightly to her left, her lips gently pressed against Jason's neck and her right hand lightly caressed his face before moving down to unbutton his shirt. Jason sighed when the warmth of her breath touched his skin as she gently nibbled on his neck. One-by-one she unbuttoned his shirt and inched her lips, kiss by soft kiss, under his chin. She placed her wine on the floor and straddled him.

"Those early morning workouts are paying off," she said as she rubbed her index fingers slowly around the edges of his pectoral muscles.

Staring into his chocolate-brown eyes, she moved toward his face and kissed him. With both hands lightly holding his face, she spread her lips and pressed them softly against his. Jason's mouth parted slightly, and their warm, wet tongues met. She pulled away, smiled, and again stared into his eyes.

The leaves rustled outside the porch door, though there was no breeze. A twig snapped and Kara straightened. The two looked at each other before glancing at the flimsy door.

"What was that?" she whispered. Her heart raced as she slowly stood, as though any sound might cause something outside to stir. She looked at Jason and pulled him by the hands. He placed his finger to his lips to signal her silence.

He stepped slowly to the frame of the door, her close behind. She heard footsteps outside the porch and a metal trashcan beside the driveway overturned. The clanging caused her to grab Jason by his shirt. His hands ran alongside the door and he flipped a rusted light switch which turned on a single, yellow bulb outside the porch.

He stood frozen as if worried the slightest movement would bring the source of the noise to the porch. He pointed to the ground near the trashcan. "It's just a raccoon," he said with the sound of relief. The scraggly creature retreated to the darkness, seemingly unbothered by the ruckus.

"Are you sure?" Kara asked.

"Positive. See, there he goes." Jason kicked the bottom of the door. "Get out of here," he said as the raccoon scooted away. "Well, I guess wildlife fun is just one of the amenities they offer up here."

"Let's go back inside," she said. "I feel a little creeped out."

"Yeah, maybe it would be a little cozier inside."

They stepped into the kitchen.

"You wanna listen to the radio?" Kara asked. She pointed to the counter. "There's an old looking contraption but maybe it works. Let's see if we can find a station that plays something besides backwoods music. I'll even settle for talk radio."

Jason plugged the cord of the moon-shaped radio into an outlet beside the refrigerator. He turned the knob of the green plastic dial to the left, and then slowly to the right. "I can't get any stations," he said as static filled the air.

"Is it too much to hope for a television?"

She walked into the den area and finished her glass of wine in one quick gulp.

He wrapped his arms around her. "You okay?"

"I just feel uneasy. What do you say we go find a motel?"

"Let's not overreact. Besides, we have no clue where a motel is, and we've already paid for this place. Just take a deep breath.

Everything's fine."

"Maybe a hot shower will calm me down. Surely this place has hot water."

While Kara showered, Jason brushed his teeth.

"You doing better now?" she heard him say as lukewarm water splashed against her back.

"Yes. It's going to take me a while to loosen up in this place, I guess."

After Jason showered, he slipped on a pair of gray pajama pants and a 49er's T-shirt. Kara stepped to the bedroom window.

"Looking for something?" he asked.

"Are you kidding? It's pitch black. There could be some giant, one-eyed head staring back at me on the other side of this glass and I'd never know it. I guess they've never heard of blinds in this part of the world."

She opened the closet door. "Great. No spare blankets. I was going to toss one over the curtain rod."

"Pull the curtains together."

"They aren't large enough to cover the window. Besides, they look so flimsy they'd probably fall to the floor if you touched them."

"Come lie down and let me take your mind off things."

He took her by the hand to the bed. Placing her head on the pillow, lying above her, he kissed her. Her lips were rigid and taut. She closed her eyes and forcefully pressed her lips to his, rolling him over on his back. Kissing his neck hard and fast, her lips moved quickly to his face to generate some semblance of passion. She bit his lower lip forcefully, sighed, and took his hand in her hands.

"I just can't do this," she said as she rolled over and onto her back, looking at the window. "I'm sorry," she said running her hand through her hair. "But this is like something out of a Freddie Krueger movie."

"Let me turn off the lights. Nobody can see us if it's dark."

"You must be crazy. I'm not lying in the dark in this place. The light stays on."

Jason held her to his chest. "This isn't exactly the way I envisioned the evening."

"I know." She rose up on her elbows. "I'm sorry." She let go a soft sigh. "Let's just try to get some sleep. Maybe tomorrow I won't be so jittery."

Jason left on the kitchen and bathroom lights and Kara buried herself under the covers. The long day tired them. Jason fell asleep quickly, and soon developed a rhythmic breathing pattern. She lay in silence and her eyes glanced about the room while the sounds of the old cabin evaporated into the cool air.

Did we lock the kitchen door?

The floor creaked as she lightly stepped along the dark hall. Her heart raced as she pictured a farmhouse scene from *Night of the Living Dead.* Goosebumps rose on her forearms when she noticed the pull latch on the kitchen door was unfastened. Moving slowly, the creaks of the cold floor beneath her feet made her more nervous. She tried to pull the latch, but the door stood slightly open. Holding her breath, while a rush of cold air slipped through the door and the jamb, she tried to push the door shut. Perhaps years of rugged weather had warped it, and its bottom brushed against the floor. Lifting up on the door by the knob, she finally slammed it shut.

There.

The porch door, eight feet away, jiggled. She stopped, prayed the breeze was the reason. She breathed easier as it went silent.

She slipped back into bed to toss and turn, surrounded by the unfamiliar sounds of the mountain night. Though Jason lay beside her, he may as well have been a thousand miles away. Slowly, her thoughts began to fade, and as she drifted off, muddled whispers filled the room. She rose up on both elbows and her heart pounded.

She looked to the bedroom window and for a brief second a silhouette gave shape to the darkness. Again, faint whispers invaded the room. If she could only sleep, she'd have a haven to hide from her fears. It was all she could do to slip from under the covers and out of bed.

She slowly tiptoed to the window and glanced out into the smothering darkness. Nothing. The whispers faded amid a serenade of crickets. Returning to bed, Kara nudged her way inside Jason's arm like an interloper in a soulless world.

Eventually she nodded off.

Two

He stepped along the narrow trail, dawn carving light from the dirt and the underbrush. He walked as though in a dream, carefully stepping as if the land beneath him might fall away into some world not yet entered. The smell of embers and sugar hung heavy in the air, and he loved the aroma. Not for the fragrance, but for the concrete evidence the souls of Iron Mountain still stirred in the bottom of the white lightning brewing in the distance.

Below him, in the concave bend of the mountain, the fire glowed. Rolls of smoke rose through the hardwoods, melting into the foggy morning like two celestial beings becoming one.

He stepped off the trail and worked his way down the steep slope toward the still. He heard voices. Voices of men at work at a vocation as old as the hills. Men who carried on tradition. Men who knew no other form or means of survival. And in those voices was a certain dialect and dialogue he couldn't speak, though he yearned to do so. But foreign tongues cannot speak the language of this land of 10,000 hills, no matter how hard they try. No matter how long they stayed on Iron Mountain.

When he got close enough to see the fire, and the three men pouring the moonshine into mason jars, he sat. He watched, rubbing his hand through his oily beard, observing them like a child at a carnival sideshow. He watched them work their trade, these men who seemed as though there was no distinguishing the day before from the day that would follow. A trio of habit they were, as though it gave proof to their undocumented lives.

He inched closer, hiding behind the hell's laurels that grew thick in that hardened land. The leaves of the laurels were so deep a shade of green they looked black in the early light. There was a fourth man sitting on a tree stump, a rifle lying across his lap. Their duties were not only regarded as admirable in those hills, but essential to the balance of life on that mountain.

As the skies lightened, he sat in silence and listened to the wind blow through the treetops above him. He imagined himself working the still, accepted and as natural as the giant poplars that populated the land. Sullen, he slipped back, away from where he'd come. His boots pressing against the trail, and a breeze rattling the leaves on the elms and poplars the only sounds.

As he headed home to a shack deep in the backwoods, he heard a grunting sound in front of him. He removed his Bowie knife from a sheath held by a thick, leather belt, wary. The angry squeal didn't bode well for a quiet walk home. The ferns tossed about in chaos, and when he stepped closer, the boar charged full speed ahead. The coarse-haired black beast, over two hundred pounds, picked up speed as she approached. Her tusks protruded like some ancient beast that roamed the land a millennium ago.

He braced himself for the impact, his knife gripped tightly in his large hand. When the boar charged for his legs, he tried to leap above it, a pirouette that kept the beast from hitting him full on. Her tusk cut through his canvas pants and sliced his calf. The impact brought him to his knees, and the sow turned and drove her head into his midsection, knocking him on his back.

The boar was above him now. He tried to ram his knife into her head, but it glanced off her rugged hide. She lowered her head and he blocked her with his forearm before she could make contact with his face. Straddling him, she drove downward, trying to use her tusks as a weapon.

He put the blade to her neck, pushing upward on her snout. When it punctured her skin, she squealed. The wound seemed to enrage her, and she moved her head from side to side trying to drive him into the dirt.

He pushed deeper, his powerful hands keeping a firm grip. Her tusks scraped against his cheek, and the warm blood ran down his beard. Still he held his ground, and she started to waver. He was able to push her off and he rolled her on her back and forced the knife downward in her chest. She thrashed about, her grunts labored. When he forced the knife into her heart, she collapsed.

He watched the blood pour from her chest onto his hand, and for a moment, he kept the knife buried deep just to see if he could feel the final heartbeat. To see if, through some transference, he could feel life leave her and, perhaps, enter him before fading away forever.

He gutted the sow, and with his large hands, dragged the boar home.

Three

Kara was submerged in peaceful sleep. She slept in that hour when fear retreats with the darkness, when shapes reemerge, providing reassurance a familiar world has returned.

For three hours, she'd slept hard, with little movement. She woke when Jason accidently stubbed the rocker with his toe. "What was that?" she said, startled, rising up on both elbows.

"I'm sorry. I smashed my toe against the chair. Didn't mean to wake you." He sat in the rocker and rubbed his aching toe. "This floor is cold as ice."

She struggled to focus her eyes, to uncloud her mind. Morning had softened the grimness of night, and realization set in she had made it through. "What a freaky evening. I was creeped out big time."

"You okay now?" He moved to the bed and sat beside her, rubbing his hand through her hair.

"Now that it's light, yes I am." She checked her watch. "Doesn't look like it's nine a.m., does it?" She looked out the window. "Is it cloudy?"

"I can't tell. The fog's so thick I can hardly see the trees."

"Well, I'm cold. Come warm me."

"No problem," Jason said as he slipped under the blanket, his body covering hers. He gently tickled the right side of her neck, just slightly below her ear. "Did you sleep at all?"

"A little. I had the willies because it was just too eerie."

"How about breakfast in bed?"

"Aren't you sweet?" She rubbed her hand along his face. "Come on. Let's cook together."

He kissed her softly on her forehead. "Let's get at it. I'm starving."

Wearing the T-shirt and cotton pajama bottoms she slept in, Kara removed a wooden brush from a side pocket of her purse and began brushing her dark-brown, shoulder-length hair. She took a puff from her asthma inhaler, slipped on a pair of well-worn, fuzzy, green slippers, and headed to the kitchen.

She heard him sneaking from behind, the cold floor creaking as he walked. He kissed her neck as she broke eggs in a cast iron frying pan.

"Now this is the way to fix breakfast," Kara said as she lowered her head to allow Jason easier access. Lifting the soft hair away from her neck, he nibbled on her skin. She looked out the window at the lifting fog, unveiling a deep, dark mountainside with its seemingly endless depth of undisturbed backwoods.

"What do you want to do today?" Jason asked as they sat at the wobbly kitchen table. "These eggs are awesome, by the way."

"Let's ride the country roads. We'll do the John Denver thing. I'd like to take some pictures while we're here." Photography was a passion she'd developed four years prior at Queens College.

After breakfast was over, she rinsed off the dishes and put them on the counter.

Soon they were dressed and out the door. Jason wore dark-blue jeans, a black sweater, and a charcoal-gray fleece jacket.

"You've got this sexy, city-boy-meets-outdoorsman look going on," she said.

"Dressed to impress, baby," he said as he opened the passenger door of the two-seater. He smiled at her through the windshield as he made his way around to the driver's side. Sitting behind the wheel, he reached over and kissed her on the cheek. "I love you."

She smiled. "I love you too."

He backed out of the tight driveway, carefully inspecting the view from both side mirrors so as not to scratch his car. The German automobile may have been pre-owned, but he spent a lot more time cleaning it than her late model SUV.

As he made his way to Shady Valley Road, he reached into the glove compartment. "Okay, Miss Navigator, which way are we going?"

"Can we ride back through Doe Valley? It's as beautiful as I remember."

"Sure. And then let's drive north above Laurel City. It's a pretty stretch leading to Damascus."

"How do you remember the names of these towns and

mountains?"

"My parents loved the mountains. So we vacationed throughout East Tennessee and Southwestern Virginia. My dad would tell us the names of every river, stream, gully, town, village, or General Store. He seemed fascinated by the setting. Remember, he grew up across the state line in Boone."

As they wound down Shady Valley, Kara spotted a small clearing of land where a malnourished heifer scavenged for food. She pointed to the sad looking bovine as they slipped around a sharp, S-curve.

"Watch out," she said, reaching outward at the dash as Jason applied the brakes. A large man, dressed in faded blue dungarees and a stained khaki shirt, twisted barbwire at the bottom of a post at the road's edge. Amid the sound of screeching tires, the man straightened and stared at them as they passed. He wiped the brow below his unkempt silver hair with the back of his forearm.

"These country bumpkins must not think cars belong on the road," he said. "Maybe if we were on a mule and cart we'd fit right in." He glanced over his shoulder briefly as did Kara.

"The crazy fool's just standing in the road," he said. "He's lucky I didn't hit him." The man looked at them, expressionless. "Scary looking dude," Jason said as they pulled away.

The final traces of fog dissipated and the morning sun made its way above Snake Mountain, which ran parallel to Iron Mountain on the southern side of the valley. Spring was upon the land, and the hardwoods cast a bluish-green aura when viewed from the highway. A hilly slope of sweet grass and white pines seemed to shorten the distance from the glen to the tall slope that was Snake Mountain.

"It is absolutely beautiful here," she said. "Too bad our cabin isn't in the valley, It's a pretty as place as I've ever seen."

"I'm sure at night this place is just as spooky as where we're staying. I think it's just the mountains in general."

"I guess."

Kara spotted a faded, ivy-covered metal sign nailed into the side of a neglected, faded red barn. "Johnson's General Store two miles away," she read. "Let's stop there for some coffee. Think they have cappuccino?"

"I'm betting it comes in one flavor only—black. Only one way to find out."

They pulled up in front of the store alongside an old, green

Chevy pickup. Kara looked beyond the truck to a phone booth, its glass cracked and covered with weeds. She removed her sunglasses and squinted at the scene in front of her. Two gray benches, in dire need of paint, sat on either side of the front door.

They slowly exited the door and she noticed the gas island, with two pumps labeled *Esso* in faded blue, located fifteen feet from the front door. A crooked sign in the window beside the front door simply read "Open."

The inside of the store was musty and tight, even though the ceiling rose twenty feet. The floor was dark, well-worn wood, dusted with grit. Shelves, three rows high, lined the back wall with loaves of bread, various assortments of hard candy, and six packs of sodas that Kara never heard of.

A freestanding shelf, four rows high, stood in the middle of the store, lined with pork and beans, potted meat, and three jars of pickles. Four yellow cans of motor oil lined the front shelf.

Three elderly men sat behind a three-foot high counter. Two of them were stationary in oak rockers; one wore faded blue overalls, the other khaki pants and a navy-blue, short-sleeve shirt. They engaged in light conversation while the third man, decked in dark-gray dungarees and a flannel shirt, leaned one cheek on a wooden stool.

Ridley's Feed & Seed hats were the caps of choice for the men in the rockers; County Co-op the hat for the man on the stool. A brick of cheddar cheese sat inside a glass container on the counter next to the elbow of the man on the stool. Beside the glass container was a small radio that played a song strong in fiddle and mandolin.

"Bobby Joe came home drunk one night," said one of the men in the rockers. "He'd been battling the croup and went out for a little healin' medicine. Well, when he stumbled home into the kitchen later that evenin,' Burdie was a prayin' at the table, sayin,' 'Lord, please fergiv' my drunk, sick husband.' Bobby Joe removed his hat and said, 'Burdie, don't tell Him I'm drunk. Just tell Him I'm sick." The men laughed heartily and the young couple approached the counter.

"Morning," Jason said to the man on the stool. "How are y'all doing?"

"Mornin', young fella. Beautiful day, ain't it?"

"Yes, sir, it is. Say, do you have any boiled peanuts?"

"Sure do. It's in the refrigerator beside the pop machine."

"I see it. Thanks."

They walked to the refrigerator located against the front wall, and Jason opened the heavy door by the silver metal handle, removing a cold, brown bulging bag of peanuts from the bottom shelf. Beside the peanuts were containers of worms and various types of fish bait. The middle shelf contained a dozen bottles of soda pop. Beer lined the top shelf.

"I think I'll search for the coffee pot," she said, inhaling. "I can smell it brewing."

Jason pointed toward a silver pot by the cash register. "There it is."

"Can I please have a cup of coffee?" she said at the counter. "With cream and sweetener too, please."

"We only have sugar, ma'am," the man said as he rose from his stool. "Folks 'round here usually drink their coffee black. And when they do add somethin' to it, it ain't likely to be anything artificial." The man's face wore the look of a hard life, though the deep crevices crisscrossing his face didn't diminish the handsomeness of his ice-blue eyes.

"That's fine. Thanks."

"Are you young folks just passin' through?"

"No, sir," Jason said as he stepped to the counter with his soda and peanuts. "We're renting a cabin up on Iron Mountain. Just here for the weekend."

"The one up Shady Valley Road? Fella from Nashville named Grayson owns it."

Jason nodded. "That's the one. It's very secluded. Doesn't look like it's been used lately. Is it rented much?"

"No, not for a good while. Not since…"

One of the men sitting on the rockers cleared his throat and looked at his buddy in the second rocker.

"Since what?" Jason asked.

Kara, who was looking at a ceramic ashtray carved in the shape of Tennessee hanging from a post behind the counter, studied the eyes of the man.

"Well, not since…"

"Yes?" Jason asked.

"Son, it's not my place to say. Maybe you should ask Mr. Grayson."

"How long has he owned the cabin? It could use some

upkeep."

"Grayson is a federal agent from Nashville, and he took ownership of the property during a raid on a still about six or seven years ago. I think he was hopin' to parlay the county's campaign to make Iron Mountain a destination for tourists into some extra cash."

"I've never spoken to the man," Jason said. "I made our reservation on the Internet."

The front door opened.

"Hey, Sherm," the customer said. "The gas pump handle's stuck again. Lend me a hand?"

"Sure thing. That'll be two dollars and sixty cents for the drinks and the peanuts. You can just leave it on the counter. Y'all have a nice day." He left the counter to help his customer and the men in the rockers hid behind false smiles.

Jason put three dollars on the counter and walked out the door. As they got in the car, they noticed the old man pointing at them as he talked to the customer at the gas pump.

"Wonder what that was all about?" Jason asked.

"I don't know."

They drove on, soon returning to the land of rolling valleys and gentle streams. The peanuts made for a good midmorning snack. Jason stopped along the roadside from time to time so Kara could take pictures. In no particular hurry, they were content just spending time together.

They drove to Damascus, a quiet town tucked away on a winding stretch of highway near the southwestern corner of Virginia. Main Street was the only road that contained commerce. The side roads were graveled streets with houses and small barns.

Jason parked in front of Louise's Smoky Mountain Antiques, a rustic store fashioned out of a log cabin. When they got out of the car, they looked north to where Main Street crossed Simms Creek before curving out of sight in front of a farmhouse on a grassy hill.

"Isn't this place beautiful?" Kara asked. She took several pictures of the view down Main Street. "Here, go sit on that bench outside the hardware store."

Jason walked to the bench, and sat, looking at Kara.

"Don't look at me," she said. "Look at the church across the street so you won't look all posed up."

"You're a bossy woman, aren't you?"

She clicked five photos of Jason in rapid succession. "I'll

show you 'bossy' if you don't stop yammering. Now look at the church and keep your mouth shut or I'll be forced to spank you."

"Now you're talking." He posed, GQ style, and Kara snapped a few more photos.

She took his hand and led them around the antique store. She smiled when he placed his hand to her back. He appeared as though he was entertained, but antiquing was not typically his idea of a fun time. She, on the other hand, loved it, and he seemed content to allow her to take as long as she wanted. Perhaps he was gathering brownie points for later.

Lunch was spent at Benny's, a buffet-style restaurant with a sign above the register claiming, "The best pulled pork east of Graceland."

After they finished eating, Jason asked, "You want to go horseback riding?"

"Maybe tomorrow," she said as rubbed her foot against his leg under the table. "Why don't we go back to the cabin and finish what we started last night on the porch?"

Four

Terry Timmons held the steering wheel with one hand and the cell phone to his ear with the other. Timmons had been on the Tennessee Highway Patrol for only eight weeks, and he was hoping for a little more excitement than riding the back roads of Johnson County.

"Babe, I'm about to lose my signal," Timmons said as he began to climb the backside of Iron Mountain on the Damascus Highway. "I'll call you in about two hours when my shift is done."

"You be careful, Terry," the voice on the other end said. "I don't like you riding on those old deserted roads alone."

"I'll be fine, Amy. Nobody really on the road today except for me. Besides, I'm always packin' heat."

Timmons tossed the phone on the passenger seat and noticed a faded blue truck on the side of the road. A man was changing the front passenger side tire and Timmons pulled off in front of the truck.

"Afternoon," Timmons said as he approached the vehicle. "Need some assistance?"

The man knelt by the truck, turning the tire iron in the jack, and shook his head. He kept his eyes on the flat tire as the jack lifted it off the ground.

Timmons bent at the waist and examined the tire. "That's a doozy of a flat you got there. What'd you do, roll over a bed of nails?"

The man kept to his task, and when he lifted the flat tire off the wheel, his massive hands covered the width of the tire. Without speaking, he placed the flat on the ground beside the spare, and took hold of the spare with no struggle.

Timmons looked at the truck. "Now, this is an oldie but goodie. What is it? Seventy-one? Seventy-two?"

"Seventy-one," he said with no sense of emotion, placing the lug nuts on the wheel.

Timmons grabbed the flat. "My daddy was a truck fanatic. He'd find old models and restore them. We had a seventy-two for years. Painted candy-apple red." Timmons walked to the back of the truck. "Want me just to set her in the back?"

Timmons felt the truck lower slightly as the jack rapidly clicked, and he placed the tire in the back of the pickup. Timmons noticed a duffle bag in the cab, a bundle of plastic ties hanging loosely at the mouth. Beside them a sheath containing a Bowie knife. When he stepped away from the back of the truck, he noticed the license plate was missing.

"Helluva knife." He looked closely at it, noticing bloodstains. "You been skinnin' with it?"

"Wild boar. Attacked me yes'tiday mornin.'"

"You don't say. There's a lot of them around."

The man nodded.

A deep-red scratch under the stranger's left eye. "Looks like he sliced you a bit before you got him."

The man shrugged.

Timmons glanced below the bumper. "Where's your license plate?"

The large man placed his arm on the bed of the cab, holding the tire iron. "It fell off." He turned his chin toward the cab. "Got it in the glove compartment."

"Well, there's a fine for not displayin' your tag. I wouldn't want to add a ticket to your day after havin' a flat tire, so waddya say I let you take the plate out of the glove compartment and stick it in the back window behind your seat for now? If you promise me you'll get the plate holder fixed by tomorrow, we won't worry about that fine."

The man looked curiously at him as though he wondered what language Timmons spoke. The man wore faded green overalls, a dirty beige thermal shirt, and a gray, sweat-stained hat. His eyes were dark as coal. His oily beard smelled of soured water.

Timmons nodded toward the front of the truck. "Go ahead and get that license plate."

"Hands are greasy. Mind gettin' it fer me?"

"You say it's in the glove compartment?" The man nodded and followed Timmons, standing behind the officer as he opened the passenger door. He looked in the glove compartment, which contained only a flashlight and a pair of dirty work gloves. "Ain't no plate in here."

The tire iron crushed the side of Timmons' skull above his ear, spraying blood across the passenger window. He slumped onto the seat, and the man grabbed him by the collar, lifting him from the cab. Timmons' eyes rolled back in his head and he fell hard to the ground as the man slung him out of the truck. Timmons was face down, and he moaned and moved his feet. When the tire iron dug into the base of his skull at the spine, Timmons went limp.

~ * ~

Dust trailed behind the car as Jason darted up the driveway to the cabin. The afternoon sun draped Iron Mountain in a blanket of olive. Though the treetops were alive with color, the thick hardwoods shielded the cabin from any direct sunlight. A rustling of leaves was the only sound, and the air took on a damp chill.

Jason's heart raced. The thought of making love to Kara had him charged and ready, like a corralled bull about to be set free in a cow pasture. They walked quickly from the car to the cabin. His hand held the curve of her butt cheek as Kara opened the door. Once in the kitchen he tossed his keys on the table.

"Let's take the wine to the bedroom," Jason said while opening the refrigerator door.

"I don't want wine. I want you."

She led him by the hand, down the hall, and into the bedroom. The double bed, with a white sheet, and magnolia print bedspread intertwined across it, lay waiting. She lifted his wool sweater over his head, tossing it on the rocker. Kicking off her shoes, she peeled off her pink turtleneck, letting it fall beside her on the floor. She playfully pushed Jason onto the bed. His back felt the coolness of the sheets. His feet touched the floor.

"It seems like forever since we've done this," she said while rubbing her nails along his denim covered thighs.

She was his best friend, and he loved her without reservation, but he would be the first to say the physical attraction between them was the straw that stirred their marriage. Since their third date, he'd lost all inhibitions pertaining to the animal-like attraction he had for her, and she'd reciprocated. That's why the weekend getaway was of such importance. Jason wanted, needed, to rekindle the passionate flame that their careers had partially doused.

Straddling his waist, she slid her soft hands along Jason's

torso, beginning at his hips, working her way up his chest. As her hands made their way along both sides of Jason's neck, she pressed her lips firmly to his waiting mouth, parting them with the force of her tongue.

Pulling away, she sat and slowly removed her bra. She smiled, her eyes staring deeply into Jason's, letting him know in no uncertain terms she was in charge. He rubbed his fingers along the edge of her jeans just below her bellybutton. As he began to unsnap the bronze button, she placed her hands on his and shook her head slightly.

"Let me do it," she whispered.

She stood, turned away from Jason, and slowly slid her jeans to the floor. Bending slightly to remove the jeans from her feet, she revealed a black-silk thong. Jason rose to a sitting position, took her by the hand and guided her so she sat on his lap. Touching the curve of her back, he gazed into her eyes and the mere sight of her, the feel of her skin, made tears well. He placed his hand to her cheek, searching her eyes carefully as though it held answers to questions about the possibilities of boundless love.

"I love you," he said tenderly. "All my heart. Everything that's within me."

"Baby, I love you too."

He kissed one cheek, and then the other, his gaze never straying from her eyes. "I know this sounds corny, but I truly feel like I am the luckiest man on earth."

She simply nodded and pressed her lips to his. He placed his hand to her chest feeling her heartbeat and smiled when her sigh brushed against his face. She pressed her hands to his shoulders and guided him so he lay on his back.

Rubbing her breasts against his chest, she kissed him softly on his neck. She rose up on her knees and elbows so that the only parts touching him were her breasts and moist lips. She kissed his neck and chest, slowly inching her way down until her tongue made contact with his navel.

"Let's get rid of these," she whispered, pulling on Jason's jeans until she was able to slide it off his feet. Smiling, she slid her thong down her legs and stepped out of them.

Jason reveled in her. There was with no hint of constraint in his lovemaking, and every corner of the bed surely felt the heat of their bodies. Moans echoed through the cabin as he lost himself in her eyes.

He touched the tender beads of sweat on the arch of her back. As his breathing returned to normal, his body spent, she lay across his chest, his arms gently caressing her.

"I am so in love with you," she whispered. She slid beside him, his arm resting on her forearm.

"Do you have any idea what those words do to me?"

"I have some idea, but why don't you tell me?"

He rolled on his side and ran his fingers along her forehead, brushing her soft hair away from her face. "When you tell me you love me, it validates my existence. You are the perfect counterpart to my heart and soul."

She sighed and touched his face. A tear fell from her eye. "Baby, you just won my heart all over again. I couldn't ever imagine life without you."

In the late afternoon quiet, they drifted off to sleep.

~ * ~

Jason stirred, awakened by the sound of breaking glass. Lying on his side, facing the wall, he sat up on his elbow and looked about the room. He rubbed his hand through his hair and yawned. "Baby, you rearranging the furniture in there?" he called out.

A faint cry answered him. He hopped from bed and quickly slipped into his jeans before walking down the hall. Once in the kitchen, he noticed shattered glass on the floor. The refrigerator door was open.

"Kara?"

The door to the porch was open and the wind brushed against his exposed chest when he looked through the screen to the backwoods behind the house. "Kara?" He opened the screen door and glanced to the side of the house by the trashcan. He hurried back into the kitchen, and closed the refrigerator door. "Where are you?" he called out as he walked down the hall.

Confused, he went to the front door to see if she was retrieving something from the car. Moving around to the back of the cabin, he stopped in the cold of the room, hearing nothing.

"Hey, this isn't funny." He returned to the kitchen through the porch door. "Baby? Kara!"

The silence of the cabin surrounded him.

He burst through the front door, checking the car again. He looked down the narrow driveway. Nausea rushed through his gut.

His body rotated, searching, listening, breath heavy as he panted, small wisps of pale white coming from his mouth. He pushed the thumb of his right hand into the palm of his left, rubbing in a circular motion as though he were trying to remove the skin. He always did that when he was confused; when he was worried.

Circling the cabin, the thick woods unfamiliar. "Kara!"

He sprinted up the driveway and called out again. "Kara" echoed through the trees before dissipating into the air, as was his confidence that he'd spot her walking along Shady Valley. The curves of the mountain highway were tight, bending in either direction, limiting his view.

"She's okay," he said softly. "She's okay. God, let her be okay."

The breeze turned bitter. Clouds gathered, turning the horizon above the towering trees into a hovering, opaque ceiling. Standing in the middle of the slender dirt road, he looked for signs of movement. The rustle of the wind stirred the forest, all about him a dizzying landscape of random movement. The isolated activity surrounding him left him lightheaded. He ran his hand through his sweat-laced hair, and his eyes welled with tears. Should he run? North or south?

He bolted back down the driveway. Ferns pushed against the rugged mountain floor as the wind roared in sporadic waves like an angry sea around him. The treetops rattled above him like the bones in some ancient burial ground.

By the time he made it back into the house his body was shaking, a combination of fear and bitter cold against his bare upper body. Looking once more throughout the cabin, room-by-room, hoping she was playing some sort of evil joke on him.

His phone was on the small nightstand beside the bed and he dialed 9-1-1. "Son of a bitch," he yelled as he noticed it had no signal. He slipped on a sweater and found his sneakers by the rocker. His wallet and keys were on the nightstand as well and in a moment he was out the front door.

The car bumper scratched a knotty maple as he backed the car out of the driveway. Once on Shady Valley, he whipped his head left, and then right. Which way? Where should he go? He struggled to breathe, and opened the door, vomiting into yellow grass lining the roadside. Fighting to breathe as he got back in the car, wiping his mouth with the sleeve of his sweater, he spun out so quickly the car narrowly missed a row of mountain laurels on the side bank.

Pulling onto Highway 47, he turned left, and looked about for something—anything. The trees and mountain laurels formed shapes and figures, making him think he spotted her everywhere. He sped toward Johnson's store half blinded by the vision of her looking into his eyes as she sat on his lap just minutes earlier, her tears after they'd made love a confirmation that she loved him with her entire being.

He smashed the top of the steering wheel with his fist. Why did he not awaken when she did? He should have been by her side, clinging to the soft aroma of her perfume.

He fishtailed into the lot of Johnson's store, jumped out of the car, leaving the door open. Once inside, he found the three men occupying the same positions they'd held earlier.

"My wife's disappeared," he yelled as he ran to the counter.

"What'd you say?" the man asked, sitting as before on his stool.

"My wife. She's gone. Right out of the cabin. I searched inside, outside, everywhere. She's gone. I had no cell signal. You've got to help me." His hands shook as he grabbed the man's elbows.

"Easy, son. Stay calm. She probably just went for a walk."

"No sir. No way. She was scared of that place. Wouldn't have stepped outside without me. I heard a noise in the kitchen. When I walked in to see what was going on, there was broken glass on the floor, and the back door was open. She was gone."

Reaching for a black rotary phone on the counter, the man dialed 9-1-1. A local operator transferred him to the sheriff's department in nearby Laurel City.

"Sheriff's Office, Anderson speaking."

"Barry, this is Sherman Johnson, and I got a young fella in my store who says his wife is missing."

Johnson returned the receiver to its base. "Sheriff's on his way."

Jason stepped outside to wait. Pacing frantically, he slid his hand through his hair as an eighteen-wheeler rumbled by from the south. Off on the western horizon, Sugar Mountain's skyline rose like ocean waves of emerald to its mighty peak. The sun, well on its downward slope, cast menacing shadows, a validation he was in a distant land with no certainty of returning home with the woman he loved.

Johnson walked outside and offered Jason a soft drink.

"Tell me what happened, son."

Jason took hold of the open bottle but only held it in his hand. "I was in bed, taking a nap." His voice was unsteady. "I heard glass shatter. You know, the sound it makes when it hits something at high impact. I hurried to check it out, make sure Kara was okay. I saw the glass on the floor. And just like that..." He snapped his fingers. "She was gone."

Johnson looked down at his feet, removed his cap, and scratched his forehead. "Damnedest thing. Just like last time."

Jason looked at Johnson. "Excuse me?"

"Last summer," Johnson began timidly, as though guilty for keeping a secret. "There was a couple staying at the cabin and the young lady ran off, or disappeared, or somethin'. We heard they never found her. They were from Boston, New York, or some Yankee town, and we ain't heard diddly about it since." In a reassuring tone, he said, "Son, I'm sure your young missus is okay. You need to believe that."

"That's what you meant about the cabin this morning. Why didn't you tell us?"

"It's not my place to be scarin' folks." He looked downward. "It's just not my place." He turned and walked back into the store.

Jason waited for fifteen grueling minutes, and then leaned his head in the door of the store. "I can't sit around doing nothing. Tell the sheriff, if he ever gets here, I'm going back to the cabin. Tell him to hurry."

Jason ran to his car, and a brown-and-tan Crown Victoria spun into the gravel lot. Laurel City Sheriff was written in black on the side doors. A short, stocky man slowly exited, placing a Royal Mounties style hat on his nearly bald head. He pushed his sunglasses, rimmed with silver, up the slope of his nose with his forefinger. His white, short-sleeve shirt looked far removed from the days when it fit, and his belly hung over his belt. A black, leather holster held a pistol on his right side.

Jason ran to the squad car. "What the hell took you so long? My wife's missing, and you take your country-ass time like you're here to fetch a cat from a tree."

"Easy, mister, I drive a car, not a helicopter." The officer opened a notebook and retrieved a chewed pen from behind his left ear. "I had to drive eleven miles to get here, and part of that was putterin' behind Percy Taylor's hay-filled truck. Now tell me what happened."

"We were up at a cabin on Iron Mountain," Jason said.

"And..."

"Did you say Iron Mountain? The Grayson cabin?"

"Yes, we're renting it for the weekend."

Reaching into the squad car the officer removed the radio handle. "Barry, get down to Johnson's Store. Round up the others."

"Ten-four," echoed fuzzily through the speaker. "Be there in fifteen."

"Son," the officer said. "The quicker we move, the better our chances are of finding her."

"Okay."

"Tell me exactly where you were when you last saw her."

"The kitchen. I mean the bedroom."

"Well, which was it?"

"She must have gone to the kitchen while I took a nap. When I heard glass breaking, I hurried to the kitchen to see what had happened. The refrigerator was open and glass was everywhere. She was gone."

"Did you have an argument?"

"What?" Jason asked in puzzled tone. "No, we didn't have an argument."

As Jason talked, the farmer he'd sprayed with pebbles that morning by the roadside pulled into the gas station. Slowly exiting his mud-stained, older model Ford truck, the farmer glanced at Jason from the side of his eyes as he walked. Their eyes remained locked on each other until the farmer disappeared through the front door.

"Son, are you listenin' to me?" the sheriff asked. Jason continued to stare at the door. "Try to focus."

"I'm sorry," he said. "It's just that guy who walked into the store was a guy we saw this morning. He stared us down when we drove by, and he did the same just now."

The sheriff turned but the man had already entered the store. "Well, that's nice to know, but why don't we get back to figurin' out what happened to your wife."

"The more time we waste with stupid questions, the longer she's missing. Shouldn't you organize a manhunt or something?"

"Son, we'll do that as soon as my boys get here. In the meantime, it's crucial that you help me so we don't go in blind to the situation."

"I'm sorry. It's just been a hell of a day."

As the sheriff resumed questioning, the farmer exited the store. "That's the guy," Jason pointed. "Maybe he knows something."

"Who you talkin' 'bout?" the officer asked as he turned. "You mean Roby?"

"Can you just ask him if he's seen anything?"

"What gives you reason to think he knows anything?"

"He must live close to the cabin. We saw him no more than a mile from it this morning. And he sure looked pissed at us when we drove by."

"Roby?" the officer called out. "Hang on a sec." He walked toward the man, Jason following closely behind. "Can I ask you something?"

Roby Greer, with floppy-brimmed, gray velvet hat, stood six-foot-six. "Ask me what?" he asked as he continued toward his truck.

"A young lady disappeared at Grayson's cabin on Iron Mountain just a short while ago."

"What's that got to do with me?"

"Try not to sound so concerned, hillbilly," Jason sarcastically responded.

"Son," said the sheriff, holding his hand upward in front of Jason. "Ease up."

Greer explained he'd spent the day fishing in Maymead, a crossroad between Boone and Elizabethton. After the sheriff thanked him for his time, the farmer quickly drove off as two squad cars arrived. Four men quickly exited the car.

"Son, let's ride to the cabin," the officer said. "Let's retrace her steps." Looking at one of the officers, he called out, "Barry?"

"Sir?" snapped Barry Anderson.

"Call for backup from Carter County, and you and the boys get the squad cars up the cabin road. Cover the Shady Valley side. Check the dirt roads, barns, outhouses, and henhouses from the cabin to this gas station. And call Knoxville for a chopper. Adams?"

"Sir?" Gilly Adams asked.

"Call Brushy Fork Prison. We need search dogs. Ask for them blue tick hounds. Those things could track Elvis flyin' a UFO."

"Will do."

"Mister," the sheriff said, looking at Jason. "Describe your wife for me. What was she wearing?"

"She's five and a half feet tall. Dark-brown hair and brown eyes. She weighs about a hundred and ten pounds."

"What she was wearing?"

"Huh?"

"What was she wearing? I need a description of the clothes she had on."

"I'm not sure. The last time I saw her, she wasn't wearing anything."

"You don't say."

Jason slid in the passenger seat of the sheriff's car.

"Name's Buford Lawrence."

"Jason Lisle."

"We're gonna do everything we can to get her back for you, Mr. Lisle. I promise you that."

After what seemed like forever, Sheriff Lawrence pulled onto the long grassy driveway to the cabin, blue lights flashing. Gray clouds dropped like a cast net on the mountain, speeding dusk's approach.

Jason jumped from the car, looking about the yard. "Kara," he yelled with his hands cupping his mouth. When he didn't hear a response, he ran into the house, Lawrence's clunky footsteps close behind.

"I'm guessing this is where she was last," Jason said as he pointed to the broken glass on the kitchen floor.

"Can you get me an item of her clothing? I'll need it for the dogs."

He went to the bedroom, and grabbed Kara's sweater lying crumpled on the floor. He saw the jeans, and wondered if she was wearing any clothing at all. If she grabbed a T-shirt Jason wouldn't know it. He could smell the fragrance of her perfume on the sweater and he clung tightly to it for just a moment. He picked up Kara's inhaler and walked outside. Lawrence appeared to be looking at the ground for footprints.

"This is her inhaler," he said, displaying the plastic container. "Kara has asthma. It's a mild case but if she goes more than a day or so without it, she's going to struggle."

The deputies arrived within ten minutes and Lawrence approached them. Jason watched as the sheriff talked to them through their windows, pointing one north to Shady Valley, and the other south. Tires screeched as both cars pulled out of the driveway.

Five

When the phone rang at Charlie Swanson's desk, it was never good news. The clock read five minutes past noon. Charlie closed the brown bag that held his turkey-and-Swiss sandwich and tossed it on his desk.

"Knoxville Police Department. Missing persons. Swanson speaking."

"This is Sheriff Buford Lawrence from Laurel City."

"Hello, Sheriff. What can I do for you?"

"We had a young lady disappear yesterday on Iron Mountain. I got a feelin' it's related to the Patricia Darby case."

Though Laurel City was a two and half hour drive from Knoxville, smaller towns such as Elizabethton and Johnson City didn't have the manpower, or the jurisdictional reach of Knoxville.

Swanson reached in a desk drawer and removed a manila folder from the stack. "You did say Patricia Darby, didn't you?" he asked while shutting the drawer. "Iron Mountain?"

"Affirmative. Both ladies vanished from the same cabin."

"We've searched for that Darby gal the last eleven months," Swanson said. "We've come up empty with not much hope in sight."

"Well, you better get up here. It's happened again."

"Will do."

Swanson walked up a flight of stairs, folder in hand. He tapped on the smoky-glass door leading to Thomas Jordan's office.

"Hey, Tom," he said as he opened the door. "We got another missing girl up on Iron Mountain."

Thomas Jordan leaned back in his chair. He wore blue jeans, a button-down white polo dress shirt, and a red and navy tie. He'd rolled his shirtsleeves to his elbows. His dark hair was neat and trimmed and parted on the right side of his head. "Talk to me."

"Seems she disappeared from that cabin in Johnson County. Same one as Patricia Darby almost a year ago."

"Charlie, hand me that folder." He scanned it quickly. "Looks like you've screwed up my hopes for a peaceful afternoon." He took a sip of coffee. "Not much to the details of this case. Weren't there any leads? Fingerprints? Any clues?"

"No, sir. It was as though she vanished from the face of the earth. Nothing to go on. No leads. And trying to get help from those mountain people was like dragging a confession about the missing canary from a fattened cat."

"I've heard stories about that mountain." He finished the last of his coffee in a large sip. "Bring my car around, would you? I gotta make a call, and then I'm headed to Johnson County."

~ * ~

Jordan dialed his home number.

"Hello," the sweet voice said.

"Hey, angel," Jordan said.

"Daddy," she hollered. "When are you coming home? Can we go to Mr. Potter's store and get some maple syrup candy?"

"There's nothing in the world I'd rather do. But I've got to take care of something really important. I should be back by late tonight. We'll go tomorrow, okay?"

"Okay, Daddy." He heard the disappointment in her voice. "You want to talk to Mommy?"

"Yes, baby."

"Okay. Bye, Daddy. I love you."

"I love you, too," he said with a smile.

After a brief pause, "Hey, babe."

"Hey," he said.

"I don't like the sound of that 'hey.' What's up?"

"I've got to go to Laurel City. A woman disappeared on Iron Mountain."

"Isn't that something the local police should tend to?"

"Not in this case. She's the second one to vanish from the cabin in less than a year."

"Oh, my."

"Anyway, I'll be home late. Kiss Jessie for me, okay?"

"You got it," she answered. "I'll keep the bed warm. Love you."

"You, too."

"Tom?"

"Yes?"

"Be careful. Daddy used to tell us scary stuff about Iron Mountain."

"Don't worry."

~ * ~

They sat at a tiny wooden table in a small kitchen. Smoke from the woodstove cast a pale veil of white above them. A knife and a quarter of a sliced apple lay on the table.

"He done screwed up big time," a slender man with a faded khaki cap said. "He killed a state trooper."

"What the hell?" the other asked. "He shouldn't ever be on the highway. Dumb son of a bitch. Where did this happen?"

"Damascus Highway. Said he was loopin' 'round Stoney Creek. Ain't but a half-mile stretch. But he got a flat tire and had no choice but to pull over and change it. Trooper stumbled on him and got out to help."

"What did he do with him?"

"Drug him off to the woods and buried him."

"No witnesses?"

"He said nobody drove by. But somebody's gonna come lookin' for him soon. And when they do, they's gonna snoop ever'where. We cain't just shoot 'em when they come."

"Well, not necessarily. We got a right to defend our land. Where's the patrol car?"

"Settin' off a loggin' road a mile off the highway."

"Drive it to the cliffs. Burn it, and roll it off into the trees below. We got to make sure they ain't got a clue where to look."

"What about operations? We need to shut it down for a few days?"

"No. It's business as usual. Besides, those troopers know the reputation on Iron Mountain. They ain't gonna take a chance on gettin' their heads blown off."

"What about the boy? He's gotten a little carried away."

"Let him keep on a keepin' on. We want everybody afeared of comin' on our mountain.

~ * ~

The ride to Iron Mountain moved like a molasses roller coaster as Jordan's black SUV journeyed eastward through the Blue Ridge Mountains. His mind compared the circumstances revolving around Patricia Darby's disappearance with the little he knew about this new girl. Same location. Roughly the same time of day. No clues, no motive, no body. At the time Darby disappeared, he was assigned to two other murder cases, as well as attempting to settle a territorial war between rival gangs in East Knoxville.

Three long hours later, Jordan's vehicle pulled in front of a one story brick building. In white lettering on the front of the building, "Laurel Springs Health Department." In front of the building was a sign held by prongs that looked like ones realtors used to advertise homes for sale. The sign read, "Laurel City Police Station."

"Sheriff," Jordan said with a nod as he approached Lawrence's desk. "Detective Thomas Jordan."

"Nice to meet you," Lawrence said. "Buford Lawrence. How was the drive?"

"Terrible. Can't you do somethin' to straighten out the roads 'round here?"

Both smiled briefly.

"Any sign of the girl?"

"None," said Lawrence. "Understandably, her husband is climbin' the walls. I've got my deputies combin' the county, and we've had a chopper and hounds looking for her. The only person we know of anywhere near the cabin yesterday was Roby Greer."

"Who?"

"A local farmer. Mr. Lisle says he was giving them creepy looks or something when they drove by him on Shady Valley. I talked to him to see if he noticed anybody comin' or goin' from the mountain, but he said he was fishin' when she disappeared."

"Let's take a look at the cabin. We might need to talk to Mr. Greer as well."

"Let's go," Lawrence said, snatching his hat and keys.

Sheriff Lawrence maneuvered his squad car through the mountain roads like Dale Earnhardt. As they climbed Shady Valley Road, Jordan spotted the swift waters of Muddy Branch running toward the mouth of Roan Creek. Knee-high patches of wild phlox and yellow grass flanked the water.

According to Lawrence, the police force in Laurel City ran five deep, and other than him, all younger than the age of twenty-five. Experience was not an asset for the force, but he claimed the energy of youth made up for it.

"What's up with the realty sign in front of the police station? You split quarters with the Health Department?"

Lawrence shook his head. "Our little town ain't got much, and they felt it best to put a sign out front rather than replace the writing on the wall. Health Department is two blocks away."

"How long you been a lawman?"

"Twenty-six years. Began as a deputy, working under Blackie Carson. Carson had been the county magistrate for almost fifty years, going back to the early days when there was no police station. For the first twenty-two years, Carson was a one-man outfit. He finally persuaded the town council to add a deputy to the force, and they got me."

Jordan nodded and glanced out his window. "This is pretty country."

The trip to Iron Mountain was Jordan's first. When Patricia Darby disappeared, it was assumed it was an isolated case. Weems Phipps led the investigation of the case, but retired on New Year's Day. The case hadn't been assigned to another investigator. That was, not until it was dropped on Jordan's desk.

"Around here it is. But the higher you climb, the darker and deeper it becomes. Ain't too pretty then, in my opinion."

"I hear the people who live up here aren't the friendliest bunch."

"You heard right. Folks back in these hollers despise the outside world. Been that way since these mountains were constructed by God Almighty, I s'pose."

The car worked its way up Shady Valley and pulled into the drive leading to the cabin. Slowly, Detective Jordan exited the car. He removed his dark sunglasses because the thick trees of the mountain blocked the afternoon sun from finding its way to the cold floor. His eyes scanned the cabin and the surrounding woods. Without uttering a word, he walked to the side porch door of the cabin and into the kitchen. Two deputies stood at the kitchen table, nodding at him. He was too consumed in thought to acknowledge.

Jordan looked at the broken glass and the refrigerator door.

"We checked for prints," Lawrence said. "None found, though that don't surprise me. Even if we'd found any, if it were one of Iron Mountain's own, there'd be nothing to match in the database. These boys up here ain't ones to head to town. No doctor visits. No trips to the DMV. Certainly not jail. We stay clear of them best we can."

"How'd the Lisle's find this place?" Jordan asked. "To rent,

I mean."

"I think it's on the county website," Lawrence responded. "You know, the Internet. I don't know much about computers, so I try to stay away from them. Anyway, about two years ago the County Council decided it would be a good idea to snatch some of the tourist crowd from Boone. They started a campaign to get more people in the area, which has pissed off the locals up here. Though this cabin is the only one on Iron Mountain available to tourists, some have been built in Doe Valley. Folks like to stay in the valley, but they come up Iron Mountain to hike, maybe set up an overnight camp."

"What's the attraction? To hike, I mean."

The Appalachian Trail crosses the mountain on the northern slope. It ain't uncommon for hikers to get shot at. Now, they mighta stumbled across a still, or maybe they were just gettin' a warnin' to stay off the mountain."

Jordan walked slowly through the den and paused to look at the picture above the couch. "Bears. I love bears."

"Those bears are just like this mountain," Lawrence said. "From a distance, they look all warm and fuzzy. But once you get close enough, you find out they're meaner'n hell."

After looking at the disheveled bed, Jordan walked outside. A gentle breeze ruffled the knee-high ferns for just a moment before becoming silent again. He lightly brushed his hands through the underbrush at the edge of the driveway. As a deputy drove up the narrow path, Jordan turned his head so that his left ear faced the patrol car. "Mr. Lisle should've been able to hear a vehicle riding down this driveway."

"Yep. He said he heard nothin'."

"So, if she wasn't driven out of here, did she leave on foot? These trees are a little tall to be climbing."

"I don't know how she left, but it was the same with Patricia Darby. It's like they both just vanished in thin air."

"Whoever did it knew what they were doing. Quick and silent."

"Quieter'n a speckled trout in Doe Creek."

"Where is Mr. Lisle staying?"

"In town at the Valley View Motel, although I think he's spending most of his time ridin' the back roads. Guess he's hopin' she'll magically pop out by the roadside somewhere."

"I'm gonna need to speak with him. Did you say Mr. Greer lived in Shady Valley?"

"Not far from it."

"Let's pay him a visit."

~ * ~

Lawrence pulled onto the steep dirt road that led to Greer's farm. It was a narrow, windy road, with weed-filled banks tight on either side. In the distance, Iron Mountain stood like a jagged, charcoal-gray wall. Though spring had made its way to the mountain, the hardwoods along the crest stood barren and singular, the trees like wooden beings whose sole purpose was to watch the valley below.

The squad car passed a small, faded-brown barn beside the road. Its collapsed roof provided just enough sunlight to allow Jordan to spot a slender mule inside. The old gal was chewing on long strands of decaying hay, briefly raising her head as the car drove by like a disinterested party.

Greer's house was modest at best. It was made of shingle siding faded to a shade of gray so light it was almost colorless. The house was located against the base of a sharp hill at the foot of Iron Mountain. Leafless poplars and hemlocks with reddish needles bordered the back of the house. Along the sides, weeds rose to the windowsills, resembling small trees in their unimpeded growth.

Above the front porch was a small overhang, barely wide enough to shade the front door and the living room window. There was no yard to speak of. As Lawrence's car pulled up to the front of the house, a black, mixed-breed hound and a black-and-tan German shepherd bolted from underneath the flimsy porch.

"His dogs are bigger than his mule," Jordan said. "How 'bout you let 'em chase you to the barn, and then I'll slip up on the porch?"

"Not likely."

The dogs circled the car as the men remained inside. A loud whistle pierced the air, and the dogs immediately sat.

"You can get out the car now," Greer shouted in a gruff voice from beside the house. "They won't move less'n I tell 'em." His face, like worn leather, revealed a man as hard as the rugged Appalachian soil.

The men cautiously exited the car as the hounds growled.

"Buford," Greer said, nodding slightly.

"Roby," Lawrence acknowledged.

"Mr. Greer, I'm Detective Thomas Jordan." He extended his hand, but the offer was ignored. "We're here about the missing woman at the Grayson cabin."

"I told Buford here yes'tiday I don't know nothin'."

"That may be true. But you do live near the cabin. You do know the people and the landscape. Correct? Maybe you have some ideas that could help us. A young woman is missing. She's the second one to disappear from the cabin in the last eleven months. And since it's my job to find out what happened, I thought it'd be fun to bring in as many experts to the table as possible. Toss ideas about."

"Ideas? You want ideas? Look around. You got any ideas how to make life easier for this old mountain man? You ride up here, hidin' the smugness behind your sharp sunglasses, wearin' your fancy clothes, and what I bet is life on Easy Street. And you come here askin' for ideas. I got a couple of ideas right now, but out of politeness, I'll keep them to myself. Now if you'll excuse me, I got work to do."

"Mr. Greer," Jordan said, "what you or I wear plays no part in this. We have a young woman's life at stake, two women to be exact, and all you're concerned about is how slighted you are by the sunglasses I wear. That don't exactly speak well of your sensitivity to others, does it?"

Greer frowned. "Unless you boys intend to help me plant the seeds sittin' in my barn, I suggest you let me get back to work." Reaching his hand toward his mouth, he inserted his thumb and index finger. The shrill whistle put the dogs to motion and they sprinted to their master's side. "Good day, gentlemen." Greer turned and walked away.

Jordan, hands on hips, turned, scanning the deep woods around Greer's house. "I don't think he cares too much for me," he said with a twist of sarcasm. They walked back to the car.

"He don't cozy up to strangers," Lawrence said.

"What's his situation? Wife? Kids? Appears he lives alone. And with a disposition like his, he deserves to be."

"He ain't exactly been walkin' around with a rabbit's foot in his pocket."

"How's that?"

"His wife ran off a while back. Heard she took off to Oregon to live with her sister. Couldn't take him anymore; couldn't handle the state of affairs of the family. They had two sons; both dead."

"No wonder he's bitter. What happened to his boys?"

"One died fishing at Watauga Lake. Burley was his name. He was just twenty-five years old. He and Roby were in a small fishin' boat. Burley fell overboard, apparently hitting his head. The engine blades chopped his face so bad he was completely disfigured. Needless to say, it was a closed casket funeral."

"And the other?"

"Died in jail across the state line."

"Interesting," Jordan said as he craned his neck upward to view the mountain skyline. "That sure explains the foul disposition."

Jordan assessed the situation on the ride back to town. Greer certainly had more than his fair share of tough blows in his life. Who wouldn't be soured with the world? How would he fare should something similar happen to his family? He guessed the outcome would not be handled with sweet disposition. So, it made sense Greer be allowed the courtesy of feeling like life had shortchanged him. And with the hard life of surviving in the rugged Appalachians certainly weighing him down, it would be a heavy burden on anyone.

But in this particular case something didn't sit right.

Six

Jordan lay on his back, staring at the ceiling. He tried to limit his twisting and turning so as not to awaken Marty. Arms behind his head, he inhaled deeply, slowly. Marty, curled in a fetal position, cuddled a pillow. Jordan loved to look at her when she slept. He ran his fingers through her sandy blonde hair, pulling it away from her face.

Marty opened her eyes.

"Staring at the stars?" she whispered groggily. She slid closer to him, removing the pillow bundled between her legs, placing her head on his chest. "You need to let that stuff go when you're home. Especially when you should be sleeping." She rubbed the dark hair on his chest, and laid her leg across his thighs. Her skin was soft and warm.

"I can't help it. No telling what's happened to those two girls. Can you imagine what it's like for their husbands? Their families? I'd be going crazy if it happened to you or Jessie."

She patted his chest. "I'm sure it's a nightmare."

"What makes it worse is the lack of concern by the people who live there. I can guarantee there won't be any candlelight vigils outside the cabin by the locals. These women are totally on their own as far as Iron Mountain is concerned."

"Well, that was before you came into the picture. As of now, the great Thomas R. Jordan has come to save the day." She tickled his ribs gently and kissed his chest.

Rising up on her elbow, she caressed his face. "Now, let me take your mind off of the situation so you can get some rest." She slid on top of him, gently kissing his chin. She removed her orange Vols T-shirt, and her slender figure carved a sexy shape in the darkness. She lowered her head to him, her warm lips pressing against his waiting mouth. In the darkness, for a brief while, the burdens of Iron Mountain faded.

When the sun made its first appearance through the bedroom window, Marty glanced at the clock. Jordan was dressed and putting his shoes on as he sat at the edge of the bed. "Morning."

"Hey," she said softly. "Up early, aren't you?"

"We need to talk."

"I already know what you're thinking," she said matter-of-factly. "You want to stay in Johnson County for the investigation."

"You know me too well."

"It's not like it's the first time this has happened. That's part of my job, dealing with the things that come with your job." She extended her hand and he cupped his hand around it. "Jessie and I will be okay. You just be careful. Iron Mountain is a dangerous place."

~ * ~

Jordan sat at the kitchen table, rubbing his hand through his neatly trimmed hair. Though the sun had cleared the eastern skyline above Clark Mountain, a thick layer of slate-colored clouds hid it from view. It was a wintry sky, though the clouds showed no signs of rain. He watched small patches of pale-white clouds hover close to the mountainside like feeder fish alongside a whale. He forced a smile as Marty poked her head in the doorway of the kitchen. He'd heard the stories of Iron Mountain. Whether they were legend or fact, he didn't know. For the first time in his career, he had an uneasy feeling.

"Hey, good lookin,'" she said, placing her hands on his shoulders. "You be careful out there on that mountain."

He placed his coffee mug on the kitchen table and placed his hand on hers where it rested on his shoulder. "Always, baby. Always."

Jessica scooted into the room, slipped around Marty's leg and leapt into her father's waiting arms. "Morning, Daddy."

"Morning, sunshine." He rubbed his fingers through her blonde locks.

"Can we ride the carousel today?"

"I can't, sugar. I gotta go off for a while."

"Oh, Daddy," the precocious six-year-old said. "Please? Plllease?"

"I can't. While I'm gone, you have to promise me you'll take real good care of Mommy."

"I promise."

"When I come back, we'll ride the carousel at the mall and I'll buy you a scoop of chocolate ice cream the size of your head."

"You're the best." She pushed the hair away from her face and kissed him on his cheek.

"You are such a pushover," Marty said as she removed a mug from the cabinet.

~ * ~

Forensic reports from the cabin showed prints and human hair from Jason and Kara only. The hounds came up empty in their attempts to find a path where Kara and her assumed abductor left the cabin. Lawrence and his men searched the outlying areas, engaging the help of volunteers in an effort to find at best a clue that would lead them to keep the hope Kara might still be alive, or at worst, to find her body. Lawrence tried to manage the balancing act of keeping those in the county alert without sending them into panic mode.

Jordan set up camp at the Valley View Motel, but spent most of his time at the Laurel City Police Department. The suspect list stood at zero. Lawrence and his men speculated the kidnapper was most likely an inhabitant of Iron Mountain, and Jordan had no reason to think otherwise. To remove both Patricia Darby and Kara Lisle from the cabin without any sign showed the kidnapper was very familiar with the area. The folks on Iron Mountain were savvy in the ways of their deep forests, and if they knew who was responsible for the abductions, they'd never turn in one of their own.

Jordan set up a mini-control station of his own in his motel room—walkie-talkie, CB radio, a map of Johnson County pinned to his wall. He hoped to give Jason, whose room was three doors down, at least some comfort from knowing the investigation was going full blast. He could only imagine what kind of torment Jason was enduring.

"Mind if I come in?" Jordan asked as he tapped his knuckle on the open metal door of Jason's room. Jason straddled the front left corner of the bed with his elbows on his knees, his face in his hands.

"Umm, yes. I mean no. Come in." Jason seemed to avoid eye contact with Jordan as though his red, puffy eyes might come across as weak.

Jordan removed a straight-backed chair out from underneath an octagon-shaped table next to the bed. "You holdin' up okay?"

"Not really."

Jordan had more in mind than just easing Jason's mind. "How long have you and Kara been married?" he asked as he sat. He handed Jason a plastic cup filled with black coffee he'd fetched from the motel restaurant. "This weekend was our two-year anniversary. What an anniversary present, huh?"

Jordan sighed and glanced out the door. The dusk blurred Iron Mountain's crest into the evening sky as though they were one seamless entity. "Tell me about her."

It didn't take long for Jason to pour his heart out. He'd fallen for Kara on their first date. He'd never had a serious girlfriend before, preferring to spread his love around, so to speak. But Kara changed all that.

The one thing that encouraged Jordan was when Jason talked of Kara's toughness, honed from her days playing high school basketball. It just might help her survive whatever the abductor was imposing on her. That was, if she was still alive. Jason guaranteed Kara's spunk was more than enough to handle the situation. At least that's what his words said.

Jordan listened to Jason for almost an hour before he retreated to his room to plan the next step, the next move.

Seven

Rachel opened the back of her white Tahoe, and her black lab came barreling out. The sun was making its first appearance above Doe Mountain, and she was anxious to explore the new land. "Come on, Sam," Rachel said as she patted her leg. "How about we take a walk? Is that what you want, big fellow?"

Sam stretched his body and his belly touched the ground. The forty-five minute drive from the hotel in Boone seemed more than long enough to suit his fancy. The large-pawed dog waited for Rachel to attach his leash, his tail wagging like it was on fire. She hesitated over leaving her vehicle on the deserted dirt road, but there was no other choice.

She removed her cell phone from her pocket, debating whether to check in and make sure Alex hadn't let one of the kids burn down the house while cooking breakfast. The idea became moot when she looked at the phone and zero bars appeared on the display. She returned the phone to her pocket.

This was Rachel's chance to get away from it all. She loved her family and life in Atlanta, but she needed a quiet weekend to herself. She wasn't sure what made her ride westward from Boone that morning. The daughter of an outdoor photographer, she developed a love for nature when she was a child. She instructed Sam to sit and knelt beside him, petting his neck as her eyes scoped the countryside.

As the sun breathed shape and depth to the land, God orchestrated a new canvas of colors and design. Some might argue the design was no different from the day before, identical to the landscape from a thousand years prior. But in that familiarity Rachel saw the newness. In that simplicity of the trees, in the ferns along the mountain floor, she knew were slight variations never seen before, and never to be seen again.

Sam pulled forward, and she let him lead the way. Bursting

with energy as they began their trek, he forced Rachel to jog lightly. "Slow down, Sam." She smiled and tugged lightly on the leash. Sam was taking a liking to his new backyard, and the feeling of freedom looked like it recharged them both.

Climbing a narrow, dirt path, Sam pressed his nose to the ground. He soon caught the scent of small game and pulled Rachel hard as he tried to climb the steep, gritty road. She grasped the leash handle and decided to let Sam follow the scent. He rambled thirty yards before stopping on a dime. He lifted his head slightly, and his ears stood at attention.

"What is it, boy?"

As Sam stared into a group of ferns, she zipped the jacket pocket that held her phone. Her bracelet caught the zipper's fastener, breaking the clasp. *That's just great.* She carefully picked the charm bracelet off a dampened clump of fallen leaves, while holding tight to the dog's leash. *I shouldn't have worn it.* Since the pocket with the phone was zipped, she placed the bracelet in the other pocket.

Walking quickly to the edge of the ferns, she tightened her hold. Slowly she reached down in front of Sam, lightly moving a crooked limb from a red spruce with her foot. Leaves flew and sticks scattered when a brown rabbit leapt from behind the bush. With tiny, trembling legs, the hare sought the shelter of the underbrush and headed northward. Sam bolted for the furry creature, and Rachel lost her grip on the leash. She reached in vain to grab the handle. "Sam! Come here, boy. Sam!"

The usually mindful dog disregarded her command. He pulled away, engaging in full pursuit. "Sam! Come back here." Her commands were fruitless, so she joined the chase.

The rabbit stretched the distance from Sam quickly, scampering under brush and fallen limbs for protection. Sam maintained a full trot while she dodged low-lying limbs from white pines and hemlocks, trying to keep up on the sloping terrain.

The distance between her and her dog widened, and her breath became labored, sweat building on her lower back and neck. Her heart pounded from the physical exertion combined with the thought of her dog running away. She scurried over two hundred yards of rugged landscape before running out of steam. Sam was nowhere to be seen.

She stopped, bent, hands on her knees, and tried to regain her breath. Lifting her head, she looked for signs, listening for Sam's familiar bark. "Sam!" she shouted again, a bit of panic in her voice. She was a bit disoriented; she hadn't paid attention to the trail she blazed while searching for Sam. "Here, boy. Sam!"

She wondered how much ribbing she would have to take from Alex for having to run Sam down through the woods. He didn't want her to make the trip in the first place. She wanted a break from the children, but he preferred she go somewhere less secluded like a B&B.

Tracing footsteps proved difficult as the ferns and underbrush wove a seamless blend of green and brown. The trees were too thick to use the sun as a directional marker and she couldn't pinpoint its exact position. The wind stirred the branches above her head, and the mountainside seemed to come alive. Mountain laurels, thick and dark, dotted the rugged terrain, their green leaves taking on a blackish hue. The isolation made her sweaty body turn cold.

She lifted her long auburn hair away from her face. Slowly turning, looking, listening. "Sam!" she shouted again. She battled between wanting to take off running, in no particular direction, and cowering behind the trees until Sam returned.

A twig snapped to her right. Seeing nothing, she froze, holding her breath, praying Sam had found his way back to her. Her head turning left and then right. Almost tiptoeing, she stepped through the knee-high underbrush covering the mountain floor. Something moved to her left. She stopped behind a thick locust, and very methodically moved her head around the side of the tree.

A squirrel jumped out from behind a fallen maple. "Oh, shit."

Breathing a sigh of relief, her hand clamped to her chest, she took a step from around the tree. As she did, a large, clammy hand covered her mouth from behind.

"Don't do no talkin,'" the voice from the shadows said, pressing a sharp object to her back.

Rachel froze for a second, and then she tried to scream. Fear compressed her lungs. She struggled to breathe. Her eyes opened wide, and her heart beat so hard the pulse pounded in her neck.

"Get a move on."

Rachel, in shock, just stood in her tracks.

"Move, I said."

The stranger pushed her forward, and she fell to her knees. His large hand took hold of her arm, and he yanked her to her feet.

"Don't make me gut you right here and now. Now move your ass." Downward over steep mountain terrain they walked, the object still pushed hard against her spine. *Please, God, don't let him hurt me. Please don't let me die. Please, Lord.* His breath was warm on the back of her neck, and her stomach roiled. She smelled his oily skin, his soured beard, and the stale aroma of sweat on his dank jacket. His hand, still covering her mouth, was calloused and cold.

As they walked down a ravine, rushing waters roared. She stumbled and he jerked her up by her collar as if she was a ragdoll. She tried to turn her head to look for Sam, but he again placed his hand to her mouth, pressing so tightly her head was immobile. She tried to observe the surroundings in front of her, committing it to memory.

He pulled her to a stop. Intense pain charged through the back of her head. Everything went black.

~ * ~

Rachel placed her hand to the base of her neck. A cold draft drifted along the dirt floor below her. She struggled to regain her bearings, her sense of being. Surrounded by darkness, the only light slipping underneath a door in front of her. The light distorted her ability to judge the distance between her and the pale slice cutting through the darkness. *Six feet, maybe eight.* Pulling herself up, still groggy, the dire situation was an awakening force. Quickly she reached in her pocket for her cell phone. There was no signal.

Turning the phone away from her, she used the light emitting from the display as a lantern. Calmly, she estimated the room to be about seven feet across and perhaps ten feet deep. Woozily, she tried to stand but her leg burned from the steel shackle encasing it. She pulled and the chain held firm, bolted to the wall. Sliding toward the door, her hand stretched for the black metal knob. On the damp floor she tried to spy underneath the door, but was unable to get a glimpse of anything on the other side. She searched around the small quarters of her prison with her cell phone again. Three small shelves containing six mason jars lined the back wall. A rat scurried behind the shelves.

Footsteps from beyond the door grew louder. Rachel held her breath, and she backed away from the door. A padlock was yanked open on the other side, and the doorknob slowly turned. The silhouette of a large man filled the doorway. She sat motionless as though by sitting still, he wouldn't see her. He reached down and unlocked the shackle.

"Git up," the figure commanded.

"Please don't hurt me," she said. "I have a family. I have children."

"It ain't your family that interests me."

"You want money? I'll give you all I got. Please, just let me go."

"You're gonna give me all you got. That's for damn sure. But it ain't gonna be in the form of currency." His open hand smashed against her cheek, knocking her into the shelves. Lifting her up by her hair, he said, "Git up."

With a vice grip on her left wrist, he pulled her out the door. They walked a few steps down a dark hallway, up a stairwell, and out into waist high weeds. Her face was numb, and the chill in the air pricked her face like needles. She tried to pull away, and he grabbed her by the arm. As he snapped her back in line, her bracelet fell from her pocket. She tried to reach for it but he yanked her elbow.

They moved along a path that looked seldom used, and Rachel struggled to study her surroundings. Her eyes glanced about while trying to keep her head as still as possible. She fought the urge to scream but who could hear her pleas for help? She wanted to break free and run.

Could she outrun him?

They walked a crooked path up a hill to the back door of a rickety wood porch. The small shack, tightly encased by hardwoods and mountain laurels, sat on a gray slab. The porch floor creaked as they walked across it. The stranger's grip tightened as he led her through a tiny kitchen where dirty dishes and plastic cups filled the counter and sink. A musty smell permeated the unkempt house. He pulled her into a small bedroom off to the side of the kitchen. Her heart pounded, and her stomach knotted like a clenched fist. Tears filled her eyes when his clammy hands pulled on the back of her jacket.

"Take that coat off," he said, matter-of-fact.

"Please," Rachel pleaded. "Please don't do this. I won't tell anyone. Just let me go so I can see my family, my children."

He threatened to slap her and she fell silent. He yanked off her jacket. "Take off them dungarees."

Towering high above her, his eyes like wet coals, he stared downward at her hips. "You can take 'em off," he said, his lips hidden by his matted beard and moustache, "or I can take 'em off fer you." He removed the Bowie knife from his belt sheath.

The tears flowed and Rachel attempted to focus on her family, her children, separating her mind from her body. With the front of her right shoe, she pushed down on the back of her left shoe, forcing the still tied, white sneaker off her foot. A white footie remained. She lifted her right foot upward, untied the shoe and slid it off. She unbuttoned her jeans and pushed them below her knees, pulling each leg off one at a time. She pulled down on her sweater to cover her panties.

He moved closer and placed the sharp knife under her chin. Her heart felt like it would explode. Clutching the collar of her sweater with his right hand, he cut the thick wool, splitting the sweater as he cut downward. She trembled as the cold blade slid between her breasts, along her stomach, until the sweater completely separated. Her chest began to heave and tears rolled down her cheeks and she turned her head and stared out the smoky bedroom window. He placed his calloused hand to her chin and tried to guide her face so that she looked at him, but she tightened her neck with all her might, refusing. He may have been in control of her body but not her revulsion.

He smiled and slowly moved the back of the knife down her stomach until the point edged just below the top of her panties.

"Please don't do this," she pleaded, trembling.

The last thing she heard was the rip of the silk material. Everything turned cloudy and horrifyingly distant.

~ * ~

Cold and trembling, Rachel lay curled in a fetal position on the cold dirt floor of her prison cell. She heard the doorknob turn, and immediately pulled back away from the door. "No, please," she whispered to herself. The silhouette of a woman appeared, a spindly shape carved by the light from the hall. "Oh, God," Rachel cried. "Please help me get out of here."

"Here," the soft voice said, placing a metal tray on the floor. "Eat this."

"Are you crazy? I don't want food." She tossed the tray, knocking the contents on the earthen floor. "You've got to get me out of here. I'm begging you."

"I cain't stay. Cain't stay another minute."

"You can't leave me here. Please help me. Please." Like a

caged animal, she swept her hand toward the figure before her. "Get me the hell out of here." Anger rose within her, and she kicked at the cold dirt under her. She yanked on the shackles, her body naked and cold. Teeth clenched, but fear in her heart, she said, "I've got to get home." She pounded her fist. "I have *got* to get home. God, woman. Don't just stand there like an idiot."

"Just do what he says. If you don't wanna die, do what he says. I best go. He'll beat me if he knows I done spoke at you."

"You can't leave me here. You can't!"

Rachel reached for the woman's sweater. It was worn and frayed. Pulling away, the woman grabbed the rickety door handle. The door slammed shut. The metal loop of the lock snapped into the chamber. Rachel was surrounded by darkness again. She pounded the cold floor.

"Help!" She pulled on the shackle as though she could free the bolts from the wall. "Somebody let me out of here!"

Kneeling on the prison floor, sobbing, her body quaked. With her face in her hands, she looked at the ceiling, pleading for God to rescue her. Why had she come to the mountains alone? Her husband was right. She had jeopardized her life, and probably ruined her family's as well.

In the dark, the dampness, and the cold, the silence began to suffocate.

Eight

Bud Crosswhite flipped off the alarm switch, seven minutes before it was about to ring. For thirty-seven years he'd set his alarm for five-thirty. And for thirty-seven years, he woke before the alarm could sound. He wasn't sure if it was because he disliked the shrill sound of the alarm, or he thought Earline deserved a little more rest. Earline often asked Bud why he bothered setting the alarm in the first place, especially on Saturdays during horny head season.

The icy waters of Doe Creek were known for some of the best trout fishing east of the Mississippi. People came from all over in search of the rainbow and brook varieties. The inhabitants of Doe Valley were fond of those fish as well, but during the short run of springtime, there was only one fish worth pursuing—horny heads. The fish, so named because of horn-like spikes located on and around its head, were native to Doe Creek. Though they rarely grew more than eight to ten inches, they were worthy fighters. A tastier fish a skillet never fried.

Bud closed the bedroom door behind him and headed for the kitchen. Decked in saggy green, long-handle underwear, his first order of business was to make coffee. His lower back tightened as he reached for the jar of coffee grounds on top of the refrigerator. Years spent in the tobacco fields had taken its toll, and rising each morning to face the day was getting harder and harder. But Saturday fishing made it a little less painful.

Murle emerged from his room in camouflage overalls. The teenager's tussled brown hair was soon covered by his faded Mountain Co-Op cap.

"Mornin,' Pop," he said, his boots held under his armpit.

"Mornin.' You's a wantin' corn bread or grits with your fish?" Fish for breakfast in Doe Valley was as common as eggs and country ham.

"Corn bread I s'pose. Think I'll go 'head and set the poles in the truck."

Alongside the kitchen was a concrete slab porch that served as part storage facility, part den. Two fishing rods, one Zebco and one Waterking, were perched above the porch door in a gun rack. A shelf beside the gun rack held a small tackle box. A burlap sack, used for carrying the fish retrieved from Doe Creek, lay crumbled in the corner next to an old GE top load washing machine.

From the kitchen window Murle looked ghost-like, his silhouette moving toward a tiny stream located thirty feet from the house. At the edge of the stream Murle lifted the rusty can from the icy water. The sky above him was a faint shade of purple, and the darkness looked in no hurry to yield to the coming morning. Bud watched him place the can in the back of the truck, before noticing the slight outline emerging between massive Iron Mountain and the starless sky.

Talk was limited at the breakfast table and they ate sloppily. Both drank whole milk from jam jars. Their plates were wiped clean with warm cornbread and left on the table when they were through.

As Bud's truck rolled quietly down Pandora Road, the sun made its first appearance above the skyline of Snake Mountain. Long shadows, stretched along the west side of the mountain, slowly retreated as the valley awakened. A soft breeze stirred up fallen leaves left from a brutal winter, swirling the brittle leaves under Bud's beat-up Chevy as he rambled on. Bypassing the usual fishing hole, he drove deeper along the twisting road than normal. Recent rains had chased the horny heads closer to the springs of Doe Creek, and Bud wasn't about to let tradition or stubbornness stop him from finding the fish.

On a hunch, he pulled the truck off the road and onto a protruding patch of devil's apple. Murle retrieved both poles from the bed of the truck, inspecting the lines and hooks to make sure they weren't tangled. Bud lifted the bait can carefully from the cab of the truck.

The sloshing of rubber boots was drowned out by the furious rush of water over age-worn rocks, the water churning white as the stones forced it skyward in controlled chaos. The roar of the creek was as much a part of the stream as the water and the rocks, as if all three were dependent on the other for existence.

They entered a stretch of stream forty feet wide where water chestnuts lined the shore. On the far side, an aged birch tree hugged the stream's edge, its trunk stretching parallel over the water for ten feet before bending skyward. Half its trunk was submerged in the creek. The stream ran about two-and-a-half feet deep, making it a struggle to wade far from the bank.

Bud and Murle stood side by side in the water initially, but after a few minutes, Murle moved downstream. He never seemed to anchor in one spot, even if he was having success. Casting his line, the worm zipped across the water, thanks to the BB-sized metal weight attached near the hook.

On Bud's second cast, the pole jerked forward. Pulling the head of the pole toward him, he turned the reel quickly with his thumb and forefinger. Within seconds, a seven-inch hornie leapt into the air, trying its best to break free of the hook buried deep in its mouth. Bud carefully guided the threshing fish from the water, taking a firm hold of it and removing the hook. He placed it in the burlap sack anchored in the water by a piece of twine tied to a rock.

Murle moved further downstream.

"Set still ever once in a while and you'll have better luck," Bud said.

Murle shrugged and headed toward a fallen willow lying in the water, its branches twisting like streaks of lightning on a Kansas summer night. Bud watched as his boy stepped delicately around the downed tree to access a deeper pool in the creek. He eased over the base of the willow, steadied himself, and drew back his rod.

"Watch that oak behind you," the father said. "Might snag your hook."

Murle looked behind him as he prepared to cast, and Bud grinned, anxious to see Murle cast successfully from such a precarious spot. Murle leaned toward the fallen tree.

"Lord amercy! Pop, come quick!"

Bud reeled in his line as he worked his way to his son. He placed his pole on the bank and entered the water beside the downed tree.

"You okay?"

Murle had dropped his pole, standing in the water like a statue.

Bud reached down, pulling back a limb from the tree, and spotted a blue-toned body lying face down in the water. The corpse's left arm had snagged on a limb of the willow. "Oh my God. Son, back on out of the water. Go on, now."

The boy said nothing, his eyes wide as silver dollars, staring in patent disbelief.

"Son, did you hear me? You don't need to see this. Go call the sheriff."

He backed away from the fallen tree, his eyes fixed on the woman's body. Slipping in the water, he finally made it to the bank. His pole floated downstream. Bud heard the truck sputter to life, and tires squealed as Murle turned the truck around and sped away.

~ * ~

Sheriff Lawrence, doughnut and coffee in hand, opened the door to the Sheriff's Department as the phone rang. "Get that, will you, Barry?" The phone continued to ring. "Barry? Damn, where's that boy?" Lawrence grabbed the receiver. "Sheriff's Department. Lawrence speaking."

"Help! We need help!"

"Calm yourself down a second. Who needs help?"

"This is Murle Crosswhite, Sheriff. Me and Pop were fishin' in Doe Creek near the Shoun's place, and we found a body in the creek bed. Pop sent me back to call for help."

"You say near Shoun's?"

"Yessir. Near the old bean barns."

"I'm on my way," the sheriff said as Deputy Anderson walked in.

"Sorry I'm late, sheriff," Barry said. "I had a flat, and the spare was as smooth as a basketball."

"Never mind that," Lawrence said. "Call the coroner and EMS."

"Why?"

"Bud Crosswhite and his boy found a body in Doe Creek, up at Shoun's while fishin.' I'm headin' out there now."

"I'll meet you there." He picked up the receiver and dialed the coroner's office.

Lawrence jogged to the squad car, his belly shaking under his shirt like a giant gelatin mold.

The ride from town to Doe Creek was a nine-mile trek, and the highway was clogged with farm machinery and pickup trucks. Lawrence debated whether to turn on the siren and crank up the blue lights, but he chose not to. *What difference would it make? The body couldn't become any more dead than it already was.*

He turned off the highway onto Pandora. The sun shone so

brightly across the valley it paled the blue sky, dimming as well the yellow grass and wildflowers. A picture of mountain serenity, though it was anything but along Doe Creek. Lawrence followed the dirt road a mile or so until he saw Bud sitting on the side of the bank. Bud rose when Lawrence pulled beside him.

"Sounds like you got a helluva fish story here, Bud," Lawrence said as he approached the bank.

"I'll show you where the body is. It's all swole up. She ain't wearin' nothin.'"

"How's Murle?"

"He was shook up pretty bad. He's at home with Earline."

"Well, let's have a look."

He followed Bud along the bank to the fallen tree. Bud pointed at the willow and Lawrence waded in alone. As he studied the position of the body, he wondered if she had floated downstream or tossed in the water where she lay. Seeing no apparent wounds on the back, backside, or legs, he placed his hand in the water, sliding the wet hair on the body's head.

"Looks like she was strangled."

"Strangled, you say?" Bud asked, squatting on the bank like a catcher awaiting a pitch. "I'll be damned. I'll just be damned."

"Don't know if that's what killed her. I better notify that detective from Knoxville."

"Who?"

"Detective Jordan. He's workin' the case of that gal what disappeared from the cabin on Iron Mountain." He glanced up toward Iron Mountain, standing tall in stoic meanness, and waded to the bank. His instincts told him either Patricia Darby or Kara Lisle had been found, and not in the manner he was hoping.

Jordan was on the phone at Lawrence's desk talking with forensics when the call came over the radio. Jordan was out the door in minutes.

Johnson County EMS and the coroner soon arrived. News of the naked body spread quickly through the sleepy mountain valley. Death was certainly something they were familiar with, though this one was highly irregular.

~ * ~

Her frail fingers placed the buttered bread on two green plates. She filled two jam jars with milk. It was all he would allow her to fix to keep the girls alive. She walked out the back door and down the path to the prison cells where Rachel and Kara were kept. As she made her way through the weed-laced path, she spotted something sparkling in the sunlight. She had never seen anything so beautiful. She rubbed her fingers across the tiny heart-shaped charm. She clasped the bracelet onto her bony wrist. It sparkled as she held her arm up, palm facing skyward.

~ * ~

Jordan pulled off the dirt road at the scene. He flashed his badge, and Deputy Adams motioned him through the barricade. Dressed in dark blue jeans, a white button-down shirt, and black blazer, his shades fought the glare off the creek. There were over fifty onlookers. Some pointed at Jordan, and all eyes seemed to be on him as he walked. He glanced at them. They looked as though they were observing a sideshow at a carnival instead of a crime scene investigation. The deputies kept them at a distance, which they seemed content with.

Jordan walked into the stream, disregarding the rush of cold water in his black loafers.

"Who have we got here, Sheriff?" He squinted slightly.

"I think it's Patricia Darby," the sheriff replied. "The body is badly bloated, but look at this." The sheriff lifted her left foot from the water.

"A tattoo," said Jordan as he took hold of her leg.

"The left ankle," Lawrence said. "A red heart with a 'P' in the center. Darby's husband described the tattoo to us the day she disappeared."

"Any clue how long she's been here?"

"Hard to tell. Bud Crosswhite says he ain't fished these parts in two years, and not many folks have a need to come this far upstream."

"Let the medical examiner do his thing. I want blood tests, pathology reports. I want to know if she was raped. I want it all."

"Check the marks on her neck," Lawrence pointed out. "Looks like rope burns."

Jordan looked at the quarter-inch indention across her throat. "She was definitely choked. But, was she already dead?" He pointed to a gash across her throat. "Here's a knife wound. And a second one under her ear. Lawrence, let's get dental records. Call Jim Parkinson from forensics at East Tennessee State."

"Yessir."

While Lawrence's men looked for clues at the scene, Jordan nodded to the direction of the road.

"Where's this go?"

"Pandora Road?" said Lawrence. "It heads northwest up the mountain. Ain't hardly travelled anymore. It was built years ago when Johnson County was the bean capital of the world. Now, it's used mostly by moonshiners and meth peddlers. Well, and the occasional fisherman like Bud."

Jordan headed for the car, and soon the bumpy road took him two miles along the creek, dead-ending where a chestnut-laced spring fed into the stream. He stopped the car and looked at the rush of water, observing, studying. Removing his wet socks and shoes and placing them on the hood of his car to dry, he grabbed an old pair of khakis used for trout fishing from the back of the SUV, and slid on rubber waders. The waders were more to provide insulation from the chilly water than to keep his clothes dry.

Doe Creek was running shallow but hard. Jordan chose an elbow-shaped bend which, though deeper, had calmer waters, making it easier to gain his footing while stepping into the stream. The waders, though well worn, blocked most of the artic chill of the waters beating against his legs. Most, not all.

Grabbing a low hanging limb, he steadied himself and moved upstream. The sun reflected off the water so even with sunglasses on, Jordan squinted. Though he'd spent years fishing the creeks of the Appalachians, this spot was as beautiful as anything he'd ever seen.

The creek, now fifty feet wide, was deep and gentle, delicately bent around a steep slope of the mountainside. As the creek began to straighten, the water spilled over a staggered waterfall that spread the width of the creek. In dead center was a heart-shaped rock, twenty feet wide, flanked by rows of smooth, step-like rocks that pulled the water around the giant centerpiece, sending it rapidly down jagged gray rocks before entering a serene pool.

For a moment, the sheer beauty of the place made him forget the reason for his visit.

He took a deep breath, closed his eyes, and touched the chilly water with each hand. He opened his eyes and began looking for signs. To his right, and then to his left, the bank quiet and tranquil. The limb of a dogwood skirted the water on the left bank, just below a second waterfall. Wading slowly, he reached for the limb and untangled a blue bandanna. He examined it for a moment and reached into his shirt pocket, removing a plastic bag. Carefully, he dropped the bandanna into the bag, and returned the bag to his pocket.

Moving out of the water above the falls, he reentered the creek where the water was slow and quiet and sat against a large rock, looking at his surroundings like a hawk searching for field mice. Slowly he turned his torso. A shiny object, dangling from a reed by the edge, caught his eye. He waded to the shimmering item. Loosening it from the reed, he removed a silver earring, a loop two inches in diameter. The lock on the earring clamp was stained with blood. He removed a second bag from his inner pocket and placed the earring in it and sealed the bag.

Jordan exited the water through the reeds, and began looking at the ground beside the bank. Two small, tire marks led from the reeds to a path with heavy undergrowth. He walked alongside the tracks as the path moved into dark woods. The undergrowth became thick, the grass and bushes reaching his waist. The path of the vehicle evaporated as the trail melted into the trees.

He drove back down the dirt road, finding Sheriff Lawrence and the coroner talking beside an orange and white EMS truck.

"Open those doors," Jordan said.

The coroner pulled the doors and slid the gurney out, exposing a black plastic zippered bag. Jordan unzipped the bag so he could see the corpse's head. He looked at the ear.

"What the hell are you doin'?" Lawrence asked.

Sliding his index finger under her left earlobe, he noticed a tear.

"I found this upstream," Jordan said while removing the bag with the earring in it. "I believe it was ripped off her ear as she was put in the creek."

Moving her head to reveal her right ear, he found the matching earring.

"I'll be a suck-egg mule," Lawrence said.

"I saw some tire tracks on the bank near the earring," Jordan said. "They vanished into the woods. Sheriff, find me a guide. Someone who knows this mountain like his own face. I need to know more about the area. Need to know more about what we're dealing with. *Who* we're dealing with."

"I know just the guide. Bet I can get 'em here tomorrow."

"You tell him to meet me here tomorrow morning at nine. On second thought, make it eight. We got a killer to catch."

Nine

He had their life mapped out. He was a planner in the biggest sense of the word. And after he fell in love with Kara, he knew theirs would be a perfect world; two children, a dog, a cat, and in that order. The first child would come three years and nine months after the wedding date. The next child would come exactly two years after the birth of the first. At least that was the plan prior to the trip to Iron Mountain. Now, Jason couldn't think of anything but the present. The future meant nothing; not until Kara was safe again.

Nine days had passed since her disappearance. He'd become quite familiar with the back roads of Iron Mountain, scouring the countryside, looking, calling her name. He couldn't sit still in his motel room, knowing she was out there somewhere in all that expanse of mountain. It was his idea to come to the cabin in first place. And so he searched, looking carefully from the road into the windows and screen doors of old shacks and houses where untrusting eyes stared back.

Jason paced the faded green linoleum floor of his motel room. The Valley View was Laurel City's lone motel, located a mile west of town, where Highway 47 entered Doe Valley. A two-wing building, it stretched out on both sides of the small office and restaurant like aviator wings.

The motel walls closed in and Jason walked about restlessly waiting for news. He snatched his keys from beside the rotary phone and walked to his car and rode west on Highway 47 into the night. The stars illuminated the moonless sky in a way that carved Iron Mountain into a massive silhouette of blackness.

Should he drive up Shady Valley again, the dark of night notwithstanding?

Low on fuel, Jason pulled into a place named Dewey's. It had one gas pump out front. The pump island had no cover—just a silver and white pump, a water spigot, and an air hose. Removing his wallet, Jason noticed the dusty pump had no ability to process a credit card. So he flipped the silver arm on the side and refueled then walked inside Dewey's to pay.

To the left was a small counter littered with lottery ticket boxes, a jar of pig's feet, and pickled eggs. In the middle were shelves of dry and canned goods. Beer and sodas lined the refrigerators against the back wall.

As Jason paid the woman behind the counter, muffled music came from behind him. The sound came through an open door across the room that led into some sort of honky tonk.

Maybe a few beers would help.

Maybe the person who'd taken her was there, bragging about it, and Jason could beat him within an inch of his life after he found out where she was. He certainly didn't want to go back and stare at the four walls of the motel room. He parked beside the Chevy and shut off the engine. Rapping his fingers on the steering wheel, he took a deep breath. *Why the hell not?*

He repositioned his car in front of the bar. There was a wooden door with a poster-board sign advertising cheap beer. Several pickups and a '60's Chevy were parked out front.

Inside the dingy joint, there was a square room with a small bar, four round tables with chairs, a pool table, and a jukebox. He looked about the place, and into the eyes of everyone there, looking for signs. Guilt, fear, smugness. Surely someone's eyes held the answers.

Two men playing pool stopped to watch Jason walk to a stool at the bar. A woman at the jukebox, wearing a tube top and a frayed jean skirt, tapped the glass while deciding on a song. Two men sat at the bar arguing whether Richard Petty was still the king of stock car racing.

"What'll you have?" the man behind the bar asked.

"A beer. Any kind will do."

The man opened a can and set it on the musty counter. Jason took a quick swallow and looked at the mounted boar's head on the back wall. One of the men playing pool walked outside. *Walking after Midnight* played while Jason chugged his beer. A few more patrons entered and Jason watched them through the mirror located behind the bar. He rubbed the ring of the beer can as the song continued.

He ran his hand through his hair. Maybe he missed

something back at the cabin. A clue, a sign. What if she was near the cabin when he took off to Johnson's General Store? Maybe he was looking too far away and not paying attention to the immediate surroundings. Was there a shed behind the cabin? He couldn't remember. He was working on his third beer when two men walked up beside him.

The men ordered a beer and stood at the bar, their elbows on the counter. They tipped the scales around two-fifty each, tree-trunk solid. One of them, a dark-haired man with a straw cowboy hat, wore a black and gray flannel shirt with the sleeves torn off at the bicep. He had a large, brass belt buckle and worn, work boots. His partner was shorter, with a big belly hanging over his brown belt. He wore no hat and his hair was long and stringy, his beard scraggly and his face with pockets of acne scars.

After taking a sip, the man wearing the hat said, "Well, looka here, Jakob. We are in the company of city folk."

Jason looked straight ahead.

"Hot damn. Willie, I believe you're right. Fancy jeans; leather jacket. I'm sure that's his sports car outside. Hell, he oughta be buyin' us all a round o' drinks."

"Hey, boy," Willie said, turning so he faced Jason. Jason took a sip and glanced at his beer can. "Where's your hospitality? Don't you know since you's a visitor to our cozy establishment, it's your rightly duty to buy us locals a drink?"

He looked at the barkeep cleaning mugs behind the bar.

"Are you deaf, boy?" Jakob asked. "My brother's talkin' to you."

He removed a ten-dollar bill from his wallet, tossing it on the counter. "Buy your own damn drink." He turned toward the door.

The brothers towered over Jason as they stepped in front of him.

"Out of my way, redneck," he said, moving to his left to sidestep the men.

"What's with the hostility, city boy?" said Willie. "You pissed because your lady friend up and left you?"

"What the hell do you know about it?" He shoved Willie into the pool table. Jakob grabbed Jason from behind, pushing him forward until his face was flush against the green velvet tabletop of the pool table.

"Git your slimy face off my pool table, shitass," said one of the men playing pool. The player pushed his stick against Jason's neck. "What the hell you doin' in here, boy? They don't serve wine and cheese here." He rammed his stick into Jason's side. "Jakob, take your boy outside. We's tryin' to master the game of billiards."

Jakob pulled Jason from the table, spun him around, and punched him in the ribcage. He fell to the floor while the bartender turned away and continued cleaning beer glasses. Willie's boot drove into his hip, and when Jakob pulled him across the floor by his jacket, he left a trail of blood on the floor. Outside in the parking lot, Willie pulled Jason to his feet and punched him across the jaw.

Jason's knees buckled. Rage stormed through his veins. He slammed his hands into Willie's chest, knocking him back to where Willie struggled to keep from falling. "Where's my wife, you country ape?" His hands were clenched, readying himself for Willie to charge. He wiped the blood from his mouth with his sleeve and then placed his fists in front of him.

To his left, Jakob stood. "Might want to worry more about yourself," he said, removing a knife from a sheath on his belt. While Jason eyed the knife, Willie hit him again, dropping him to his knees.

A combination of blood and tears trickled from Jason's eyes, though the tears were not from fear. Inside him was anger, a frustration, foreign to him. Disoriented, he contemplated which brother to lunge for. He wanted both, and for a moment, imagined what he could do with a baseball bat to their skulls.

"Git up, son." Jakob handed the knife to his brother and seized Jason by the collar of his leather bomber jacket, lifting him to his feet. Pushing Jason against a green pickup, they stood nose to nose. Jakob's breath was warm and putrid. His brown teeth, clinched tightly, were partially hidden by the matted hair of his beard. His cold, intimidating eyes cut through Jason. He slapped Jason's left cheek, the sting reverberating across his face.

"I got a good mind to let Willie carve on your face," he said. "He ain't had that kind of fun in a long while. Waddaya think?"

"Do it, you fat bastard. I don't give a shit." He spit in Jakob's face.

Jakob backhanded him, and took hold of his shirt with both hands.

"I wouldn't mind slicin' him up some," Willie said.

Jakob laughed. "If we see your lady friend, we'll take good care of her. Real good care of her." He rubbed his hand across his crotch and grinned.

Jason grabbed Jakob's shirt at the shoulders. "You son of a bitch." His fist bounced off Jakob's neck.

"Sumbitch?" Jakob slapped Jason's face again. "City boy callin' *me* a sumbitch."

"Let me carve on him, Jakob," Willie stepped beside Jakob and placed the knife to Jason's chin. "Is that what you want, city boy? Want me to give you an Iron Mountain shave?"

Jakob slammed his fist into Jason's midsection, sternum high, and his knees buckled. "Answer him, boy." Jakob forced Jason to stand, and again pushed him against the truck. "Answer him." He refused to respond, and Willie's fist landed flush against his chin, dropping him to the pebble-laced ground. His vision was cloudy and blood had filled one eye so that he couldn't see. He wondered briefly if the man working the store next door had called the police.

Willie squatted till his knee was close to Jason's head. "Tell you what, boy. This is your lucky day. We're gonna let you leave. But next time we won't be so friendly." Jason, blood coming from his mouth, stared back, saying not a word. "Now get the hell outta here."

Jason gingerly rolled onto his hands and knees, shook his head, and slowly stood. The brothers watched Jason stumble to his car. With blood dripping down his leather jacket, he drove slowly back to the Valley View.

Ten

"We need food supplies," he mumbled in between bites.

"We's 'bout out," she agreed, scrubbing plates in a metal sink.

"Go to the shanty. Should be some preserves in the springhouse. Check the cabinet for lard cans. Might be some meal still in 'em."

"I'll fetch some after I feed them gals."

"Don't give 'em no more than they need. Just enough to keep 'em alive."

After she gave Rachel and Kara biscuits and buttermilk, she made her way down the slope to a small shack hunters used during bear season. She moved quietly to the shanty, located a half-mile to the east, and for a moment looked northward toward Holston Mountain, contemplating. But he'd find her if she left. She knew he would.

The warped wooden door was difficult to open. Cold and drafty, the smell of stale urine and rotting wood hit her when she entered, though they were familiar odors. Across the cold floor she walked, to the pantry where she found five jars of fig preserves on the bottom shelf. They were covered in dust, but looked edible. She couldn't be choosy, so she placed them in a burlap sack.

In the cabinet was a one-gallon can of meal. She struggled to lift it into the sack. The food supply weighed heavy on her when she laid the coarse burlap across her bony shoulder. She scanned the room for anything worth taking, even though she didn't have the strength to carry much. She rubbed her forehead and walked out the door, moving slowly as she headed back to the house.

~ * ~

Jordan sat in his SUV at the edge of Pandora Road. Doe Creek carved a path between hills seemingly untouched by time. Like unraveled twine, the shallow, swift-moving creek wove around banks of yellow grass and hardwoods. The water slipped under a rickety, ivy-covered wooden bridge, eliciting memories of his childhood days in nearby Damascus.

The youngest of four boys, he grew up on a small farm where days were long and the workload hard. Being the youngest awarded him no special favors. He was expected to work just as much as the others. His father often reminded him and his brothers at the dinner table, saying, "If you expect to eat, expect to work." Chore lists were long and done without exception, illness or injury being the only way out. And those were closely scrutinized. Excusable injuries were those of the broken bone variety; illness mandated fever well over a hundred degrees.

Jordan loved to fish, and was fascinated by the sleekness and power of rainbow trout. Countless times he'd stand on the covered bridge above Backbone Creek on the way to school to watch the trout run downstream. The times he just beat the tardy bell were too numerous to count.

A bony knuckle tapped on the driver's side of Jordan's window, bringing his trip down memory lane to an end. As he lowered the window, a weathered face leaned in.

"You the detective?" said a voice that sounded hardened by years of smoking.

"Mornin,' ma'am," he said. "Can I help you?"

"Buford said you's a needin' a guide."

"Yes ma'am, I am. I'm just waiting on him to get here."

"Ready when you are."

"'Scuse me?"

"We can't get much done with you sittin' in that car. So, you need to get off your ass and foller me."

"Ma'am, this is a serious situation I'm dealing with. I don't have time for…"

"Name's Emma Douglas. I lived my whole life in this neck of the woods, and I'm the best guide in the county. You gettin' out the car, or ain'tcha?"

As a man who had spent sixteen years investigating crime scenes, interrogating witnesses and suspects, he had seen it all: gruesome bodies; terrifying criminals; shifty informants; untrusting recluses hiding in city alleys. But he wasn't quite prepared for this elderly version of Annie Oakley. Her slender body moved, stilt-like, toward a light-gray station wagon years removed from its last washing. The pseudo-wood grained panels on the sides of the doors drooped like banana peels.

He removed his shades from the dashboard and got out of his car.

Approaching the passenger door, the heads of a floppy-eared basset hound and a black chow poked out the backseat window. The chow bared his teeth in a vicious growl. The basset hound barked wildly.

"Hush up," Emma shouted. Turning toward Jordan, she said, "Don't worry none 'bout The General and Dan'l Boone. They won't hurt you. Not 'lessin you try to get frisky with me."

"I don't think that'll be a problem."

"Don't be so sure. I'm quite the catch."

"I'm sure you are."

They entered the front seat from opposite doors, sitting amongst dog biscuit boxes, partially used Kleenexes, and six cans of Skoal. Her hat, a crème-colored apparatus with a white, fuzzy bill and earflaps turned upward, rested just above her eyes. Before cranking the car, she slid the hat up her forehead, revealing curly salt-and-pepper hair.

"Well, I see you're a neat freak," he said.

"I see you're a smart ass."

Jordan shook his head and scratched his eyebrows.

Emma talked of how she lived all her sixty-two years in Doe Valley, two miles from the foot of Iron Mountain. She had survived over thirty years on her own after her husband Eb was killed in an explosion at the lime kiln. She became a guide to pay the bills and feed her three children, and was considered an expert tracking anything from bears to lost hikers throughout Johnson County. And based on the way she spoke, she was proud of her achievements and high status in the outdoor community.

"What's on Iron Mountain you're so anxious to see?"

"There's a killer on the loose."

"No shit."

He looked strangely at her and continued. "Two women have been taken from a cabin on Iron Mountain. Found the body of one in Doe Creek off Pandora Road near Bryson's Spring. Tracks lead from where her body was placed in the water to a trail that slips up the mountain."

"That trail follers the crick right to the footsteps of Iron

Mountain." Her hands moved through the air as if she were guiding the creek herself. "The crick then turns west, and the trail moves up deeper into the mountain."

"Who lives up there?"

"The folks of Stoney Creek. They keep to themselves, and they sure don't take to visitors. There's stills up in them hollers. They also say they's them things called meth labs. Ain't rightly sure what that is. A rough, rough area. Meaner'n a bag of snakes. You think whoever threw that gal in the crick lives on Iron Mountain?"

"I don't know, but I sure plan on findin' out."

"Well, let's get a move on then."

Emma's car rambled along Pandora Road. Jordan instructed her to stop at the spot where he found Patricia Darby's earring. The General anxiously leapt through the window. Old Dan'l, the basset hound, was content waiting for Emma to open the back door.

Dressed in green dungarees, a khaki hunting shirt, and faded, untied leather boots, Emma opened a can of Skoal. She pinched the soft tobacco between her right thumb and index finger, pushing a thimble full between her brown, lower teeth, and her chapped, lower lip. The strong odor of menthol quickly evaporated in the mid-day breeze.

"Well detective, what say we do some hill climbin'?"

"Think you're up to it?"

Emma laughed and turned toward the creek. "Crazy city folk. Never had much use for you."

The dogs led the way, with Emma and Jordan close behind.

The clouds thickened, and the sky held a dark, solemn tone. What began as a light breeze turned into a chilly wind. Jordan slipped his sunglasses into the side pocket of his jean jacket and followed Emma up the winding trail.

"We got snow movin' in," Emma said.

"This late in the spring?"

"The wind's blowin' straight in from the north. There'll be snow on the ground by nightfall."

"You can tell that by the direction of the wind?"

"Yep. Well, that and this here ankle." She lifted her foot. "It hurts like a toothache right 'afore a snow. And right now, it feels like it needs a root canal."

"That a fact?"

"Yep. So we better get our asses a movin.' That is, lessin'

you want to get snowed in with me."

"Maybe some other time."

Emma led the way on a trail that cut a path along the eastern side of Iron Mountain. The pair began the climb, leaving the spot where he found Patricia Darby's earring. The dirt trail, littered with marble-size gray rocks and barely wide enough for an automobile, rolled into a tight valley, known to the locals as a "holler." The slope of the trail rose gently skyward at first, splitting the creek and small hills of brown, spotty grass where cattle grazed. A makeshift fence of poles made from locust tree limbs, bound by wire, hugged the trail to keep cattle from slipping away. Scraggly bouquets of unknown weeds surrounded the base of the knotty posts.

Rundown shacks, built for the sole purpose of survival, dotted the hollow. The roofs were made of rusted tin, constructed in a steep V-shape. The exterior walls of the shacks were a dreary mixture of wood and peeling shingles that resembled brick façade wallpaper. Small porches were filled with washtubs, milk crates, and makeshift rocking chairs. Steps leading to rickety porches were made of light brown stone. Tiny, wooden outhouses with crescent moon door carvings bordered the back of the houses not far from wells covered with tin slats.

As Jordan walked, curious eyes peered at them from cracked, dirty windows. Faces with no expression, like souls with no eyes to the future, and none set to reflect on the past. Two children, most likely brother and sister, ran barefoot along the creek bed in pursuit of a wild hen. He guessed them to be seven, maybe eight-years-old. Their clothing was identical; baggy, gray wool pants and brown flannel shirts. Jordan smiled at the girl. Her dark brown eyes stared untrustingly back. Her face was dusted with crusty mud, and her Dutch-boy hair was tussled.

A woman called from the house and the children ran to the safety of their shack as she opened the front door to let them in. She closed the door just enough to hide from view yet still watch the strangers.

"These people look like they've led hard lives."

"It's always been this way 'round these parts. Barely enough food to survive on. It's the way life is. I ain't livin' like Donald Trump myself, but I don't have it near as bad as these folks. And it'll git worse the further up the mountain we go. Most of these people have never left the mountain. Up yonder is Donnie Ray's shack. He's a distant relative, though I cain't rightly remember how we're related. He's lived there by himself for over forty years. His wife Vernie died durin' childbirth. He ain't got runnin' water. No electricity. Just like most of these folks."

"No electricity?"

"Ain't never had it, and if they did, they ain't got no way to pay fer it."

When they passed Donnie Ray's house, he stepped to the doorway. Bone thin, curved shoulders, sunken chin. His hair was thin, combed across a bald crown.

"Emma," he nodded.

"Waddaya say there, Donnie Ray?"

"What brings you up this way?"

"Just passin' through. Tryin' to make a buck."

"I heard that."

"Takin' this city boy for a stroll up Stoney Creek."

"Stoney Creek," he repeated. "I wouldn't if I was you. Why don't you visit a spell?"

"I cain't, Donnie. But I'll come back with a custard pie next week if the creek don't rise."

"Well," was all Donnie Ray said.

Donnie watched them from the porch as they walked on, a look of eternal despair in his eyes. Jordan wondered how people like Donnie Ray endured life. How they found the strength to face each day, and what drove them on to face a new day other than the basic instinct of survival?

The slope of the hollow rose and fell in a fairly smooth fashion as they stepped closer to the shadow of Iron Mountain, and the small hills moved in shape and direction around them. They came upon a patch of thick poplars and locusts on the left side of the trail, and it led into an isolated hill that rose sharply skyward, five hundred feet tall at its crest. The knoll looked barren except for the jade-colored grass that blanketed it, as though God Almighty draped the grass upon the hill like a bed sheet tossed across a mattress.

From where he and Emma stood, the only backdrop behind the hill was the pale sky, making it appear that nothing except gray space existed beyond it. On top of the hill was a single holly tree at the edge of a small graveyard. The silhouettes of tombstones against the insipid horizon stood out in two-dimensional shape.

"Any idea who's buried up there?" asked Jordan.

"The Shoun family. The Shouns owned land throughout this holler for a hundred years or more. Only a few of 'em still alive. They say when Venus is just beyond the curve of the waxing crescent moon, you can see the shadow of Jeremiah Shoun walkin' 'round. He was killed one night by some men from Stoney Creek. Talk was that he was carryin' on with a gal up there. He was found gutted, hangin' from that holly tree."

"Killers ever caught?"

"Hardly. In them days, no lawman would dare set foot on Iron Mountain, and more specifically, Stoney Creek. Not if he had hopes of sharin' a meal at the dinner table with his kinfolk ever again."

The slope of Iron Mountain began to rise dramatically, and the hollow melted into towering white pines and oaks at the base of the mountain.

"The trail gets steep now, and you're gonna have to watch your footin.' At some point you'll need some assistance, and laurel limbs are the easiest to grab hold to, but they ain't everywhere on the mountain. So, just grab whatever you can."

Jordan sat on a nearby, lime-laced boulder, tying his left boot string, and making sure his gun was securely fastened above his ankle. He double-knotted each boot, and then zipped his jacket.

"How long you gonna rest on that rock?" she said as she removed a fresh pinch of snuff from her pocket. "It ain't gonna stay daylight forever. This ain't Alaska you know."

"Give me a second. I don't do this kind of thing on a daily basis."

"This ain't nothin.' You oughtta try climbin' it from the west side. It's so steep you feel like you're walkin' up a skyscraper. I ain't lyin.'"

"Where's that smoke comin' from?" Jordan asked as he pointed to light plumes drifting above the thick tree line along the western skyline. The smoke curled up into the mountain breeze in swirling rings before dissipating into a fog that had quickly formed.

"That's Stoney Creek Holler."

"Lead the way."

"Okay. It's your funeral."

Eleven

The fog thickened into dense, smoky clouds that skirted the treetops. As the billowy bands erased the skyline of Iron Mountain, only the steep slope of the mountain identified north and south. They walked in silence, Emma sure in her steps. The General and Dan'l looked as though they'd had enough. They stretched their tired paws on a patch of grass along the creek bed, in essence throwing in the towel. Doe Creek began to veer west, and the incline of Iron Mountain was about to become almost vertical. Maybe in their younger days the mutts could have made the climb. But with them long in the tooth, Jordan gathered they would sit this one out.

Though leaves had returned to most of the hardwoods, the backdrop of clouds darkened their texture, making them look similar, color wise, to the rugged bark of the trees. After a half hour of climbing, Jordan stopped to catch his breath.

"Good Lord," Jordan asked as he took hold of a limb of a white pine. "Why do these folks live so far away from civilization?"

"That's the way they want it. They don't need nobody; don't want nobody. They got that hair-brained notion from old Gaines Logan."

"Who?"

"Gaines Logan. The Hermit."

"Hermit?"

"Yep. The feller what lived forty years on Iron Mountain with nothin' but a steer, a dog, and a rattlesnake."

"Forty years? Sounds like Donnie Ray."

"Hell, son, you don't understand. Where Donnie Ray lives is considered city to the conditions on Iron Mountain. Donnie may live alone, but he ain't isolated like Gaines was."

"Since this Gaines fellow was born and bred up here, maybe that's all he knew."

"No, sir. Weren't born here. He was born in Doe Valley,

same as me. It was in the late 1800's. Was an orphan boy, and he stayed with various kinfolk. He worked at an early age, and he pocketed away money when he could 'cause he never knew if he'd be put out on his own at any moment. When he turned twenty-three, as the story goes, he took the money he'd saved and headed west. He met a couple of men on a train headed to Missouri I believe it was, and they robbed and beat him."

"You don't say."

"He figgered the world was evil, so he came back home and took to buildin' a small shack and a tiny barn on top of this mountain. Forty years. My great-uncle, Satch Lowe, found him dead in his bed, his dog lyin' on his chest."

"Sounds like something from a book of tall tales."

"But this man's story weren't no tall tale. He came down off the mountain twice a year. My grandpappy had a small store along Doe Creek. Gaines traded corn and taters to Pappy for flour, lard, and dry goods. One day Pappy asked Gaines why he liked livin' all alone on the mountaintop. Gaines told Pappy 'there weren't nothin' like sleepin' under the chandeliers of heaven.' Gaines said Iron Mountain was so big it could hold back thunder, that lightnin' couldn't reach over its top."

"Old Gaines sounds like he was an odd individual."

"About a mile up above Stoney Creek is a gravesite where they chunked him in the ground by his favorite hemlock. They put up a nice tombstone, and tossed his pots and pans into a slab of concrete so people would remember him. And there's others just like him livin' up here. No stores. No interferin' with the outside world."

"Sounds like we'll have a fun time with these folks."

"Yep. Now it's time to turn up the fire under your shapely fanny, city boy."

He looked at his watch, knowing Jessie was about to start her dance class. He smiled, thinking how cute she looked in her pink dance outfit.

After an hour of climbing the trail, they entered a slender gorge that gave them a reprieve from the extreme climb. On a trail three feet wide, littered with leaves, they crossed a tiny stream that, compared to Doe Creek, looked like little more than a drainage ditch.

"Where's this water come from?" he asked. "Is this is Stoney Creek?"

"Stoney Creek ain't a creek at all. It's more legend of a large creek that carved out the valley between Iron and Doe Mountain. Did you know the Appalachians are the oldest mountains in the world?"

"I think I remember reading that in my school days."

"Well, this here creek comes from a spring up near the peak. It's the only source of drinkin' water on the mountain."

"It's not exactly rip-roaring, is it?"

"It ain't much to look at now, but it cranks out at its source like a fire hose. It leads up to the holler."

The creek sliced a path from the mountainside, a vein of continual motion and then rose sharply, but the terrain alongside it was maneuverable. After they climbed a thousand feet, they walked into a small opening littered with bundles of copper tubing and cast iron barrels. The aroma of a woodburning stove permeated the rapidly cooling air.

"Emma, why do these people have stills? Prohibition ended seventy years ago. I'm sure it's a lot easier driving to the liquor store for the folks in this county. Cheaper too, I'd imagine."

"Well, it's a bit of a ride so it would take some effort. But mostly it's all about doin' what their daddy's and granddaddy's done. Some swear by it, sayin' there ain't no comparison. It's like eatin' a meal in your granny's kitchen instead of some truck-stop diner that offers up a meat and three veggies. Some say that it's like the old days, meetin' runners creekside to get a mason jar of hooch."

"Then what's with the meth labs?"

"Well, some of the younger generation's got what they say is 'a pulse on the community,' and that this meth is a right popular way for folks to chase their blues away. From what I gather, it's a sight cheaper too. But, Lord, I've seen the results of a few 'uns who've got all caught up in it, and it's plum scary."

"It's bad stuff, Emma. Sad thing is, it's spreading everywhere. Dangerously addictive."

"Well, I say they should just stick to the haticol. You know, moonshine. Other than some cobwebs in the brain the followin' day, white lightning is pretty harmless."

They neared the top of the mountain.

"Are these mountain folk as mean as legend has it? Do we need to be worried about getting shot?"

"You stay close to me and you should be okay. I need to tell you about the man who runs the show up here. Name's Bum Whitfield, and he calls the shots. Bum is the self-proclaimed mayor of the 'holler.' The others just fall in line. They do what he says. If not, they find themselves an early grave."

The stares of untrusting eyes again followed them, this time from six wooden shacks scattered among thick poplars and hemlocks and elms. The homes, similar to the ones they'd passed far below, had no sense of placement. Two homes were less than twenty feet apart, facing the southern side of Doe Valley. Three others faced east, almost in stepping-stone order. The last home looked down at the others, built between two Norwegian spruces close to eighty feet tall.

A small gathering of men sat in circular fashion in front of the home located highest in altitude on the mountainside. Buckets, two tree stumps, and a three-legged chair provided the seating on the sunken porch of the house.

With Emma leading the way, they walked guardedly toward the men. A pair of mangy dogs, neither distinguishable as to breed, began circling the intruders.

"Easy, boys," a voice yelled from the porch.

The dogs fell in line behind Emma, most likely due to the smell of her dogs. To Jordan's left an elderly woman sat on a rocker in front of what looked like a woodshed. She stared glassy-eyed at him, with no sense of facial expression. Mangled strands of briars and orchard grass hid her to the waist, and light plumes of smoke from her corncob pipe drifted above her head.

"Afternoon, Bum," Emma said to the elderly man who sat perched on the three-legged chair so that it leaned against the house. "How you boys a doin'?"

"Who's your hikin' buddy?" Bum asked.

Jordan half-smiled and walked slowly to the tin-covered porch where Bum sat. "Thomas Jordan. I'm a detective from Knoxville." Jordan reached toward the porch and extended his hand.

"Detective?" Bum said with obvious mock respect, making no effort to shake Jordan's hand. "A real life detective. Ain't that somethin' boys? Should we salute?" A handful of men, easily spanning three generations, chuckled.

"That won't be necessary," Jordan responded, smiling as he made eye contact with the men as they stood. "But I could use your help."

Bum rose from his chair, and moved to the front rail of his porch. Looking down at Jordan he said, "What kinda help?" Bum wore baggy pants made of some blend of wool. His long-handle shirt was a brownish hue, and the collar was visible thanks to a gap caused by a missing button from his dark flannel shirt. A gray felt hat covered most of his stringy, silver hair. He spit a wad of tobacco juice off the side of the porch, chasing two brown hens away from the steps.

"A woman's body was found yesterday near Shoun's. Was floating in Doe Creek. Seems like she was placed in the water about two miles upstream."

"A body you say? Sounds mighty serious."

"I'd say quite serious. A second woman is missing as well. So you can understand my desire to ask folks around these parts if they know of any suspicious goings on." He paused. Had his words fallen on deaf ears? His intent wasn't to solicit answers. Rather, to let them know that he was a man dead intent on solving the crimes. "Something that could help us in finding who did these awful things. To help make sure this person pays for his indiscretions."

"Hell, maybe it's the gal in the crick you should talk to."

The men laughed; a laughter that seemed more forced than genuine. The elderly woman beside the woodshed regarded them all with curiosity. No other women or children were in sight, though they probably viewed the scene from small windows and cracked doors.

"Yeah, maybe so," Jordan replied, a smile with the same smirk as Bum's. "But, it'd be more fun to get the information from you if I could."

While he waited on Bum to speak, he spotted Roby Greer retreating inside the doorway to the shack below Bum's.

"We don't know nothin' 'cept what goes on up here. Ain't none of our business what happens in the valley. Ain't nobody else's business what goes on up here."

"Well, it *did* happen up here. The women were taken from a cabin on Iron Mountain. So, if you only know what goes on up here, then you sound like just the guy I need to talk with."

Bum squinted one eye, studying Jordan as though he were trying to understand some deeper purpose inside the detective's head. "You know,"" Bum said, "it's the attitude within a feller's soul that controls the doors that open, and those that don't."

Emma stood fifteen feet behind Jordan and cleared her throat.

"Mind if I have a look around?" Jordan asked. Had he planted the seeds of discourse in the so-called leader of Iron Mountain?

"There ain't nothin' to see."

"I'll just check for myself."

Bum walked off the porch, and when he stood in front of Jordan, the other men circled uncomfortably close around the detective.

"We don't like your kind snoopin' 'round here. Nothin' personal." Bum's eyes stared steely into Jordan's.

Jordan held his ground, and returned the stare into Bum's hazel eyes. "My kind? What exactly is *my* kind?"

"The kind that thinks a badge gives him free rein to trespass."

"You might run the show up here, and that's all well and good in your little world. But, there's a killer loose, and my hunch is he's among us."

"Shitfire. Ain't no killers up here. We're peace lovin' folk."

"I hope for your sake you're right."

"My sake? You might want to show a little more concern about your own well bein.' Now, why don't you slide back on down the mountain? Don't mess around where you don't belong."

An Iron Mountain wall erected, Jordan could get no further. With a nod, he turned and Emma followed him to the thick brush and out of the clearing. The spinster sat in her rocker, with an emotionless expression, yet a strange sparkle in her blue eyes. Jordan stepped close to the woman. She wore a green bonnet tied tightly around her face and under her chin, with a curly ball of gray hair appearing below the round bill of the hat.

"God will judge both the wicked and the righteous," she said in a raspy voice that seemed to take all of her power to force words from her mouth. Her chin bobbed up and down as if she were chewing on something. It appeared as though her long nose and chin would touch. She had a thin clump of black hair on her chin, and she rubbed it with her hand.

"Ma'am?" Jordan asked. Emma stayed on the path they'd walked as though she was afraid to hear what the old woman had to say.

"He'll judge us all. There will be a time to account for every deed."

"Is there any specific deed to which you're referring?"

"Don't set your sights on the dead. They cain't be helped no more."

"But their death can be avenged. And that's my aim."

"Don't feel sorry for the dead, for they be happier than the livin.'"

"How do you figure?"

"The good book says so. You need to study it up some. Hold the words close to your heart."

"Do you know anything that can help me? Do you know something about the girl who was found, her throat slit from ear to ear?"

"Again, it's not the dead to feel sorry fer. Though the best of all is them that ain't yet been. They ain't seen the evil that's been done in this world."

The woman put her pipe in her mouth, took a long draw, looking off to the distance as though the unborn called for her attention.

"I told you those folks were crazy," Emma said when they began to walk away from Stoney Creek. "You talked to one who ain't got no clue what reality is, and the others you got riled like a nest of hornets."

"Part of the job. What's above these old shacks?"

"Nothin' much. A couple of stills, maybe. Why?"

"I want to slide up above and have a look around."

"Let's go then."

"No, not you. I want to go alone."

"I ain't leavin you up here," she said. "It will put your life at hazard. Not to mention you'll get lost surer than shit. I got a reputation to uphold, and if I let you stay up and freeze to death, break your neck fallin' in a ravine, or worse, gettin' your skinny ass shot off, my days of bein' a guide is over. Besides, my ankle says the snow is commencin' to fall, so I can't leave you here in good conscience."

Reaching in his jean pocket, he removed four, twenty-dollar bills from his rear pocket. "Thanks for your time, Emma. Thanks for the company."

"You don't know what you're gettin' yourself into. This ain't the city streets of Knoxville."

"I'll be okay, Emma. Thanks for escorting me up here. But

now it's time for me to earn my paycheck."

"Suit yourself."

She disappeared into the thicket.

Twelve

The loud, constant rush of water was a beacon and Jordan found the narrow stream. He followed it northward. Above him, poplars and maples rocked in the wind, so straight and mighty in their path he became small and unaccountable, a man out of place and out of touch with the land he travelled. He'd heard stories when he was a boy, his father gathering him and his brothers around the fireplace to talk of the old country. As he walked the mountain, he sensed the ghosts of the early settlers around him, the trees the fiddles of the dead, playing a haunting song as the trees rocked and swayed. He imagined the souls of men who'd spent their lives searching for light in the darkness of that mountain walking alongside him.

As he made his way along the creek toward the mountain's jagged crest, there was movement below him. He conjured up the dismal tune of "Bury Me Beneath the Willow" in his head, thinking back to the nights his mother swayed in the darkness to the song when she thought no one was watching. He was a country boy, but the nature of country rose up around him to where the relativity of it had new meaning. The smell of sweat, the aching in his joints, and the weariness of his soul a result of walking in a land where he was not only a novice, but unaccountable in the ways of hard life and survival.

The smoke-filled shacks stood below him and he buttoned his jacket. The strengthening winds rattled the trees, and the late afternoon temperature dipped into the thirties. The sky, looming lower and darker, warned of the oncoming storm; a warning Jordan ignored. Gripping sturdy white pines and maple limbs, he struggled to remain upright on the sharp incline of the mountainside as he surveyed the land. The mountain gave full warning of its wrath, but could the visitor heed it?

Jordan scoped the rugged terrain, and turned his head

skyward to a hawk's cry. The bird appeared as a black silhouette against the backdrop of the ominous clouds as it lit on a craggy poplar limb. It called again, a majestic witness surely more in tune with the past than the present. In that past was the blood of the new beginning gathered from the ones whose bones now lay below the land, the ones who laid the very existence of life upon that mountain. Jordan pushed on, and came across a slender dirt trail that snaked its way along the mountainside. As he neared the crest, he entered a land where mountain laurels bunched together in smothering, evil groupings. Approaching cautiously, Jordan moved closer. A wooden door, resembling entrances to old mineshafts he'd seen on television, was hidden by the laurels. He walked slow and deliberate to the door and lifted the splintered board that served as a handle. As he did, a faint voice called out from the other side. Jordan drew his revolver.

The dank chill of the dark, musty cavern cut him to the bone. Taking out the small flashlight he carried on his belt, Jordan dipped his head and entered the pitch-black cave. A steady drip from seepage overhead bounced off a tin can. He maneuvered around the cave among broken bottles and trash, approaching a splintered plywood door. An open padlock hung on a black metal door hinge.

Jordan entered slowly as the creak of the rotting door echoed into the darkness. Peering through the narrow opening, a lantern hung from a hook, dimly illuminating a pair of shackles hanging from the stone wall. A woman's moans filtered through the cavern corridor. Moving twenty feet further into the cave, a light slipped from underneath another door, and he approached it. He turned his head as he stood at the entrance and a sob resonated. Jordan opened it slightly and in the room a naked woman stood, bound in shackles. Her dungeon was no wider than ten feet, while the depth from the door to the back wall was perhaps a dozen feet.

There were wood beams, two beside her, one above, that held the shackles that squeezed her wrists. The angle of the shackles from the beams forced her to keep her arms up as though she was being crucified. Whether done so by accident or for torture, the shackles kept her in a position where her knees couldn't quite touch the ground. Her oily, brunette hair covered most of her dark, morose eyes. Her grimy face wore bruises about the cheek and chin. She barely raised her head when Jordan entered.

"Please, no," she said with a whimper. "Please."

He returned his gun to its holster. "I'm not going to hurt you. Tennessee Bureau of Investigation. Everything's going to be okay." As he reached and touched the shackle on her arm, he heard a noise behind him.

A spindly young man stood at the door, pointing a sawed-off shotgun at Jordan. The man's sullen face showed no fear. Rather, a smile emerged, revealing brown teeth, the top two curved to the right. He wore a brown cap that conformed tightly to his head.

"Take off that gun belt, mister."

Jordan slowly unbuckled his belt and dropped it on the earthen floor.

"Git on over agin' that wall."

Jordan backpedaled to where another set of shackles hung.

"Turn 'round and face the wall."

The man stepped closer and Jordan slowly turned around tracking the mountain man's posture and movements.

"Raise your hands."

Jordan lifted his arms toward the shackles.

"Fasten your arm in."

As Jordan reached to grab the shackle, he spun and backhanded the stranger across the face. The men wrestled for control of the gun, both shells blasting simultaneously into the ceiling. As thick chunks of earth fell about them, the stranger ducked behind a stack of wood crates and grabbed a Broomhandle Mauser. He fired two quick shots from the bulky pistol at Jordan, who bolted through the doorway.

Jordan stumbled as two more shots zipped past his right shoulder, forcing him to turn deeper into the cave. He dropped low and fumbled his way with hands extended into the darkness. Beads of sweat under his hairline intensified the musty coldness of the cave. Moving quickly into the blackness, he followed the cave downward as it snaked deeper into the mountain, the footsteps behind him the sound of his opponent closing the distance between them.

Trying to move as quickly as possible in the dark, Jordan caught the edge of a protruding rock with his knee. He stumbled to the rigid ground and turned as the silhouette of his stalker neared. Pushing himself against the jagged wall, he nestled into a small recession of the cave, biting his lip to lessen the pain, pulling his knees inward.

The width of the cave was no more than ten feet wide, and he was immersed in the shadows. The mountain man stopped, close enough that Jordan smelled his sweat. Jordan's heart pounded, but he convinced himself there was no way was he going to die in that cave at the hands of some mountain inbred.

The spindly man looked about in the darkness as though he sensed his prey was nearby. Slowly, he turned toward the darkness that hid Jordan and stepped forward.

"Come on outta there,'" he said with a bit of a laugh. "Time to face what's a comin' to you."

Jordan looked straight ahead, his palms sweaty, ready for an opportunity to overtake the man. He slid his right hand along the cavern floor to brace himself against the rocky wall, the heat of the gun barrel warming his chin.

He swept outward at the pistol with his right hand, moving it as the gun discharged. The blast knocked rocks and dirt on top of both men, and he lunged into his attacker, ramming him against the wall. The gun fell into the darkness.

Jordan elbowed the man in the throat and dodged a kick to his injured kneecap, and they tumbled onto the cold floor. He drove his elbow into the man's chin, smashing his head into the cavern wall. As he slumped to the cold floor, unconscious, Jordan moved back up the cave. Fighting through the excruciating pain running through his bloody knee, Jordan made his way through the darkness.

He hurried through the prison door, sweat sliding down his dirty face. The woman in shackles was slumped and still. Jordan raised her head. Her eyes opened but were foggy. "Look at me. I'm going to take you out of here." She moaned, and appeared as though she tried to focus on him. She tried to stand but didn't seem to have the energy. He spotted an ax leaning against the wall and decided to use it to break the shackles.

"Look out," she cried.

He dodged left as a sling blade narrowly missed his skull. The blade landed in the cavern wall, and he tried to grab his weapon lying on the ground, but his adversary kicked it away. The detective slugged him in the stomach, and again a second time for not making sure the man was out cold when he elbowed him deep in the cave. The mountain man hit Jordan's chin with the empty shotgun and they tumbled into the crates. Jordan fell on top of him, wresting the gun away. The stranger tossed dirt in his eyes and fled for the door.

Brushing away the gritty soil from his eyes, he gave pursuit as the man bolted to the entrance of the cave. More prudent, he knew, to release the victim inside and get her to safety, he couldn't pass the chance to catch the one who might hold the answers to why evil roamed freely on the mountain. Stepping into daylight, to the path he had taken earlier, there was no movement. To his right, the man climbed a twisty, narrow path.

Slowed by his injured knee, he struggled up the trail. The path climbed upward for over a hundred yards, and sight of the man lost as the mountain curved inward. The trail began to level out as the pursuit led him to the peak of Iron Mountain.

The clouds enveloped the trees in such a strong mist that visibility was limited to forty feet, making him feel as though he were running among the clouds. He moved northward and though the land was more maneuverable, the ferns and underbrush were thick on the mountain floor, constantly brushing and raking against his bleeding knee. A strand of briars grabbed hold of his pant leg, the barbs burying deep into the wound. Nausea built in his stomach as he carefully pulled the strand from his wound. He looked above him and took a deep breath, his head spinning. After his leg was freed, he took off toward a patch of laurels, mist isolating them like wayward calves.

He came to the edge of a cliff, below it an expanse of cloud and treetops. The end of the line? His eyes moved about. To his left, and to his right. All was quiet in that void until he heard someone cry out. Below him the young man clung tightly to the limb of a white pine in the smoky gray.

"Hold on, son," Jordan said as he knelt.

The drop off from the cliff into the mist went on for hundreds of feet among craggy rocks sticking out of the mountainside. Small trees and the roots of larger ones intertwined the rocks. The drop was steep but the blanket of clouds distorted the distance. The stranger, eyes wide and glassy, tried to tighten his grip. Jordan spotted a dogwood tree, and twisted a limb from the base until it broke. He lowered himself several feet until he knelt on a protruding clump of rock formations. Now within eight feet of the tree limb precariously holding the dangling mountain man.

Like some Appalachian trapeze artist, he swiveled his legs to adjust his grip and and lowered the dogwood limb. "Grab hold of this." The stranger removed one hand from the white pine limb.

Jordan inched closer, biting his lip to lessen the pain of his bloody knee. The pine branch cracked, bending downward. He kicked slightly to pull himself closer.

"Don't move. Grab the limb and I'll pull you back up."

The man grabbed the dogwood just as the limb of the white pine broke completely, falling to the rocky bottom below. The detective braced himself for leverage. "Hang on. I got you." The pain in his knee shot down to his foot as he pulled backward, lifting him upward. As he inched him closer to the top, the man began losing his grip. "Stay calm. I got you. Hold on for just another minute." As he spoke, the man's hand slipped. Jordan looked helplessly as the body tumbled down the rocks and limbs jetting out from the mountain. He tumbled over and over until the clouds swallowed him.

As quickly as he could, he hobbled back down the path to the cave entrance. The flow of blood had turned the pant leg crimson. He stumbled into the cave door, back down to the entrance of the prison cell.

Opening the door, he called out, "It's okay. You're safe now."

He stood motionless. The shackles were empty.

Thirteen

The water rushed along the narrow path of dirt and rock, a continual hum that cut the silence of the hollow. She knelt beside the stream, a cloth bag of clothes beside her. She removed a bar of lye soap from the bag and dipped it in the icy water. A blood stained pair of jeans in her hand, it was time to wash away the evidence. Arthritis slowed the scrubbing of the denim, and for a moment, it looked as though it would not come out. She wrung the jeans, fighting through the pain in her fingers. She looked at her wrist and rubbed it. The bracelet was gone.

~ * ~

Jordan removed his jacket, shirt, and T-shirt outside the entrance to the cave. Tearing the T-shirt, he tied it tightly above his injured kneecap. A bitter wind slammed against his back as he quickly put his shirt and jacket back on. Snow swirled, and Jordan had to move quickly before either blood loss or the freezing temperature got the best of him.

He descended the trail, hobbling to lessen the pain. Though he smelled smoke from the shacks of the hollow, he couldn't see it. The low clouds made sure of that. Besides, he certainly couldn't go back to Stoney Creek for help. Retracing his path, he made his way down the mountain. The snow spun through the trees, though only a dusting covered the ground. As he reached the bottom, a familiar bark echoed from below.

Emma sat on a large rock beside the stream, petting The General.

"I was 'bout to give you up fer dead," she said as she snapped her ear flaps together under her chin. "I figgered if the boys up Stoney Creek didn't get you, the butt-cold temperature would."

"I told you I didn't need you. Thought you went home."

"Well, lookin' at that leg o' your'n, I think you're still in need of my services."

"I'm okay. Really."

Emma knelt in front of Jordan and looked at his bandaging technique. "Good work. Cain't see no blood, so I'm guessin' you'll live to see another day. Set on this rock. Dan'l will take care of you till I git back."

"Back from where?"

"Alister Moody lives about a mile from here. His boy's got one of them four-wheelers. We'll use that to git you outta here afore you freeze to death."

Emma reached into her coat pocket and tossed a brown medicine bottle to Jordan. "Sip on that whilst I'm gone."

"What is it?"

"Well," she laughed, "just a little corn squeezin.'" Placing her fingers to her mouth, a shrill whistle cut the air. "Mr. General, it's time to go." Emma took to the road, her dog by her side.

Emma returned in less than an hour on the all-terrain vehicle, The General chasing from behind. The cold air, combined with Emma's elixir, eased the pain in Jordan's knee. He slowly straddled the vehicle, and the dogs ran behind as the pair headed for Pandora.

He retrieved a walkie-talkie from his car. Emma placed the dogs in her car, waved to him, and sped up the mountain road on the four-wheeler. Turning on the hand-held device, he said, "This is Thomas Jordan. Put me through to Lawrence, over."

"Ten-four," a young deputy's voice said.

"Lawrence here."

"Sheriff, I need your help."

"Name it."

"I'm down at Doe Creek near Pandora Road. Send an ambulance. Bring the coroner too."

"What happened?"

"I'll tell you when you get here."

"Be there in twenty, over."

When Lawrence and his men arrived, Lawrence immediately motioned to the driver of the EMS truck that followed them.

"You okay?" Lawrence asked.

"Never mind me. We've got to get on up the mountain."

"What happened?"

"I found a cave above Stoney Creek. Found a girl held captive there."

"Is she alive?"

"She was, but now I'm not sure."

"What do you mean?"

"I got attacked by one of the locals, and I got his weapon. I chased him out of the cave, over the ridge, and he fell off a cliff."

"Dead?"

"If he ain't he's a damn fine escape artist. Either that, or he sprouted wings on the way down."

"And the girl?"

"I went back to the cave and she was gone. The shackles were opened."

"Any chance she got out on her own?"

"No way."

"Well, I got some more news today that adds fuel to this rapidly growin' fire," said Lawrence.

"You don't say?" Jordan said. "Hit me with it."

"I got a call from the Tennessee Highway Patrol this mornin.' One of their troopers has been missin' for nearly a week. The last known location was Highway 91."

"Backside of Iron Mountain?"

"That would be correct. He's missin.' The patrol car's missin.' Maybe he crashed into a gully or ravine."

"Maybe he didn't."

"That's what worries me."

~ * ~

Approaching nightfall, along with the increasing snowfall, made finding the body a race against time. It would take at least two hours to reach the cave, and since the captive was no longer there, Jordan decided finding the body of the mountain man was the only option. Hopefully Lawrence or his men would recognize the man, and solve at least part of the mystery.

Snow accumulated in Jordan's hair while he described the layout where he'd watched the man fall through the clouds.

"I think I know where he's talkin' about, sir," Deputy Anderson said. "It's on the east boundary of Iron Mountain. Rough terrain. Be tough on foot."

"Take Emma," Jordan said.

"Emma?" Lawrence asked. "Where is she?"

"She won't be gone long." Jordan pointed to Emma's wagon, her dogs barking from behind the windows.

As the paramedic began working on Jordan's knee,

Lawrence and his men looked at the county map. "We can drive the backside of the mountain along Bruce Campbell's farm," said Anderson. "I bet we can get within a half mile of the cliff."

Emma walked up. "Howdy, boys."

"Emma," Lawrence said, tipping his cap.

"Emma, I chased a man to the peak on the east side of the mountain. He fell off a cliff. Can you take us there?"

"Got nothin' else to do. You boys foller me." Walking to her wagon she said, "Come on Dick Tracy, you ride with me."

Jordan looked side to side before realizing Emma was talking to him.

"Hold on," Lawrence said to Jordan. "You stay behind and let the paramedics fix that knee up. We'll search for the body."

"Just slap a band-aid on it," he said to a husky EMS member. "That's all I need."

"Sir," the paramedic said. "Looks like you lost a good bit of blood. Come to the truck with me, please."

"We'll take care of it later."

"But, sir..."

"No buts. Bandage me up and let me get back to work."

"Yes, sir."

In less than five minutes, Jordan's knee was cleaned and dressed. He hobbled to Emma's wagon. "Let's ride." Jordan and Emma led the way. Lawrence and his men followed.

Emma led them to Highway 47, where they headed east toward the unincorporated township of Butler. Jesse Long, the county coroner, was radioed by the EMS tech, and would be waiting for the search party beside the highway near the township of Rocky Gap. Long soon fell in line with the convoy, and they turned off onto a dirt road next to a rundown silo. The snow accumulated on the road, but the vehicles drove on. Driving in snow was as common as driving in the rain to mountain folk.

The winding trail cut through old tobacco fields carved out of the mountainside. The fields, neglected and, by the looks of things, forgotten, had become barren pastures where cattle scrounged for food. Pines grew tall and choked out what few hardwoods grew there. Two miles up the road, Emma pulled on to a weed-covered path.

"Hold on." She laughed. "It might get a little bumpy."

The wagon weaved its way up sharp turns and tree limbs

brushed against her car on both sides. Lawrence and the others struggled to keep up. The ambulance dropped a hundred yards or more behind as it slipped through the tight trail.

Emma rolled down her window with her left hand, her slender fingers holding tightly to the wheel. She grabbed hold of a maple limb caught in the windshield wiper, tossing it skyward. Lawrence's car swerved quickly, barely dodging the limb. A half-mile up the trail, the road melted into the woods. Emma killed the engine.

"Well, that was better 'an ridin' that mechanical bull at Percy's." She laughed at herself and got out of the car.

"Up through these woods 'bout a quarter-mile, Buford," Emma said as she opened the back passenger door. The dogs leapt from the car and circled the group.

The ambulance slowly caught up and the EMS techs began removing the gurney. The swirling snow made it difficult to see, and the deputies lowered the bills of their hats.

"Detective, with that leg of your'n bein' torn to hell, you might better stay here," Emma said. "The woods get mighty thick and the slope is so steep you can hardly pull your way up it."

Jordan nodded. "Yeah, I guess you're right."

"Let's go," Lawrence said.

The group entered the timber, the EMS tech at the back as he rolled the two-wheel portable gurney into the woods. Emma led the way, her dogs at her heels, with Lawrence and his men following behind. Lawrence nodded to his friend, Jesse Long, who was also the owner and operator of the town's only funeral home. Lawrence sensed trepidation in Long's eyes.

Folks on Iron Mountain were known to take pot shots at visitors, especially with regards to ones who wore badges.

"Stay close to me, Jesse," Lawrence said. "You'll be fine."

The thirty-minute climb brought the team to the foot of the cliffs as dusk settled in. Lawrence led the way, immersed in mountain laurels and hemlocks illuminated in white, the contrast of the wet snow darkening the trunks of the pines and hardwoods. The rocky wall of the cliff was the color of slate; jagged and fierce, as the snow had not yet found a way to stick to it.

When they made their way to the base, there was no body. Rather, a trail of blood which led from the jagged rock across the snowy ground, disappearing into a smattering of ferns.

"See where that leads," Lawrence said.

Anderson and Bacon walked into the ferns. Lawrence, hands on hips, turned his head skyward toward the top of the cliff.

"The blood trail disappears," Bacon said as he approached the search party.

Stooping over the pool of blood on the rock, Lawrence said, "He didn't make it out of here on his own."

"Whoever dragged him used his body like a whisk broom," Anderson said as evidenced by the absence of footprints.

The men searched the area with flashlights. Emma waited beside her dogs. Through the dark, they walked back to their vehicles.

Jordan exited the back of the EMS truck, noticing the empty gurney.

"We're smack dab in the middle of a nightmare, aren't we?" Lawrence said.

"Looks like it," Jordan said.

Jordan laid out a plan for the next morning. His knee would prevent him from ascending the mountain, so he described in great detail where the entrance to the cave was located. Emma drove Jordan to his car while the search party returned to town. Jordan thanked Emma for the help she provided. He hobbled to his car under snowflakes the size of silver dollars. Emma's wagon rambled down Pandora Road.

Jordan stood against his car, unwilling to call it quits for the night. He couldn't stand the thought of letting the day end without finding something substantial toward solving the case. Frustrated and cold, Jordan reluctantly opened his car door. He carefully eased in behind the wheel. He started the car and wipers brushed away the coating of snow on his windshield. Through the cloudy window, a figure stood beside a ground-hugging mountain laurel.

A sharp pain ran through his leg when he got out of the car. The lights of the SUV revealed an elderly woman in a brown, full-length dress. Her coat, a red-and-black checkered picot, had frayed sleeves covering her palms so only her stubby fingers were visible.

"You search for answers in the wrong places," she began.

"Excuse me?" he asked.

"You're searchin' for clovers in the wrong briar patch."

"Is that a fact? Where is it I should be searching?"

"Listen to the mountain. Her secrets whisper in the wind."

"What secrets are they?"

"That's fer you to figger out. She'll speak to you direct if you're willin' to listen."

"Who are you?"

With the help of a knotty oak cane, the woman stepped from beside the laurel. Her long, silver hair clung close to her weathered face, exposing shadowy black eyes. She didn't answer.

Jordan moved closer.

"That's close enough," she said. "You come to our mountain like all the others. You come thinkin' you can educate yourself to our way of life, thinkin' us simple folk ain't no match for you. But it ain't the people of this mountain you got to figger out. It's the mountain herself. And it's only she what kin tell you what you ought to know."

"I've no idea what you mean. I'm only here because..."

"I know why you're here," she interrupted. "The mountain—she holds the answers. Respect this world you don't understand, but don't trust its people. Only trust the mountain."

"Do you know who I'm after?"

"It is not for me to say."

"Help me put an end to this."

She waved her hand in front of her as if she were waving a wand. "Listen to the mountain. Gain her trust. She'll tell you what you's a wantin' to know."

"I still don't understand. How do I listen to the mountain? Is the burning bush going to make a return engagement?"

The tiny woman turned and looked over her shoulder at the cresting mountaintop in the dark sky. "Your answer lies there. Listen and she will tell you."

With the winds whipping, and the snow falling harder, Jordan turned and pointed to his car. "How about we get out of the snow and you can tell me how to listen to the mountain?"

He looked back. She was gone.

Fourteen

In the predawn light, the sun was minutes from making its appearance above Shady Mountain. The night sky had softened to purple, turning a thin layer of clouds to soft orange under that gentle sky. The clouds, narrow at the mountain's crest, widened as it spread above Doe Valley, giving the sun a colored veil from which to make its entrance.

The skyline's beauty eased Jordan's tired and troubled mind somewhat as he made the three-mile trek from the Valley View to Pandora Road. The winds were still, and smoke rose heavenward from the cherry-red chimneys of farmhouses along the highway. Sparse groups of cattle nibbled on tall grass peeking through the snow as the sleepy valley came to life.

Lawrence's fleet of squad cars sat bunched along Pandora. As Jordan pulled in behind the three vehicles, he chuckled, wondering who was keeping an eye on the town. Gilly Adams emerged from his car.

"Morning, deputy."

"Mornin,' sir. Sheriff Lawrence has already started the trek up Iron Mountain with Deputy Myers. He wanted me to stay behind and wait for you here. Anderson is verifying the tire tracks where Mrs. Darby was put in the creek. It's an ATV of some kind."

"I appreciate the update. I don't guess anybody came looking for our mountain man last night."

"I'm sure that man is already buried somewheres up in that godforsaken land."

"I'd guess that statement to be right."

"Detective, we've put in calls to nearby towns to alert them to what's going on. I talked to the sheriff at Bryson's Cove, twenty-five miles northwest of here, and he said a graduate student from East Tennessee State has been missing for three weeks. She was on spring break, and apparently went hiking up a stretch of the

Appalachian Trail. Her backpack was found alongside a recently used campsite. The spot was along the northeastern edge of Iron Mountain. The sheriff is faxing her picture and personal information."

"Good work. Any word on the missing trooper?"

"No, sir. At least nothing official has come into our office."

As Jordan tried to block out the sickening thought of another potential victim, the police radio came alive in Adam's car.

"Gilly, this is Anderson. Did Jordan show up yet, over?"

"Roger that."

"Well tell him we got us another body floatin' in the creek. I spotted it walkin' past Moses Jefferson's farm."

"We'll be there in five, over."

~ * ~

Jordan stepped into waters not more than a half-mile from where Patricia Darby was found. The nude body was face down, but didn't appear bloated. He rotated her to her side, guiding her head with his hand on her chin. Her dark, shoulder length hair covered her eyes and nose.

"I'd say it's the girl from the cave," he said while brushing her hair away from her face.

Her brown eyes had paled to a cloudy-gray, and they stared rigidly upward. Her neck was sliced from just under her left earlobe to just above her throat, similar to the first victim. Rope burns encircled her neck.

"Call the coroner."

While Adams waited for the coroner, he radioed Lawrence, who was en route up Iron Mountain, to tell him about the latest addition to the body count. Whereas the removal of Patricia Darby's body was witnessed by half the town, the removal of the recently discovered body would be performed with no audience. Keeping the discovery under wraps would hopefully keep the already tense county from going berserk with panic. After the coroner, Jesse Long, secured the body, Jordan and Adams rode back to the office. By noon, Lawrence and Myers returned from Iron Mountain.

"What did the boys on Iron Mountain have to say?" Jordan asked.

"'Bout what I thought," Lawrence responded. "Said none of their kinfolk was missing. Said they had no clue who fell off that cliff. Didn't care who fell off the cliff."

"What'd you find in the cave?"

"Not much. The shackles were gone. Just a few rickety crates and some empty cans and bottles is all."

"Damn."

"How's the knee?"

"It's just a nuisance. I'll live."

"That's more than I can say for some of the folks around here. Especially ones who decide to wander on to Iron Mountain."

Adams walked up and handed a fax to Lawrence.

"Missing girl from Bryson is Barbara Thomas," Lawrence said, scanning the paper. "Twenty-three year old coed from Corbin, Kentucky. Big hiker. She told her roommate at ETSU she wanted to spend the afternoon on the Appalachian Trail. Said she needed a break from studying." He showed the photo to Jordan.

"I believe that's the girl we just found," Jordan said.

"Call Jesse and tell him the news," said Lawrence to Adams. "We need to match up dental records, prints and such. Call Sheriff Titus at Bryson's Cove and tell him we think we've found the missing hiker." Turning to Jordan, "What do we do now?"

"We need to trace the hiker's path on the trail."

"Let's get after it," Lawrence said as he headed to his patrol car.

~ * ~

Arnie Jensen removed his hat, ran his fingers through his greasy hair, and returned it to his head. He looked across Iron Mountain like a weary traveler in search of home. Sitting in a locust rocker on the small porch, he said, "This is, by God, gettin' outta hand. He ain't supposed to be a killin' machine."

Bum spit tobacco juice off the side of the porch while sitting on a gutted butter churn. "He done exactly what we've wanted— keepin' outsiders off our mountain."

"He may be a scarin' those foreign to this land, but the law's now snoopin' 'round. They might find and destroy our cash crops. I don't like it. Nary a bit. 'Specially that detective what come with Emma."

"Shitfire." He spit again. "He messes with us, he best be ready to die fer it."

~ * ~

Lawrence's squad car headed west on Highway 47 as pale clouds hid the noonday sun. Snow blanketed the hillsides, and spruces and firs, their branches heavy with white, produced a mid-winter landscape.

His car drove along Black Bear Holler, a small stretch that bordered the west side of Iron Mountain into Bryson's Cove, Jordan riding in the passenger seat. Jordan had spoken with Sheriff Titus about the contents and condition of Barbara Thomas' backpack. As Jordan shared the information with Lawrence, he spotted the sign for the Johnson County Lumber Yard, looking to the top of the bald where tin buildings housed countless timber logs. Two cranes moved them from a giant stack onto steel trucks. Smoke billowed from the trucks into the cool air.

"This place provides lumber for the entire eastern corner of the state," Lawrence said. "Pierce Coble started it up twenty years or so ago." Pointing to a house at the base of the bald, Lawrence added, "As you can tell, Pierce is doin' quite well. Ugly as sin, but married himself a fine lookin' specimen. Twenty years his junior. Money can't buy you love, huh? I believe that to be a falsehood."

The home looked to be five thousand square feet, built of wood, similar to a log cabin. A four-car garage, a shed that housed two four-wheelers, and a playhouse were located to the left of the house, all constructed in the same style as the house.

"So what happens if you win the lottery?" Jordan asked. "You gonna leave the missus and find a young gal? You know, to test your theory?"

"I'm right settled in to the fact that I'll be a one-woman man until I die."

Jordan looked to the narrowing holler. "Is this part of Doe Valley?"

"No, but it's the same kind of folks livin' here. Hard workin' 'and honest, do anything to help a neighbor, kind of crowd. They live closer to Iron Mountain than Doe Valley, but they're just as unwelcome there as any other soul crazy enough to go on it."

"Guess Barbara Thomas had no clue about Iron Mountain," Jordan said. "Otherwise, why would a young gal hike it alone?"

"Well, the Appalachian Trail does cross the mountain, and people from all over walk it. It's not uncommon for hikers to have run-ins with the locals, but usually it's somethin' along the lines of flashin' a rifle at 'em if the hikers wander off the trail or set up an overnight camp. There's a hiker's shed a few miles off the mountain, and hikers are wise to make sure that's where they camp for the night."

"So would Barbara Thomas be killed just because she may have set up camp somewhere besides the shelter?"

"Well, we ain't sure if she even built a campfire. Just because there was one near where her backpack was found doesn't mean much. Could have been from a previous camper."

"Let's take a look anyway."

Soon the car began to climb a stretch of road that hugged the mountain in sharp switchbacks. The right side of the road shouldered walls of loose rock and boulders that climbed steeply skyward. The left side of the road looked over the tops of the tall timber on the sharp down slope. The road crept higher onto the mountain, taking them into a fog that made it appear as though they had driven directly into the clouds. The treetops above them faded to gray. When they rounded a hell-bent curve, Lawrence tapped hard on his brakes. "Watch yourself," he said as the car came to a quick stop.

Rocks were scattered along the road like marbles. A stream of chalk-like mud wound around the rocks, stretching across the road and dropping on to the treetops on the down slope below.

They slowly opened their doors. Jordan stood in front of the car, hands on hips. "Ain't this a hell of a mess."

Lawrence kicked at some of the smaller stones. "Looks like it ain't meant for us to make it to the trail. Not today, anyway."

"This isn't going to stop us. We can slide enough rocks off the road to open up a path. What do you think?"

"I think my back's gonna be hurtin' tonight is what. Let's get after it."

The men went to work, like a pair of newly sentenced chain gang members. The smaller rocks were lifted, tossed, and rolled first. With dirt-laced hands, they sweated through bowling ball-sized rocks so that the road began to look passable. They kicked baseball-sized rocks off the road with their boots, and then looked at each other as one boulder remained; a jagged rock the width and shape of a tractor tire. Lawrence leaned his shoulder against the cold gray rock. "I haven't played offensive tackle in twenty-five years."

"Time to relive the glory days," Jordan said as he lined up next to Lawrence. With loud moans, they slowly rotated the rock two revolutions, the second one causing the rock to bounce off the road, crashing into the treetops below, snapping pines as though they were sticks.

"Let's go," Jordan said as he walked to the car.

The road snaked up in a series of sharp turns for two thousand feet. At one point, on a turn bent so sharply the car could barely maneuver around it, Jordan commented he could reach out the passenger window and touch the back bumper. The fog, combined with mist from the low ceiling of clouds, thickened, and visibility was shortened to thirty feet. When the men exited the car and stepped on to the Appalachian Trail, Jordan wondered if they'd stepped in a tunnel of gray.

The men walked for nearly thirty minutes to the spot where Barbara Thomas' backpack was found. Sheriff Titus had roped off the area, though the fog made it difficult to spot the yellow tape. Jordan guessed cordoning off crime scenes was something rare for the sheriff of Bryson's Cove, much as it was to Lawrence and the men of Laurel City. Kidnapped women and bodies floating in creeks weren't an everyday occurrence. He learned from Lawrence that when someone disappeared on the trail, it was normally careless hikers who ventured off the trail by either mistake or stupidity.

To divert hikers from the crime scene, small blue arrows were painted on boards and nailed to the trees, making a semi-circle detour. Twenty-two feet away from the two-foot wide, snow-laced trail, a circle of blackened rocks surrounded a small pit. The men walked to the charcoal remains that dimmed the snow, covering it in gray.

"If she was at this campsite, why would her bag be over on the trail?" Lawrence asked.

"Good question. If he took her from here, my guess is he'd head deeper into the woods, not take her back on the trail."

"I don't think he took her along the trail. Too much of a chance that they'd be seen by other hikers."

Jordan looked along and behind two poplar logs apparently used as seats around the remnants of the fire pit. There was a ten to twelve foot cushion between the campfire and the trees, surely to prevent a fire hazard. Lawrence walked around the edge of the clearing, looking into the underbrush.

"If she went off for a day hike, with no intention of an overnight trip, would she even worry about a fire?" asked Jordan. "Her backpack had protein bars, a banana, and water. There'd be no need to set up a campfire."

"Well, the soot on her bag indicates she was in the vicinity of it. I guess she could've stumbled and accidentally dropped the bag into the pit."

"I don't think that was it."

"Maybe it was someone else's campsite, and she stopped to chat with them a spell."

Jordan stirred the coals with a stick and bit his lip. "I don't rightly believe it."

"So how do you see it playing out?"

"My guess is that it was her campsite. The killer surprised her, and carried her off like he did the others. I'm certain it's our boy all right, and if we don't find him soon, Doe Creek's going to turn red from the carnage."

Fifteen

Billy reached across the black cloth seat of his father's pickup, grasped the handle of the passenger door, and opened it. The new, bronze Chevy was gassed and ready to go. Becky, wearing a mischievous grin, stepped on the side rail and hopped in. She slid across the seat and placed both hands against his cheeks, kissing him firmly on his lips.

"Let's go before Daddy sees us," she said, turning to look out the truck window.

"Where'd you tell him you're going?" He had planned for nearly a week for this night to happen, each day slower than the last, scheming and dreaming about the chance to be alone with Becky.

"Crystal's. If they call my cell, you need to stay quiet."

"I'll be quiet as a stone. Hey, I got a little somethin' for us." He reached behind his seat and grabbed a plastic bag. Becky smiled when she saw the six-pack of beer. "Jack got it for me. Made me pay him ten bucks for it. Why don't we find a quiet spot and knock a few of these babies back. Maybe listen to some music."

"Is that all you have in mind?" She rubbed her hand along leg of his faded blue jeans.

He smiled and pulled the car on to the road. "We'll see."

The chance for romance didn't come around too often for the young couple. Like Billy, Becky was born and raised in Johnson County, and she experienced firsthand the snail's pace of mountain life. It was salt-of-the-earth kind of living. Men tilled the soil, or worked a trade. Her father worked the graveyard shift at the textile mill, which to her, was as noble a profession as being a doctor or lawyer. But she didn't want to work the mill, or learn a trade. She wanted thrills and spills like she imagined all big-city girls had.

Billy's truck rolled west. Doe Valley offered the best Johnson County had to offer in the way of secluded spots. The recent snow, however, made it harder for lovers to blend into the side roads and hideaways in the valley. The powder illuminated the ground into a dusk-like state, and Billy's bronze truck eased up Shady Valley Road.

"We're not goin' up Iron Mountain, are we?" Becky asked. "You know they found that lady's body just a couple a days ago." "I'll protect you." Holding up his left arm, he flexed his bicep. "If this gun ain't enough to do it, this one will." He opened the glove compartment, revealing a black revolver.

Billy turned onto a path where trucks once hauled trees for Tri-State Timber. The snow, four inches deep, gave the night floor a neon-like glow. He drove three hundred yards into the woods before stopping the car. He reached to the floorboard and clutched the plastic bag.

"Here," he said, twisting the top off the moist bottle.

"It ain't real cold, but it'll do," she said, and poured a third of the bottle down her throat.

Would Billy try to convince her his sole purpose for climbing the lonely mountain was to steal away some time to talk about their future together; to profess undying love for one another? What bound them was physical.

They began to kiss. The car's engine hummed and the headlights cut a path into the soft, swirling, snow falling from the trees. Heat fogged the windows as they shared their passion in the dark cab. Billy was aggressive with his kisses, and his arms clung tightly around her waist. His lips moved along her chin to her left ear. As she turned her head and sighed, a shadow cut the path of the headlights.

"What was that?" she said as she pushed Billy away. She wiped the foggy windshield with the sleeve of her blouse.

"What was what?"

"I saw somethin' move in front of the truck."

They leaned forward.

"You can't see anything through the window," Billy said. "It's too fogged up."

"I'm telling you, I saw something. Lock the doors."

"Your mind is playing tricks on you." Billy tried to kiss her again.

"Stop." She pushed him away. "Let's go. Let's get off this mountain."

Billy retrieved the pistol from the glove compartment. "Wait

117

here."

"What are you doing?"

"I'm going to prove there's no one out here so we can get back to finishing what we started."

"Then why do you need the gun?"

"Just on the slight chance that you may have been right. I don't call this gun 'the enforcer' for nothin.'"

"Billy," she said, tugging at his jacket. "Don't be stupid. Let's just go back home."

He opened his door slowly and ignored her plea. He looked at the back of the truck before turning his head toward the front. Slowly he moved until he stood in front of the headlights, his gun pointing at something—at nothing. He circled the truck, glancing at the darkness. Becky's eyes followed him as only the hum of the truck's engine cut the silence of the night. He held his arm extended and rigid, the gun pointing whichever direction he turned. Standing at the door, he again looked to the front of the truck and the gray of the woods carved out by the headlights.

"There's nothin' out there. Your mind was just playin' tricks on you."

"I know I saw something. I don't like this, Billy. Take me home."

He climbed back in the truck and closed the door and took her hands in his. "Listen to me. There ain't nothin' to be afraid of." He looked her calmly in the eyes. "Come on, baby. It's been a long time. We been waitin' for weeks to get this chance."

He kissed her neck, and at first she pulled away. She sighed, looked out the window again, and hesitantly turned her head skyward. Billy began unbuttoning her blouse with one hand while sliding her coat off with the other. The windows fogged again as their breath became heavy. He raised her skirt and slid his hand inside her panties. He kissed her furiously and she welcomed his lips. He was sliding her underwear off when she stopped him.

"I know this ain't the best timing," she said. "But I gotta pee somethin' terrible."

. He again tried to remove her panties. "Can't you wait till we're done?"

"I'm about to bust. It's the beer."

Billy slowly pulled away. "Hurry up then."

"I'm sorry baby, but I can't help it. I'll make it worth your while when I get back."

"Well, let me hold on to this while you're gone." He slid off her panties, and she smiled. He ran his hand up her thigh.

"Hold that thought," she said. She opened the door. "Be right back."

She stepped onto the cold snow and moved behind the truck. Though she had no hesitation giving her body to Billy, she was too shy to relieve herself in front of him. And so, she scurried behind a fat laurel twenty yards to the right of the truck, out of view.

When she had finished, she stood, lowered her skirt, and turned back to the truck. She smiled when she noticed her door was open. "Ain't you a real gentleman," she said as she hopped in the truck.

She screamed when she saw Billy slumped against the driver's side window. Blood poured from his neck, the tines of the pitchfork pierced deep, the handle of the tool propped against the seat beside him. His cloudy eyes were open, as if staring into the portal of a faraway world.

From behind a calloused hand grabbed hold of her hair, and pulled her out of the truck. Her shoulder and head smashed against the snowy ground. As he reached for her feet, she kicked him into a snow bank. She hopped from the ground and began running. Panic numbed her, making her oblivious to the cold.

She was right. She *had* seen something. She should have made them leave. Now Billy was dead, and she was fighting for her life. She battled the urge to throw up as she tried to block the image of his eyes, staring dull and fixed at her.

On across the angled terrain she ran, afraid to look behind her. The mountain floor could not hide her from him, and she knew it. Her only hope was that she knocked him out when he fell to the ground. The slope was slippery and she fell while trying to turn onto a small trail.

She lay spread-eagle, and didn't know what to do. Should she run? Should she listen for footsteps? She thought about the gun in the glove compartment. Could she circle around and make it back? Her breathing was heavy, and she looked, listened for, movement. She tried to suppress tears, and a cold sweat gripped her body. She decided to crawl, still afraid to look about. If she couldn't see him, he couldn't see her.

Back to the truck. Got to circle back to the truck.

She crawled to her right, below where the truck sat, its engine still running. She saw the beams cut into the snowy night. Closer she went. Almost ten yards to go. Surely, he had fled, for she heard no footsteps; saw no movement. She couldn't wait to grab hold of the gun. "I'll blow the bastard's head off," she whispered to herself. Slowly, she turned her head, holding her breath.

His clammy hand seized her by the hair.

She tried to scream, but claustrophobic fear constricted her chest.

"Git up." The stranger let go of her hair, grabbing her wrist. She pulled away. "Let go of me!" She flailed haphazardly at his forearm.

Gripping her wrist tightly, he jerked her quickly to her feet. She yanked away and slipped into the snowy ferns.

He again seized her by the hair then placed his knife under her chin. "Lessin' you wanna die like your friend, you'll quit fightin.'"

"Oh, my God. Please don't hurt me. Please don't hurt me." Tears welled in her eyes.

He pulled her onto the trail, toward the truck. She looked at Billy slumped inside the vehicle, as if willing him to miraculously come back to life and shoot the scumbag in the face.

In front of the headlights, he slapped her across her face. He grabbed her by the throat, and seemed to examine her hair in the light of truck beams. He held the knife to her chin. Though her blue eyes pleaded in silence for him to stop, it appeared to set him in a trance.

~ * ~

He had just turned sixteen, and never so much as held a girl's hand. Growing up on a farm, in a family with no girls other than his mother, he had little opportunity to be around them. He was not allowed to go to school; his father felt it was a waste of time, and cut into the work that needed to be done around the farm. Sunday mornings at church offered the only chance, though he was too shy to approach any of the girls.

So he was completely caught off guard the day Pauline Hickson walked up to him in the churchyard beside the baptism pond. Pauline was a blonde beauty, the envy of all the girls, and adored by every boy in the county.

He stammered and stumbled as Pauline invited him to her

birthday party that Friday night. She whispered in his ear how much fun they would have, and promised a hayride that evening, just the two of them. When his father dropped him off at Pauline's driveway for the party, his clothes, though ragged, were clean. He carried a yellow iris wrapped in cheesecloth, and presented it to her at the door.

He was led out back to a bonfire where a group of teens roasted marshmallows. Though he knew some of them, he considered none a friend. He sat apart on a pine rocker, watching Pauline mingle with the crowd. She brought him a glass of lemonade, and again thanked him for coming to her party. Pauline was the prettiest thing he'd ever seen.

With the help of Pauline's mother, they roasted hot dogs and ate homemade ice cream. The others mingled and chatted while he sat alone. As the crowd began leaving, Pauline reminded him about the hayride. After Pauline thanked the last guest, she walked with him to the barn. Cleveland, her older brother, sat at the reins of a tractor attached to a wood wagon filled with hay.

He was nervous as he helped Pauline on the wagon, and he smelled the freshness of her skin. Her hair held a fragrance of lavender. He wasn't sure why he was the lucky one Pauline selected, but he wasn't about to argue the point. Cleveland drove them on a dirt road that split two cornfields, and Pauline grabbed his hand. At a pair of pecan trees, she instructed Cleveland to drop them off. Cleveland turned the tractor and drove back to the house.

The crescent moon sparkled in her eyes. Smoke from the embers of the bonfire flowed up the hill from the backyard, adding a romantic aroma to the mild night air. She kissed him on the cheek, telling him she'd wanted him for some time. He didn't speak, but his heart began to beat rapidly.

She would make a fine bride, and he would take care of her for the rest of his life. She told him he was the most handsome boy she had ever laid eyes on. Her smile made him weak.

She told him she wanted him, and asked if he felt the same. He could only manage a slight nod. She said she was going to slip behind a nearby haystack and step out of her clothes. Before doing so, she unbuttoned his flannel shirt and removed it. She told him to remove his pants while she disrobed, and she would call him when she was ready. He stumbled as he tried to take his pants off, forgetting to remove his boots beforehand. Finally, he was down to his under drawers. Pauline called out, and he walked nervously to the haystack. As he approached, she warned him she was completely naked, and hoped he was as well. He shakily removed his drawers and stepped around the haystack to Pauline.

His face was hit by bright light, a host of flashlights shining at him, and he struggled to see the group of teenagers standing behind a fully clothed Pauline. Their laughter carried across the night air; Pauline's laugh the loudest. He quickly gathered his clothes, the laughter still echoing through the field as he ran into the darkness.

~ * ~

He slapped Becky's face again, taking hold of a fistful of hair when she stumbled. He drove his fist into her midsection, and then sent a right hook to her chin. Her cries seemed to only fuel his rage. Her body ached though she felt numb in the cold. He ripped her bloody shirt with his knife.

"Help!" she screamed. "Oh, God, somebody help me! Please don't."

She slipped on the snow as he rained blow after blow upon her body. He wrestled her skirt above her head, and she tried to crawl away.

"Get off of me, you pig," she said, kicking her leg at him as she pushed away from him on the snow.

With his hand grabbing her hair by the roots, he forced her on her knees and elbows. His hand still holding tight to her long hair, she cried out. With his grip rendering her immobile, screams turned to soft whimpers as he forced himself on her. Reduced to an animal. No chance to retain self-dignity.

When he was done, she dropped limply, flat on the snow-covered ground. Blows once more rained upon her shoulders, back, and buttocks as she felt the anger spewed with each punch. Blood spilled from her mouth and her tears fell onto the ivory floor. Punishment was completed when his steel blade pierced her throat.

Sixteen

The telephone rang in Jordan's room at the Valley View. He was finishing his second cup of coffee, looking at the Johnson County map. The clock radio on the nightstand read 6:43 a.m. He verified distances between the location of the bodies found in Doe Creek, the spot where Patricia Darby's body was placed in the creek upstream, and the Stoney Creek area on Iron Mountain. In workmanlike fashion, he tried to put the frustration of it all behind him so he could stay focused on finding the killer.

"Well, the fun never ends," Lawrence said, his voice dipped heavy in sarcasm. "We found another body two hun'ert yards from where Patricia Darby was found."

"I'm on my way."

He stepped outside and spotted Jason's silhouette between the curtains in his room. He sped out of the parking lot. Dawn had not broken but the skies had softened to a plum-like hue, and a reddish tint appeared above the skyline of Snake Mountain. The thick needles of the white pines cradled the late season snowfall, and yet they stood pale in that dimness of early morning. Jordan's car lights flickered in the distance as he drove up slippery Pandora Road. Lawrence opened his car door and stepped into the cold air.

"Mornin,' Sheriff," Jordan said as he exited his vehicle. "Let's have a look."

Lawrence, flashlight in hand, led Jordan along the white powder bank to a group of large rocks, two of which had snagged the leg of a naked corpse, face up in a foot of water.

"Her leg got lodged betwixt these rocks," Lawrence said. "Otherwise, she mighta floated for miles."

"Do you think it's Kara Lisle?" Jordan asked.

"No. We think it's Becky Shoun. She was reported missin' last night around midnight. Told her parents she was stayin' with a friend so she could go off with her boyfriend. The thing is, no one's heard from the boy. He didn't come home last night either."

"I would imagine they went off by way of some kind of motor vehicle. Get a make on the car they were driving. What kind of verification do you have this is the Shoun girl?"

"She's wearin' a hemp bracelet on her wrist with a shark's tooth. Her father said she got it at Myrtle Beach last summer. He's on his way."

Jordan reached under the young woman's shoulders, lifting her head above water. Lawrence shined his flashlight through the sparkling water. The sun had risen, but the water was dark gray, more reflecting the light than allowing it to penetrate. Jordan lifted the body out of the water.

"Looks like he pushed the knife through from the back of her neck." Glancing at her midsection, he said, "He beat her like a piece of meat."

"He's usin' one helluva butter knife, ain't he?" Lawrence said as water seeped over the top of his rubber boots. "Freezin' my fat ass off fishin' ladies out the creek is not the way I wanted to spend my spring. I shoulda listened to my father in law and been a tractor salesman.

"It's time to find this bastard," Jordan said. "And that's what I'm going to do, even if it kills me. So say goodbye to your family, your pet dog, and your pleasant state of mind. I need all your time and energy, cause you're sure as hell going to get mine."

~ * ~

Jordan sat behind Sheriff Lawrence's desk poring over the coroner's report. Patricia Darby and Barbara Thomas died from slashed throats. They had been strangled, most likely to get them to the point of submission before having their neck sliced. Becky Shoun died from the puncture wound to the back of her neck from a knife. There was no residue under any of the fingernails of the victims other than Johnson County soil. Lawrence walked in with Adams following behind.

"Looks like he killed them from behind." Jordan chewed on a pen. "You'd think one of them would have scratched him or got hold of his hair. But there wasn't a trace under their nails to indicate it."

"The cold creek coulda had somethin' to do with that," Lawrence said, taking a seat in an oak chair with black vinyl upholstery. He faced Jordan like a guest in his own office. When

Jordan stood, Lawrence wiggled his finger downward and Jordan sat. "As you were."

"Why do you think he beat the Shoun girl like he did?" asked Adams. "None of these others had those kind of bruises."

"Maybe she tried to fight him," Lawrence answered. "She wasn't strangled, so he might've had no choice but lay the knife to her. Lord knows she was a feisty gal."

Becky Shoun had three broken ribs, a broken jaw, her left shoulder dislocated, and her right eye completely detached.

"There's no doubt he inflicted more punishment on the Shoun girl," Jordan said. "Something about her must have set him off. If she fought, it didn't do her any good."

The room became silent when Jason Lisle walked in. His swollen eye, split lip and scraped left cheek evidence of a painful incident.

"Good Lord," Lawrence said. "What in the Wide World of Sports happened to you?"

Jason stood at Lawrence's desk as though no one was in the room but Jordan. He wore a green Charlotte 49er's sweatshirt and faded jeans. "I saw you leaving the hotel this morning. Thought you might have some news about Kara. She can't make it much longer without her inhaler. It's been close to two weeks and she's got to be struggling to breathe."

"Got nothing new on Kara," answered Jordan. "We're movin' as quickly as possible. What happened to you?"

"I got into a bit of a scuffle with the locals last week."

"Last week? Looks like they roughed you up about thirty minutes ago."

"Yep, they did nice work, huh?"

"Where'd this take place?" Lawrence asked.

"At that friendly night spot, Dewey's. I stopped at the gas station next door, and thought a few beers might ease the pain. Bigfoot and his brother came in and roughed me up."

"Can you identify them?" Adams asked.

"I can do better than that. I can tell you their names—Jakob and Willie."

"The Parker brothers," Lawrence said. "Them boys live on Iron Mountain. Didn't know Dewey's was one of their drinkin' holes."

"What started the fight?" asked Jordan.

"Don't know that they needed a reason. They knew about Kara though."

"Want me to bring 'em in, Sheriff?" asked Adams.

"You try it and they'll shoot your balls off," replied Lawrence.

"You're afraid of these men?" Jason asked. "Refresh my memory. Aren't you the police?"

"You don't understand," Lawrence said, rubbing his chin as though he were trying to convince himself he understood.

"I think I do. If you live on Iron Mountain, you get a free pass to do whatever you want without worry of punishment or retribution. And here you are, the protector of this county, and your only concern is whether they'll shoot you? Good Lord, what's wrong with you? Give me your gun, and I'll get them myself."

"Now that's enough," Lawrence said. "You have no clue about this world you've been thrown into. The law means nothin' to these people. Not our law, anyways. So you need to simmer down and let us do our business."

"So, you just let the Parker brothers go on about their business."

"I didn't say that. If they know we're after them, they'll hide out for months in places we'd never find."

"What if they're the ones who took Kara?"

"They're wily, I'll give you that. But if they took Kara, they ain't gonna be advertisin' it. They know someone took her, though. Most of the county knows it too. Question is, do they know who?"

"Well, I just don't understand how they can get away with kicking my ass."

Lawrence assured Jason that the Parkers would be dealt with, and Anderson took Jason to Doc Jacob's office to have his eye checked. Lawrence dispatched the other deputies to patrol duty. He and Jordan remained at the Sheriff's office.

"You know where those boys live?" asked Jordan.

"Yep. But I'm tellin' you, they'll shoot us if we step foot on their land. Best chance to get them is to catch 'em comin' or goin,' in their truck, away from their house. We could set up a roadblock. I don't think they'll take shots at us from their truck if they don't have the mountain to hide 'em."

"Well, somebody knows who took Kara," said Jordan. "Who killed those girls. Maybe it's these guys." He shook his head, trying to shake mounting frustration. "In the meantime, let's see if we can determine where Becky Shoun was killed. Better look for her boyfriend too."

Lawrence drove Jordan to Doe Creek to look for something to tell them where Becky had been placed in the creek. On the way to the creek, Jordan told him about the previous night and the spinster who'd given him advice on solving the kidnappings.

"Hannah Profitt?" Lawrence asked. "She's as crazy as they come."

"Never told me her name."

"Crooked nose, short, silver-haired woman?"

"That's the one. She told me if I want to find the answers, I had to 'listen to the mountain.'"

"Don't pay her no mind. She's tetched. The answers are gonna come from forensics and hard work."

Seventeen

Lawrence's squad car turned on to Pandora Road. Jordan spotted two deer standing next to Doe Creek. The doe and her fawn watched the squad car, frozen in their tracks like beasts peering at travelers from an alien world. When the car came to a stop, the deer trotted off into a thicket of birch trees that hugged the bank. Their small tracks the only markings on the thick blanket of white. The creek's rushing waters carved a path between the snowy banks, a look so pure it seemed no human had ever known the of the creek's existence. In the distance, a dog barked. On the highway a truck rambled by.

"This should be the last snow we'll see 'til November," Lawrence said. "Hope the creek is body free by then."

"It will be," Jordan said. "This heartless bastard's days are numbered."

Lawrence started down along Pandora again, the road running parallel to the fast, pure waters of Doe Creek, twenty feet from the west bank. As they rode in silence, a call came in from Deputy Anderson.

"Sir, I was scoutin' around up Shady Valley, close to Birch Gap, when a dog wandered up."

"And?" Lawrence asked.

"It's got an I.D. on its collar. Says he's from Atlanta. He sure is a long way from home."

"Got a phone number?"

"Roger that."

"Radio the office and get Adams to call and see if anything seems peculiar."

"Yes, sir. Ten-four."

Jordan looked about the creek bank. There had to be a clue, something, to point him to the killer. Lawrence pulled onto the bank and they exited the car. The sheriff gave them a cursory glance but stayed near the car in case news came back on the dog. A soft breeze swept a dusting of snow from hemlocks into the icy waters while Jordan looked along the bank. Standing a few feet from where Becky Shoun was found, Jordan buttoned the top of his navy wool blazer, tucking his red striped tie into the coat. His jeans covered all but the heel of his black boots, which disappeared into the soft powder. Could he re-create what happened? Could he get inside the mind of the person who had brought Becky Shoun to her icy grave?

While Jordan searched, Myer's voice came alive on Lawrence's radio. Lawrence, who'd kept the window down, reached in and spoke, his upper body inside the car. After a few minutes, he walked to the bank beside Jordan.

"Myers said the dog belongs to an Alex Williams from Decatur. His wife went to Boone last weekend and took the dog with her. According to Boone P.D., he's had no contact with her since Saturday. Boone P.D. says they've been searching western North Carolina for her since Monday morning."

"Tell Anderson to hang on to the dog. Let's get some hounds and see if that dog can lead us to Mrs. Williams."

"I'll call Brushy Fork and have them meet us up in Shady Valley. Shouldn't take them an hour to get there."

"What are you waiting on?" Jordan asked in an abrasive tone. Iron Mountain stood in the distance before him, powerful, majestic, reaching to the heavens.

Sam looked cold and hungry lying in the back seat of Anderson's squad car. Jordan approached slowly, and extended his open hand, palm up, through the window. "Easy big fella. Easy." Sam inched his way to Jordan's outstretched hand, and Jordan scratched his head. "You gonna take us to her, big guy? You know where she is?"

"Hounds are on the way," Lawrence said after placing the radio receiver back on the hook.

"Time to see if we can find Mrs. Williams," Jordan said. "Before she ends up in Doe Creek."

"Yes, sir."

Soon two beagles and two blue tick coonhounds exited a white van. A pair of prison guards led them out by their leashes. Myers arrived with a shirt Rachel Williams had worn the day before she disappeared. A deputy from Boone had brought the shirt to

Myers, meeting him at the state line. The beagles got a whiff of the clothing and began running into the woods. The deputies, rifles in hand, followed the guards who held the leashes of the baying hounds.

Jordan followed in Anderson's car, driving around a sharp bend and onto an old logging trail. The car trekked slowly through knee-high weeds and yellow grass peeking through the snow. Sam, looking out the passenger window, reacted to the barks of the beagles and began to whimper. Jordan stopped the car, lowering the driver and passenger windows.

Sam leapt out the passenger side and began wagging his tail. He barked loudly, crouching as if he were ready to pounce. Jordan removed a small rope from the trunk and tied it around Sam's collar. "Find her, boy."

Leaping across downed trees and skirting around thick mountain laurels, Sam led Jordan along the mountainside. Lawrence yelled for the search party to join in the pursuit. The hounds pulled on their leashes for release, but were kept close at hand.

The slope of the land was slight, a flattened bend of the mountain. The deputies moved swiftly, leashes gripped tightly, the yelps of the dogs echoing across the mountain. After three hundred yards, Sam turned into ankle deep water and Jordan followed suit. Head low, the dog seemed confused by the water. He crossed back and forth twice.

"Spread out," Jordan shouted to the other men. "Keep a distance of fifty yards apart. Move east from the creek." Turning to Sam, he said, "Come on, boy. Let's find her."

The rush of adrenaline recharged Jordan's love of the chase, of winning the game.

Sam resumed a quick pace and led the detective through dense woods. A light blanket of mist skirted through the trees, creating a chalky haze that limited visibility to less than forty yards. The winds whipped, kicking snow up from the ground. The posse moved to the right of Jordan to blanket the area. Excitement built in the frantic barks of the canines as they strained to pick up Rachel's scent. The dogs inched closer together as the mountain sloped down into a ravine.

They continued eastward while Sam slowed. His ears rose, his head turned at an angle, and his tail arched. Jordan looked to the slope, trying to follow what Sam was staring at as the mist clouded his view.

"What is it, boy?" he asked, rubbing Sam on the back of the neck. "Take me to her." Jordan wanted to find Kara and Rachel alive, but just as much, he wanted the satisfaction of getting his hands on their abductor.

The angle of the mountain floor softened again as the mountain sloped gently to the south. Sam grew more excited, and his barking became louder. The others closed in around Jordan and the Golden Retriever.

"I found somethin'!" Deputy Anderson shouted, his voice bellowing through the trees.

He had stumbled upon a shack. Jordan instructed the posse to surround the shanty, sending Lawrence and Anderson to the back. Jordan approached from the front, releasing the leash which held Sam. Adams walked inside, gun pointing forward.

"It's empty," he called out.

The one room shack was dark and dank as the gray afternoon light struggled to penetrate the grimy window and the open door. The doorway was at the front left corner. A thin tin roof, less than a foot above the doorway, held the weight of several fallen branches. No weeds grew near the house to speak of.

The officers returned their weapons to their holsters. A rotted couch sat in the middle of the open room, and two straight back chairs were pushed up against the back wall. A tiny wood stove was in the right corner. There was no running water. Beer bottles and food wrappers littered the mold-laced floor. The strong stench of urine filled the air.

Lawrence pointed to a brown sweater lying across one of the chairs. Jordan stepped over a pile of Styrofoam cups, a broken bottle of Wild Turkey, and a pornographic magazine.

"Grab the sweater," Jordan commanded. The sweater smelled musty and looked damp.

Adams and Myers had strapped the dogs to a poplar in front of the shanty. They barked restlessly.

"Looks like kids come here to party," Jordan said. He kicked a pipe from underneath the edge of the couch. A condom wrapper was beside the pipe.

"Hunters use it in the winter," Lawrence said. "Wasn't nothing more than a squatter's shack years ago. Some of the men in Doe Valley got tired of trekkin' in and out of these woods, so they

131

began setting up camp here. It was dry and they could set up sleeping bags and stock a little food." Kicking the condom wrapper, Lawrence added, "It looks like outside of bear season, this place is open season to anybody wanting to have a good time."

The dogs continued to bark, Sam's bark distinctive from the others, and Jordan sensed the agitation.

"Sounds like he's pickin' up somethin,'" Myers said. "Maybe her scent. He must have held her here."

Jordan looked into an empty cabinet located above and beside the stove. Small traces of yellow meal were on the shelf, and at his feet. He squatted and touched a bit of it with his finger. As he rubbed it between his fingers, something shone under the stove.

"What have we here?" Jordan said.

Lawrence, who stood near the couch, walked up behind Jordan, who was still in a squatting position. He opened up a small heart on a bracelet that contained a tiny picture of two children. The initials RBW was inscribed on the gold heart.

"Listen up," he shouted, walking to the door. "I want a sweep outside the shack. Circular, a quarter mile radius. Lawrence, I want this place shaken down like a dead Christmas tree. Fingerprints; hair; gotta be somethin' here."

The search party swept across the rugged terrain. The barks of the dogs sliced into the tall timber, making it sound like they had quadrupled in number. Deputies and the prison guards were spread to study the frigid ground for signs. Sam, his body weary, moved about with Jordan sporadically, running restlessly.

"We're gonna find her, boy. You can bet your wagging tail on it."

The search came up empty, though fingerprints were lifted. Lawrence made use of the walkie-talkie strapped to his belt. "Murray Jacobs is bringin' his truck to pick us up," he announced. "There's a road about a quarter mile below us. He'll take us back to the cars."

Jordan, glancing up the thick mountainside, said, "We're close. I can feel it. Let's continue the search."

"North wind's kicking up, and the dogs won't get much more," said Lawrence. "Besides, ain't a thing around here for miles. Far as I know, anyhow."

"Damn." Jordan ran his hand through his hair, his frustration mounting. "I want your men up here at first light."

"Ain't the Ol' Greer place down below here?" asked

Anderson.

"Been so long since I been up here I forgot," Lawrence said. "But, yeah, Roby's place is at the bottom of the holler."

"I think it's time to get a warrant and pay Mr. Greer a visit," said Jordan.

~ * ~

Footsteps pounded heavily on the creaky steps. Kara cowered against the wall. The door to her cell opened and he unlocked the shackle which bound her leg. He pulled her by the wrist.

"Let's go," he said. Kara's sweat pants were caked in dirt, and her musty T-shirt wrinkled. "I said, let's go," he repeated, tightening his grip.

She coughed profusely. She needed her inhaler. He pushed her through the small hallway and into the bedroom. Blood stains on the drywall behind the bed told the story of a room of terror. She began to cry.

"Git on that there bed," he ordered, brandishing his knife.

Numb, she sat on the edge, nervously hunched over.

He moved closer, grabbed hold of her throat, and pushed her on her back, staring at her chest. Slipping the knife under her chin, he tugged at the floppy shirt, slowly slicing it, moving downward until the shirt separated, exposing her breasts. He shifted the edge of the large blade over her nipples. She shuddered.

"Them pants," he grunted. "Now!" The anger raged in his eyes. "You're all the same. Stupid, lyin' whores."

He reached for her pants and dropped them to the cold floor. Exposed and at his mercy, Kara's body went limp. All she heard was the creaking of the old bed. All she could feel was the weight of him as he raped her. Time seemed to stop.

Her sobs were soft in her prison cell. She lay curled in the corner, the shackle clasped around her ankle. Her clothes lay in a heap beside her on the floor.

Eighteen

Sheriff Lawrence's office was abuzz with deputies, county investigators, and a growing group of media. Jordan studied coroner documents and lab results on Patricia Darby, Becky Shoun and Barbara Thomas. He tapped his right foot on the floor as he sat behind the mahogany desk. Kara Lisle and Rachel Williams would soon be next. The clock was ticking.

Jordan studied the situation, trying not to let the hunt become personal. Anderson and Myers had returned to the hunter's shack in hopes of finding something they may have missed before.

Lawrence ambled into the small police station, a folded piece of paper in his right hand. Flashing the paper in front of his face, he said, "Tom, waddaya say we visit my good friend Roby Greer."

"You got a warrant?"

"Yes, sir, I sure do."

"On what grounds?"

"Don't ask questions. Just get your car keys."

The black and crème squad car splashed through puddles of slush as it pulled in front of the Greer farmhouse. Greer's dogs, as if on cue, circled the car, barking and growling. The shrill whistle brought them to a halt. The farmer, ax in hand, picked up a newly cut piece of maple and threw it on a growing woodpile. He mumbled something and removed a blue handkerchief from the chest pocket of his gray overalls. Wiping his neck he looked at the squad car, shook his head, and resumed chopping. The ax seemed small in his hands. The blade sliced powerfully deep, splitting the wood into two smooth pieces.

Jordan slowly opened his door, eyeing the brown-and-black German shepherd sitting uncomfortably close to the right front tire. Slow and deliberate, he stepped onto tall weeds. Lawrence followed. The sun hid behind an ashen haze that produced a cutting glare off the few remaining patches of snow.

"Lessen you got a warrant, you boys better get off my property," the old man called out, splitting another log.

They approached carefully, Jordan eyeing the ax. The sheriff reached into his pocket and took out the paper. "As a matter of fact, got it right here."

Greer set the ax down and took to reading. It took him several minutes. He looked at Jordan who searched for fear or uneasiness in his eyes. "You think this is gonna make any difference? Ain't nothin' up here to find. You're wastin' your time."

"Perhaps. But, we just wanted to chew the fat with you some more," said Jordan. "We felt so welcome last time, we couldn't wait to come back." Jordan's tone was laced with sarcasm.

"Chew the fat," Greer repeated with a laugh. "Maybe they's a needin' to put somebody on this case that don't take it as lightly as you. Fear's spreadin' throughout the county like wildfire and you want to chew the fat with someone who ain't got a damn clue as to who you're lookin' for. Well, let's chew the fat quick-like because I got wood to chop."

Greer placed the ax against the woodpile, looking sternly at Jordan as he passed him on his way to the porch. He dropped into a faded rocker made of maple saplings and pointed to two folded, brown-metal chairs leaning against the corner beside the porch rail.

"What's on your mind?" Greer said.

"Mr. Greer, where were you on Saturday, April twelfth between the hours of two and four o'clock?"

"Fishin' Winter Creek in Maymead."

"Was anybody with you who could confirm that?"

"I fish alone."

"See anything out of the ordinary around here in the past two weeks? Seen any strangers around?"

"You're the only stranger I seen."

Scratching his chin, Jordan turned his head toward the direction of Iron Mountain, dark, dreary, smothered by low, dark clouds.

"Sheriff?" Jordan asked.

"Sir?" Lawrence said, looking caught off guard that he was brought into the conversation. Lawrence was second fiddle to Jordan and the TBI, but he wasn't there just to chauffeur him around the mountain.

"How far would you say it is from this porch to the cabin where Kara Lisle disappeared?"

"As the crow flies, less than a mile. Course, longer on foot."

Jordan nodded silently.

"Tryin' to convict me by proximity?" Greer asked.

"How much time do you spend on Iron Mountain? Specifically, in Stoney Creek?"

"I stay away from that hellhole."

"You were there last week when Emma Douglas took me up there."

"You be mistaken."

"Mr. Greer, I'm not a patient man by nature, and you're already wearing on me." Jordan looked about the farm. "What do you know about caves on Iron Mountain?"

"That they exist. This is the best you came up with? Questions about caves and how far it is from my front door to the cabin? How often I go to Stoney Creek? You're wastin' my time and yours."

Jordan nodded matter-of-factly. "Mr. Greer, you happy here? You know, on this farm? Happy with your neighbors? You got one of those, 'borrowing sugar and having cookouts' kind of relationships? Do you have that sort of closeness with folks around here?"

"Buford, where in the hell did you find this fella? I don't borrow sugar from neighbors. Cookouts? Son, look around you. This ain't suburbia. Here we live to survive, unlike you."

"The folks on Stoney Creek. Close friends of yours?"

"Got no close friends." Greer pushed his rocker back until the rim of his gray velvet hat touched the porch wall.

"Life's meant to be shared, don't you think? You live alone here. Must get lonely. Only seems natural you'd reach out to someone to fill the void." Jordan looked across the road. "Mind if we see your barn, maybe check out the chicken inventory?"

Without uttering a word, Greer rose from his chair. The dogs flanked Greer's side as Jordan and Lawrence followed behind.

The barn stood at the base of a grassy hill where six cows of mixed color grazed. Its faded red tin roof was sharply angled, and two sections of the roof, six feet long, were peeled back like the seal on a can of corn beef.

Beyond the barn, Iron Mountain formed a mighty backdrop,

charcoal gray, making the folds and curves of the mountain blur and blend so that the mountain appeared two-dimensional. To the left of the barn, a barbwire fence housed a handful of goats. The barnyard was dotted with large boulders that looked out of place; the rest of the hillside was nothing but grass and scrub trees. The goats stood on the rocks as if trying to get a good view of the men walking to the barn, although they seemed totally disinterested to the reason why. The men walked in the barn through a doorless archway. A rusted tractor faced a side wall. The scent of manure filled the air, and the warm smell of hay was the same as on Jordan's grandfather's farm. Though the glare of the sky slipped through the roof, Greer pulled a long string attached to an exposed light bulb. Jordan walked past two pens, one containing a pregnant cow, the other a slender donkey whose ears were pink with some ointment that smelled of vinegar. Several open bales of hay were piled in a corner. Greer lifted some with a pitchfork and placed it in both pens. Lawrence walked out back through a narrow doorway, the door hanging shakily by the bottom hinge.

"Is that your barn down by the road?" Jordan asked.

"Yep," Greer answered. "Ain't used much anymore."

"How many acres you got here?"

"Sixty-three."

"Sixty-three. That's a lot for one man to handle. And you take care of this all by yourself, huh?"

"Got no choice. You lookin' for part time work? Maybe I can take you on. How's your plowin' skills?"

"How old are you, if you don't mind me asking?"

"Older than you, that's for sure."

"How old was your son? Burley's his name, right?" Jordan rubbed a piece of hay between his thumb and forefinger. Greer paused, rubbed his left eye with the palm of his exposed hand, and removed his hat.

"I don't much like talkin' about it."

"I know it must be hard, but try and bear with me. How old was your boy?"

"Twenty-two."

"Was he your only child?"

"Had two boys. They're both dead." Greer picked at the cold dirt of the barn with his pitchfork.

"Your wife pass on too?"

"She took off a couple years back."

"What happened to your other son?"

"Rather not say."

"How long ago did Burley's accident take place?"

Greer squinted his left eye and looked skyward. "Four years."

"The other son? Did he die before Burley?"

"Yep."

"That's got to be tough on a man to know he outlived his children." Jordan walked through a small door that led into the goat pen. "I appreciate your time, Mr. Greer. We'll let you get back to work."

"That's all you got? Family background and such as that? Lord amercy, but if the people of this county are countin' on you to solve this crime, they are in for a world of disappointment."

"Thank you for your time."

"Can't say it's been a pleasure."

Jordan and Lawrence drove onto the highway. Lawrence looked at him. "Why did you ask him questions to answers you already knew?"

"I wanted to see his reaction. See if he flinched or said something different from what you told me."

"Did he do anything that seemed to indicate he was lying?"

"Not particularly."

"That's it then?"

"Do you know what happened to his other son?"

"Hanged himself."

He shook his head, as though he couldn't believe that so much pain and misery could fall on one family. "When was this?"

"Must've been ten, twelve years ago. Elvin was his name. Hanged himself in jail."

"Tell me why he was in jail."

"Murder."

"Good Lord. Do you know the story behind it?"

"I've heard various versions. This is what Brother John Pickens said Roby Greer himself told him one night when they drank moonshine down by Maple Branch as best as I can recall. Elvin was about fifteen when he ran away from home. He was gone about two years and had no contact with the family. Roby received a letter from the sheriff in Stevens Creek, across the Virginia border. The letter went on to tell how Elvin had stayed in trouble with the law one way or another. The letter said he was a habitual offender, and apparently, Roby had no clue what that meant."

"I've dealt with a few of those, I must say."

"Well, Elvin had been arrested on charges like petty theft, vagrancy, and drunk and disorderly, spending time in and out of jail. But the night after Thanksgiving, he killed someone."

"He moved his way up the crime ladder, huh?"

"The top rung, it sounds like. Robbed and beat a man to death. Left him in an alleyway. An eyewitness saw it happen. Anyways, a few days after the murder, they arrested Elvin and put him in jail. That night he was found hanged, a bed sheet tied round his neck."

"Damn, what a sad series of events."

"But there's another version. One of the deputies in Stevens Creek was a distant cousin of mine, and he told me that a drinking buddy of Elvin's told him that Elvin was innocent."

"How did he know that?"

"He said Elvin and he had been drinking in a beer joint next to the train station. They stayed there till closin,' and when they left, Elvin spotted a man in an alley sprawled out on the ground. They walked up to the man, and he was all beat up and bloody about his head. He said Elvin checked to see if the man was still breathin.'

"Though the man was already dead, Elvin must have guessed it wouldn't do any harm to check the coat pocket of the gentleman for spare change. When his buddy asked what he was doing, Elvin told him that the dead couldn't take money to the afterlife. When he reached for the man's wallet, my cousin told Elvin he was crazy and said he would play no part in it. He took off down the alley."

"So he was still a petty thief."

"Sounds like it. Well, a passerby apparently saw Elvin bent over the man, and when he called out, Elvin took off runnin.'"

Jordan shook his head and stared out at the hillside.

"From what Brother John Pickens said, Roby left in the middle of the night to retrieve his son's body. When the sheriff explained to Roby what had happened, he made it clear that it was not the Sheriff's Office fault for the unfortunate end of Elvin's life. The state of Virginia offered a pauper's grave, but Greer wouldn't stand for that.

Lawrence and Jordan drove back to town.

"Greer knows more than he's letting on," Jordan said as they entered the police station. "Something's not right."

"What do you mean?"

"He's pushing seventy, maybe seventy-five. Think he's physically able to tend to that old farm all by himself?"

"I don't follow you. His boys helped 'til they passed away. Now he tends to it on his own."

"Does he?"

~ * ~

Midge Roberts flipped through the cluttered file cabinet in the small storage room of the county Health Department. Glasses hung on the tip of her nose, her bluish-silver hair emitting a neon-like hue as she verified the name on the file—Greer, Burley.

"Here it is, Detective," she said as Jordan peered over her shoulders.

"Thank you so much, Mrs. Roberts," he said. "I appreciate you taking time from your hectic day to find this file for me." Midge removed the glasses from her nose, smiled, and touched the back of her bouffant hair. "What a lovely smile you have." He was laying the compliments on the best he knew how.

Midge blushed. "Well, I'll leave you be so you can look at the file," she said. "What is it you're a lookin' for, if you don't mind me askin'?"

"Just curious to see how exactly this young fellow died, that's all."

"Oh, it was a terrible death. You know, his face was so messed up they had to have a closed-casket funeral."

"That's what I heard. Did you know him?"

"A little. He came into town 'bout twice a year. Very quiet boy. Very big boy. Drove a rickety black truck. My husband, Ralph, ran the drug store, and he would come in with a list of stuff his daddy needed. Would hand the list to Ralph without sayin' a word. He'd nod when asked questions. The poor fella couldn't read. Didn't go to school. Sometimes the kids around town made fun of him. He'd act like he didn't hear them. But I know he did. Poor boy."

"Well, you've been most helpful ma'am. Ralph's a lucky guy."

She blushed again, touching Jordan on his right arm. "You stay back here as long as you need." Her black shoes clomped down the hall, fading with each step until she disappeared through the door.

Jordan examined the report, looking closely at cause of death—head trauma. The report gave no indication that suspicious or foul play had occurred. He walked up the stairs to the coroner's office, and tapped on the window of the partially shut door. Jesse Long sat in a stiff wood chair, reading a copy of True Crime Stories.

"'Scuse me, Mr. Long. I wonder if I could ask you a few questions about Burley Greer."

"Certainly. Have a seat." He closed the magazine and turned it so the front cover was in front of Jordan, as though showing evidence in a courtroom. "You ever read this magazine?"

"Can't say I have."

"It's fascinatin' stuff. Like the story I'm readin' 'bout now. It tells of how Woodrow Reece attacked a house full of folks one night outside Little Rock. He broke in while they slept. Butchered them all. Mother, father, four children." He opened the pages. "Check out pictures of the crime scene."

"Maybe some other time."

"I'll save the copy for you when I'm done."

"Thank you. Tell me, did you work Burley Greer's case?"

"Sure did. Been the coroner here for seventeen years. Burley's was the worst I ever saw. Well, before the mess we're in now."

"How well did you know him?"

"I had seen him around. Never talked with him. He'd come into town for Roby and head back to the farm."

"When you examined him, could you identify him? I heard his face was in bad shape, but if you hadn't been told who he was beforehand, could you have identified him?"

"Not really. The boat motor blade ripped his face apart. It was a gruesome sight."

"Anyone else on the boat that day?"

"Just Roby."

"Was an autopsy performed?"

"No sir. Weren't one needed."

"Nothing was done to verify that the deceased was Burley Greer?"

"Well, no. Not with his father right there. Besides, we didn't have anything to substantiate his identity with other than through

Roby. It's not like he had a driver's license, dental records, or such."

"You wouldn't happen to remember if Burley had any distinguishing features would you? Birthmark? Scars?"

"Not that I recall. Roby didn't ask me to dress the body before the funeral. Just wanted him cleaned up some and sealed in that pine casket. Why?"

"Just curious. Thanks for your time."

"Anytime."

He walked to Midge's desk and handed her the file. "Thanks, Miss Midge. It was a pleasure, and I appreciate your help."

Nineteen

Jordan lay on his bed, unable to sleep. An eighteen-wheeler rumbled by, its lights sneaking in above the curtain, and rolling across the ceiling of the old motel room. The steady rumble of the diesel rig offered a soothing respite from the quiet evening as it made its way along the dark highway. The rig reminded him of sleepless boyhood nights when he would listen to the jagged hum of trucks driving by his house on to unknown destinations along the Damascus Highway.

He'd worked many cases; solved them all. He could deal with the cold indifference of city streets. The pursuit of evil men. In those situations, the rules were as familiar as the playing field. Not now.

Now he battled a foe encompassing more than the human element, one he had no clue how to fight. He wasn't even sure where the battle was to take place. As scary as it was running through back alleys and abandoned apartment complexes in Knoxville, knowing his assailant could be waiting for him in the distance, it was ritualistic and somewhat ordinary. But now he faced a foe he knew nothing about, in a world where he didn't know the rules. It weighed him down with self-doubt, with uncertainty, and made him question whether he was the man for the job.

Dawn was two hours away, and Jordan was ready to roam Doe Creek, to hike Iron Mountain, and to talk to anyone and everyone who lived on the mountain, if necessary. The words of Hannah Profitt on his mind, he slipped on a pair of jeans and grabbed his coat from the back of the chair pushed under the small table near the motel room door.

When he stepped outside, his face tingled from the chilly air. A new moon hung in the western sky, a cosmic fingernail that cast the land in pale blue. Stars sparkled from every corner of the sky, a sea of diamonds that looked as if they would fall to Earth if God gave the heavens a gentle shake. Traces of snow clung to the corners of fields and along barns, in spots where shadows lingered during the daylight hours.

He walked into the gravel parking lot, the yellow glow from the light outside his motel room providing a dim shadow in front of him. Stooping, he picked up a handful of cold pebbles and began tossing them one by one at the highway. Were Marty and Jessica sleeping soundly? Did he enter their thoughts as often as they did his? He missed them.

He walked across the road, the sweet smell of clover easing the frustration of the night. Crickets performed a noisy serenade that somehow sounded choreographed. The scene took him back to Saturday mornings when he and his brothers would fish the creeks before sunrise. He straddled the top of a wooden fence and looked out across the valley that melted into the base of Iron Mountain.

The light came on in the restaurant, and he climbed off the fence. Myra was behind the counter and smiled when he tapped on the glass of the front door.

"Mornin' Myra," he said as she unlocked the door. "Too early for business?"

"Bring yourself on in," she said. "I don't usually lock the door, but after what's been goin' on around here, I don't feel safe."

"I understand."

"I got my first pot on the stove if you want to take a seat. It'll be ready in a country minute." The smell of hickory burning in the wood stove competed with yeast rolls rising under a giant dishtowel on the counter. The percolator bounced the coffee beans to life.

Jordan sat by the window at a red-checked tablecloth-covered, two-chair table. He picked up a green piece of paper held by a metal menu holder. Placing the paper on the table, he smiled at the uncolored outline of Tennessee. When he was a boy, he would color paper maps at the Daniel Boone restaurant. Two crayons sat in a tiny unused ashtray. Within minutes, Myra brought a cup to Jordan's table, along with a biscuit with a dash of honey.

"Tough night?" she asked. Her warm smile caused her green eyes to squint, and wrinkles formed below her eyes. Her shoulder length hair was dark with fine streaks of gray running through it like guitar strings.

"Nothin' I can't handle." He forced a smile.

"Whole county's on edge."

"I know. Can't blame them." He took a sip and studied the coffee as though he might see a vision of the killer if he looked hard enough. "Myra, what do you think of those Iron Mountain folks? Are they truly that stubborn and anti-anything that's not Iron Mountain grown?"

"Folks on Iron Mountain are a breed unlike any other. At least to my knowledge. Maybe we judge them unfairly. Nothin' wrong with being proud of your homeland, your heritage."

"They certainly seem to have a chip on their shoulders."

"They defend themselves, but I don't know them to be necessarily the aggressor. I think they are like a wounded fox. They won't attack lessen you enter their den."

Jordan thought hard on those words as Myra returned to the counter. After finishing his biscuit and coffee, he walked to the counter. "How much do I owe you?"

"You don't owe me nothin,' sweetie." She smiled and he headed back to his room.

~ * ~

Emma sat on the hood of her dusty wagon when Jordan pulled up. Despite the cold mountain air, she wore frayed khaki shorts that revealed pale, varicose-veined legs. Her brown leather boots were laced with red mud. Her brown, down jacket was unzipped.

"Well hello there, you gorgeous stack of pancakes," she said as he opened his car door. "Can't get enough of me, huh?"

"If I could find anybody else in this county who knew this area like you, I'd drop you like a lead balloon."

Emma smiled and spit tobacco juice. "Waddaya got in mind this fine mornin'?"

"I want you to take me to see Hannah Profitt."

Emma's smile quickly disappeared. "Go sell crazy somewheres else. We're all filled up here." She shook her head and looked off in the distance as though she was trying to reason some sense of Jordan's request. "You don't want nothin' to do with her."

"I think she can help us."

"I think she should be left alone. Let her scare off her own kinfolk. How do you know about her?"

"I got the distinct pleasure of meeting her the other day. Just appeared out of nowhere telling me if I want to solve this thing, I need to listen to the mountain. Well, I'm ready to listen."

"Hannah's a scary gal. I don't know who's older, her or the mountain. She's a healer woman. Some folks say she's a haint."

"Do you know where she lives?"

"Well, I know the general area. I'd say when we get close enough, we'll be able to spot her on her broomstick in the treetops."

"Will you take me?"

"You sure there ain't somewhere else you'd rather go? I get the willies just thinkin' of the old hag. The broomstick comment aside, she's known to roam all over Iron Mountain. Long ways to go without a guarantee she'll be home."

"I'll take my chances. You up for it?"

"I might have to charge you double for this one." She shook her head in defeat. "Get your bony ass in the car."

Hopping in, he said, "Where are the mutts?"

"Home watchin' Jerry Springer."

Two miles down Highway 47, Emma pulled off onto a dirt road that ran alongside a dilapidated barn. They rolled through a ditch that looked like it once contained water, now abandoned or perhaps re-routed. The road they travelled looked to be more path than road, winding around long-abandoned shacks and fields decades past their crop producing days.

Emma maneuvered the old wagon in Richard Petty fashion as it climbed the backside of Iron Mountain. The morning sun disappeared behind a dark line of clouds and the fields seemed to melt into a black canvas of thick trees.

"Okay, Dick Tracy," she said. "End of the road. We have to travel by foot from here. You all right with that knee?"

"Lead on."

As they stood at the foot of a trail that led into poplars and hemlocks, Emma pointed to a nearby abandoned house enveloped in yellow grass and infertile grape vines. The dwelling was located in front of a thick row of white pines that buffered the house from the hardwoods.

"See that old house yonder?" she asked. Tobacco juice slid down her chin. She wiped it clean with the back of her hand.

"What about it?"

"The Robinson family lived there years ago. Spinal meningitis rolled in and wiped out their four young'uns in less than two weeks."

"You don't say."

"Me and my sis snuck up behind the house whilst it was a goin' on. You could hear their screams a mile away. Weren't no cure for it back then. After they died, folks had to stand at the road to pay respects, skeered they might catch it too."

"This wasn't an easy place to live, was it?"

"The daddy, Arthur, was nice as could be, but dumber than a bucket o' rocks. He broke his arm once cuttin' a tree limb."

"What's odd about that?"

"He was standin' on the limb he was a cuttin'."

Emma led Jordan across rugged mountain terrain not fit for man or goat. The slope of the land virtually vertical in design. Rampant mountain laurels turned the terrain into a maze of narrow paths that zigzagged across the mountain. As they climbed, Jordan began to limp.

"You okay?" she asked.

"Fine as apricot wine."

"When we git to Hannah's, iffin' she's there, and I bet she ain't, I ain't a goin' inside. I'll stay close to the trail. You can talk to her as long as you k'ere to."

"Suit yourself."

They moved at a snail's pace. A thin trail of gray plumes floated from a shack a few hundred yards to the east. Two men decked in faded blue overalls stood guard over a still. They raised their rifles and aimed them at the oncoming trespassers.

"Hank and Squirrel Edmonds," Emma whispered. She raised her cap and waved it above her head. "Best let 'em know it's me. If not, they'll shoot us where we stand."

They carefully walked on. Fifty yards past the still, Jordan turned his head slightly.

"Don't eyeball them boys. Look straight ahead, city boy."

"There sure is a lure to this moonshining business," he said as he followed Emma on a slender trail.

"Moonshiners have been around Iron Mountain since the days of Gaines Logan. During Prohibition, bootleggin' was a moneymaker. Cain't grow much up here with this hard soil, and moonshine was a sure fire way to make money. Course that opened up another stable of problems: gettin' locked up, warrin' with other shiners, gettin' shot."

"But Prohibition ended a long time ago."

"The end of Prohibition slowed moonshinin' about as much as the revenuers did, which wasn't much. Johnson County only sells beer and wine, so unless you drive to Damascus or Boone, a quick ride up Iron Mountain is all it takes. Moonshine had been good to those hard-edged people, and they guard their stills like Fort Knox."

They trudged on for thirty minutes.

"Hannah's house is supposed to be just above the next ridge," Emma said while grabbing a scraggly cedar limb. "What makes you think she'll tell you anything?"

"I'm running out of options, so what do I have to lose? She talked a good game by the hemlock. Seems like she knows a lot about what's going on up here."

"More power to you if you can get her to help. Like the rest of the folks on the mountain, she don't think much of the outside world."

Hannah's shack stood in a small clearing surrounded by dark woods with heavy under brush. The wooden structure was faded gray, with a small porch held shakily by two posts. A laurel-wood rocker sat next to the door, an oak butter churn beside it. Above the door was a breadbox sized transom window. A fallen pine limb lay across the tin, auburn-tinted roof.

The bitter smell of pennyroyal filled the air as Jordan tapped on the flimsy wooden door. Emma stood thirty feet in front of the house, pacing. After no answer, he knocked again, louder. Emma looked relieved as Jordan turned and faced her.

"So much for findin' her today," she said as though trying to sound convincing. "We best git on home now."

Jordan took no heed to Emma's request, and he walked to the side of the house where he spotted a metal wash pail, half filled with water, next to a well encased in slate, two feet high.

"See, she ain't here," he heard Emma call out. "Let's head back home."

He walked behind the house, corn shuckings scattered on the ground in front of a fold up chair. The woods behind him quiet and without movement. A crow's caw was the only sound in that great expanse of forest.

He stepped to a window of the small shack and peered in through the cloudy glass. The house was dark and there was no movement. He tapped on the window and turned his ear to the glass.

Resigned to following Emma back the way they came,

Jordan shook his head and approached her from the side of the shack. "I guess you're right. If she's in there, she's not coming out. I'm sorry I wasted your time. Let's go."

A scraggly voice called out, "Kudzu is a tender vine, but it chokes the life from the strongest tree."

Hannah stood to the side of the porch beside the woods, Emma slipping behind Jordan as if to hide.

She wore baggy, charcoal gray wool pants with the pant legs several inches from reaching the tops of her worn leather boots. A long-sleeve, crème-colored thermal shirt that was soiled under her armpits covered her torso. She held a slender green vine wrapped around the base of a giant locust.

Emma back peddled, but Jordan approached the mysterious mountain woman. Hannah looked curiously at Emma, as though Emma was nothing more than a statue. She turned her eyes toward Jordan, and in those eyes, Jordan saw a piercing vision of a world no man was invited to share or made privy to its secrets. In the meeting of their gaze was the meeting of two paths, neither familiar with the course of the other's.

"Keep talking," he said calmly as he walked closer.

She snapped a piece of the vine. "Harmless lookin,' ain't no disputin' that." Hannah dropped the vine to the ground, and patted the thick trunk. "Strong, sturdy tree. Just like Iron Mountain her'sef. But it ain't no match for the kudzu vine." She reached to the base of the tree, and wrapped the vine around her gnarly hand, pulling it from the ground by its roots. "Not lessen you kill it first."

"Why are you telling me this?"

"Kudzu is fur'in to our mountain. And yet, it lives here. It kills here." A cold breeze blew, as though it carried the souls of the dead from deep crypts hidden by the underbrush. Hannah looked over her shoulder as if the winds aimed to gird her soul. "She's speakin' at you, city man, but you refuse to listen."

"If she's talking, I'm not hearing. You got a translator? Maybe you can be that for me. What does kudzu have to do with the murders and abductions taking place on Iron Mountain? A killer's on the loose and you tell me that the mountain's talking. Help me, Hannah. This isn't a game. Innocent people have been killed. Probably more will be if we don't end it."

"You know your world, I s'pose. But you's like a newborn calf here. Wide-eyed and heavy in thought as you try to decipher the workin's of this place. You try to stand, to walk. To suckle at the teat of the golden cow. You are the runt, the outcast that gets left behind to die."

"Good God," he said, shaking his head.

"Perhaps it's God you should be callin.'"

"I don't think God's going to show Himself here."

"I say here's the onliest place he shows himself. This here's his Eden."

"If this is Eden, keep me clear of hell. I'm pretty certain He's nowhere near this mountain."

Emma cleared her throat, and Jordan looked at her. She raised her eyebrows and nodded to the path from which they had traveled. "God is evident in ever'thin' you see here."

Jordan turned and faced Hannah again.

"His fingerprint is in the slope of the holler. It's in the bloom of the mountain laurel. It's in the winds that rattle the treetops. You equate God to churches and crosses. You don't see churches here because this mountain is God's sanctuary. And the choir's voice comes from the graves on the hillsides. But because you don't hear bells in a tower, you assume we're in a godless land."

There was a fire in the old woman's eyes. "We don't need a church steeple to hide behind. In your world, you fill the pews, but only to seek big homes and fancy cars. As though it's the attendance roster that makes you square with God. You step on others to git what you want, and you think you can hide behind the cross and no one will see your sins, especially God above. But He sees it. He sees it."

Jordan regarded her in some fashion as though her thoughts were not of this world. "Hannah, you're zapping my strength. I know you don't think highly of me, or anyone else who wasn't born on this mountain. But who knows if the next victim is someone you know or care about."

"Ain't my job to k'ere about others. What concerns me is the preservation of my homeland. It's the soil beneath my feet." She kicked a small chunk of rock in the grass with her boot, dislodging it from the ground. She picked up the rock, turned it over, its underside flat and exposed as though the rock had been cut in two. She placed her tongue to the rock and her spit changed the stone's surface to a profuse array of red veins. "This is the blood of my ancestors. The blood of this mountain. Through the course of time all will pass to dust and bones, but this land will stand strong. She feeds off the souls of her people, and it keeps her goin.' And it's God who will see to that."

"Hannah, you be as proud as you want about this place. But if you know something, please tell me."

"I done told you." She raised her hand, the kudzu vine wrapped around it. "The answer lies right here. Right before your very eyes."

Hannah turned and walked behind the house. Jordan glanced at Emma as though to express he had no clue what to think about the situation and then began to follow Hannah's trail. But she was gone.

"I told you she was tetched," Emma said as they began their trek down the mountain.

"What did she mean kudzu is foreign to Iron Mountain?"

"Hell if I know. She's full o' bull hockey. Best not to pay her any mind."

They steered clear of the still on the way down the mountain. Jordan spotted the abandoned tobacco fields.

"Look, detective," she said. "I know I give you a hard time, but I do hope you solve this thing."

"You got to stop calling me detective. Call me Tom. And you don't know much I appreciate your help. No telling where I'd end up if I walked on this mountain all alone."

"You'd be dead is what."

"So is that why you're escorting me up and down these slopes? You can't be doing it for the fun of it, that's for certain. And the money isn't exactly going to pay off the mortgage."

"I just know what it's like to lose someone. You know, kin folk."

Jordan stopped and looked at her, and after a moment, she must have realized she was walking alone. When she turned to see where Jordan was, he said, "Who, if you don't mind me asking?"

"My husband. And my boy. My husband died fourteen years ago. My boy…not sure. He disappeared a few years back."

"Disappeared? Like, ran away?"

Her voice began to tremble as she looked off in the distance. "He was workin' the plow on the south end of our tobacco fields. He didn't come home for lunch. Now he was a hard workin' boy, but buddy, when it was lunchtime, he was never late. Okay, so I set out to take him his meal. Found his tractor runnin,' but no signs of my boy. Thomas was his name. Just like your'n. I found a trail of blood leadin' to the crick, but no signs of him."

"He never resurfaced?"

"No. Hadn't seen hide nor hair of him since."

"Emma, I'm very sorry to hear that."

Jordan began to place his hand on her shoulder, but rubbed his chin instead.

"It beats anything I've ever seen."

"How old was he?"

"Twenty-one. Was a bit of a renegade, I guess. But, he was a good boy. Strong as a bull. He was six-foot-four if he was an inch. Had forearms the size of a mule's neck. Got his height from his daddy's side."

"Are they still investigating his disappearance?"

"Not likely. They run slap out of ideas. They got no clues."

"I'm sorry, Emma."

"Sure would like to find him. Sometimes I look off into the fields and I see him working the crops. Sometimes I hear him talkin' to me when I'm down by the crick."

He'd watched her drive away, and as he headed to the sheriff's office, he couldn't erase the look of sadness on Emma's face as she spoke of the disappearance of her son. His thoughts turned to Hannah and her talk of kudzu.

~ * ~

Lawrence sat at his desk, sharing ideas with Anderson and Myers about the deaths of Patricia Darby, Becky Shoun, and Barbara Thomas. Jordan tapped on the glass window of the door, and popped his head inside the room.

"What, no doughnuts?" Jordan quipped.

"We done ate 'em all," Lawrence responded.

"Tell me what you know about the disappearance of Emma Douglas's son."

"We searched the county for weeks. Looked down Doe Creek all the way to Lake Watauga."

"Any known enemies?"

"Not that we could find. He kept to himself. Not many friends. Just a good ole boy who liked ridin' in his daddy's truck, fishing, workin' on the farm. You know, just normal country boy stuff."

"Can you show me where he disappeared?"

"Sure. Why do you want to see it? It's not like there's evidence to collect."

"How close to Iron Mountain?"

"A couple miles."

Jordan paused. "Did you do tests on the blood samples on his tractor?"

"Sure did. Must be in the file. Where you goin' with this?"

"I'm not sure yet. But somehow I think this is all related."

Anderson rubbed his chin. "I suppose we need to follow up on everything we can think of if we want to solve this thing."

Jordan nodded. "Time to listen to the mountain."

"Say what?" asked Lawrence.

"Never mind."

Twenty

Sunset was an hour away, but a heavy fog had ushered in the night. Jordan's SUV churned along Highway 47. He was getting a preference for sunrises over sunsets in Doe Valley. At least the peaceful aura of morning eased the truth of a killer on the loose.

Jordan headed for the cabin. It was time to get in tune with the mountain, to 'listen' to it as Hannah had advised. What better way than to stay at the cabin; to stay on Iron Mountain. He debated the idea, knowing he was possibly putting himself in the sights of the killer. Marty would drag him home with a rope if she knew his plan.

He had come to the end of the line with regard to the investigation, but he owed it to the victims, and to the others who perhaps were still alive, to give Hannah's suggestion a try.

The piercing headlights of Jordan's vehicle fought, unsuccessfully, to part the misty air from the road. The narrator's voice of a *Cold Mountain* audiotape helped spell his feeling of isolation. He was an outsider and there was nothing he could do about it. Detached from his family, he felt separated from everyday life. But, the Doe Creek body count was up to three, and two were still missing. The game was on, and it was time to win; win it for the women whose lives had been forever changed.

A black bear and her cub rummaged on the roadside in an overturned metal trashcan beside a dump as Jordan sped by. The fog made it hard to see the lights in his rearview mirror. As he hugged the winding road, he spotted a pickup truck behind him quickly gaining ground. Jordan struggled to maneuver through the snake-like bends in front of him with the truck's high beams flooding his rearview mirror. He lowered the side mirrors to deflect the truck's lights. Slowing down, he pulled to the edge of the road so the truck could pass. The truck moved behind him, just feet from his bumper.

The truck sped up and tapped Jordan's car as the road took a slight downturn. He pressed the gas pedal and gained temporary separation. His hands were tight on the steering wheel. The thickening fog and the bright headlights blended into a wall of haze in front of him as he approached a narrow concrete bridge. The truck moved to its left and sideswiped Jordan's SUV, pushing him toward the bulwark. Just before impact, he pulled his wheel hard to the right, barely missing the bridge and barreling down the embankment. The vehicle hit a jagged wall of rocks along the bank, and it flipped to one side, overturning and landing upside down. The horn and alarm sounded, and the air bag exploded from the steering wheel. The front of the vehicle was submerged in a foot of water.

Dazed and upside down, Jordan searched for the seat belt buckle release as water filled the car. Struggling to move as the air bag pinned him against the seat, he unlocked the seatbelt, retrieved his belt knife, and punctured the airbag. Using the butt of his .38, he shattered the passenger window and kicked out the glass. He squeezed through the window into shallow water and the icy creek took his breath away. Righting himself and crawling along the dark bank, he pushed his wet hair away from his forehead and removed his jacket.

Sonsabitches ruined my new coat.

The whine of squeaky brakes screeched above Jordan as a truck stopped on the bridge. Jordan retrieved his gun from his shoulder holster and dove into the tall grass that bordered the creek bed. Two shadows emerged from the truck, their silhouettes looming large amid the backdrop of the truck's headlights and the fog. A flashlight's beam floated over the overturned car in the creek bed, landing on Jordan, who raised his left hand to shield his eyes from the blinding light.

"You okay?" a voice called out.

Jordan lowered his gun. "Yeah."

Two elderly men walked carefully beside the bridge as Jordan approached them.

"What in the world happened?" one of the men asked.

"I got run off the road."

"Lord amercy. You sure you're okay?"

"Yessir."

The men drove Jordan to a one-pump gas station two miles away in a small borough called Burlington. Jordan's walkie-talkie had fallen in the creek, probably becoming a late Christmas present for a rainbow trout.

"Go knock on the door, Thurmond," the elderly man said to his partner. "See if Judd's still there. See if this fellow can use his phone."

Jordan called Sheriff Lawrence, and he radioed Myers, who was responding to a report of a dead deer on the 321 Bypass. The deputy soon arrived with a blanket and a thermos of coffee. Thirty minutes later, when Lawrence arrived, Jordan was clothed in a flannel shirt and faded overalls.

"I like your new duds," Lawrence said when he walked into the dimly lit gas station.

"They're compliments of Mr. Judd," Jordan said.

Judd nodded.

"I believe one of my pals from Stoney Creek was delivering a message."

"Yeah. Best come back to the station while we get this mess cleaned up."

It took several hours to retrieve Jordan's SUV from the creek, and get things settled concerning the events of the night before. There were no leads on the driver of the truck. It was too dark for Jordan to get a make on the vehicle, and he never saw the license plate. Lawrence gave him the use of a police vehicle. After dinner, he again headed to Iron Mountain.

~ * ~

The cabin waited in dark silence, encased by the fog, similar to the night Jason and Kara first came to the cabin. With a suitcase in hand, he stumbled his way into the den and found the overhead bulb. He walked about the house and into the bedroom and stood at the window where perhaps the stranger had watched Jason and Kara; watched others before them. The ones who'd come treating the mountain like some romantic getaway.

Surely the house had seen much, but its cold walls told nothing. He walked out on the porch, looking into the endless darkness running through the hills to a world of isolation, unknown except to those who had been born upon her. In legend, and now through personal experience, the mountain was found to hold stories of life, of death; to be a world where there was little distinction between the two.

Jordan tossed three folders of information on the kitchen table and poured over the data. The only common thread between the victims, other than the obvious mistake of venturing onto Iron

Mountain, was they were female. Their ages ranged from eighteen to thirty-three. The physical characteristics were diverse—blonde, auburn, and brown hair. The same went for their backgrounds; high school senior; college grad student, young career woman, mother and housewife.

Jordan had won the praise of his superiors in Knoxville. Highly decorated, he'd helped solve every case assigned to him. But each day that passed on Iron Mountain made the solving of those cases distant memories. He glanced at his watch. Ten fifty-five p.m. Almost too tired to shower, he forced himself, out of habit if nothing else. Lugging his suitcase to the bathroom, he removed a pair of boxers and a faded Peyton Manning jersey to sleep in.

After a quick drenching, he walked into the bedroom with its barren mattress, stripped clean after Kara Lisle disappeared. Too tired to place the sheets on the bed, he removed a frayed wool blanket from the rocker and laid it across the mattress. He craved sleep, but his mind wouldn't let him find it. The situation was like a mental chessboard he tried to maneuver in his mind—the empty shackles in the cave, the incident on the road, the lack of suspects, the mysterious disappearance of Emma Douglas's boy, and the insights of Hannah Profitt.

What did it all mean?

Around three a.m. he finally slipped into a burdensome sleep. In his dreams, he chased a blurry figure between two thin rows of trees. On the outer side of the trees was only space, cliffs that had no bottom, no land below it. The path they ran was dark and he could not see the ground below him. In front of the figure he chased were faint lights of a town in some valley that seemed a thousand miles away.

Jordan slowed as he ran toward a plank of some sort, where one step off the path would send him over the edge into the blackness. The stranger slipped, and Jordan grabbed him by his shirttail. As he tried to turn the figure around to get a look at his face, the stranger jumped off the mountainside. Thunder rolled and lightning flashed around him in long, crooked veins. Below him, he heard screams of angst and terror. He looked behind him and the path crumbled. There was no escape, and the land under him seemed to chip away to where only a strip of ground a foot wide kept him from falling thousands of feet.

He woke, sat up on his elbows, his body sweaty, his heart

racing, and looked about the bedroom.

His eyes couldn't adjust to the dark. The room was still pitch black, with no light outside the bedroom window. He sat on the edge of the bed, his elbows on his knees. He rubbed the back of his neck. Down the hall he went, flipping the kitchen light and opening a slightly consumed pint of Jack Daniels he kept in his brief case. He took a long, hard drink, rubbed his hand through his hair and returned to the bedroom.

Daylight had broken when Jordan awoke. He quickly shaved and dressed then shuffled sleepily out the door. Driving the police car brought back memories of his early days as a street officer. Simpler times. As he rounded a sharp curve near the bottom of Shady Valley, Hannah Profitt stood off to the side of the road. Limbs from a red spruce crossed in front of her left shoulder and chest. She looked as eerie as the first time Jordan saw her. He looked into her beady eyes, and she returned the stare. After he passed her, he looked in the rearview mirror but she had disappeared.

Jordan rode into town. Before he stopped by the police station, he drove to Bert's Café for some caffeine to help him think clearly. Bert's Café was the only restaurant in Laurel City. It opened at five a.m., and closed at two in the afternoon, after the lunch crowd was through filling their bellies and shooting the breeze. The tiny restaurant had seven booths that lined the front window. Four small tables were located in the middle. The counter was j-shaped with six stools drilled into the floor. The worn, old-fashioned stools were silver with red cushion tops. Children preferred the stools so they could eat and spin at the same time.

When Jordan entered the restaurant, the booths were filled, most likely with the regulars, from the co-op, Jenson's Department store, and the county office. Perhaps old farmers looking for a little more conversation than they might find at home. According to Lawrence, it was a place where lies were told, jokes played, and plenty of biscuits, country gravy, and coffee were consumed.

Bert and his son, H.G., manned the grill and the counter. H.G.'s wife Sally waited tables. Lawrence told him no one outside the family knew what H.G. stood for.

Jordan grabbed a spot at the counter, and overheard a conversation about the killings. Bert slid a mug of steaming coffee in front of him while he rubbed his temples with his thumb and index finger.

"Any news about the killer?" Bert asked.

"Progress is slow. We'll catch him."

"Iron Mountain scares most folks round here. We do our best to stay away from it. Stories of Gaines Logan, and their 'us against the world' attitude—we heard 'em as young'uns and were told to steer clear of that place."

"I can see why you'd feel that way."

"I'm ramblin' on about things you probably know already."

"Not a problem."

Ed Mandrell walked in and sat beside Jordan. "What's a fella gotta do around here to get a cup of coffee?"

"Mornin,' Ed," Bert said. "Take a seat and stop flappin' your gums. The coffee's comin' right up." After filling Ed's cup, Bert wiped his hand on a dishrag and leaned in front of Jordan. "Detective, I know somebody that might can help you." He held up his index finger. "There's one man who knows everything about that mountain that don't *live* on that mountain."

"Oh yeah? Who is that?"

"Rubin Sawyer."

"Who's he?"

"He was born and raised on Iron Mountain. He left it behind when he turned a young man."

"Think he knows more than Emma Douglas?"

"Ol' Emma's a force o' nature all right. But, Emma ain't from Iron Mountain. She's never experienced what he has. What he knows. What he feels."

"Does he live around here?"

"He lives in a cabin near Powder Branch. I can give you directions right to his door step."

~ * ~

Jordan headed south toward Boone with only hope and directions on a paper napkin. The countryside south of Laurel City was sandwiched between the long, spiraling ranges of Dry Gap and Valle Cruces. Both mountain ranges lay along the eastern border of Tennessee in east to west fashion, with Dry Gap turning northward until it meets the North Carolina line. Between the towering mountains are some of the most beautiful valleys in all of East Tennessee. Stately, white Victorian-style homes stood on hillsides, their front doors facing south, as they watched over one-story brick homes in the flats of the valley. Diminutive brick homes sat side by side along the highway like giant, cherry-red dominoes.

Driving with the napkin pressed between the top of the steering wheel and his right index finger, Jordan turned east off Highway 421 onto Slab Town Road. A gravelly mix of rock and earth rolled under his tires as he crossed the Watauga County line. The road rose slowly into a quiet cove of grass-covered hills. Four horses grazed unfettered in the shadows of a dozen maples and oaks. A fifth horse, chocolate-brown with a white stripe under his neck, lifted his head to watch Jordan's car make his way through the valley.

Bert's directions were on the money, and Jordan pulled up in front of a log cabin set back about forty yards from the road. The weathered cabin sat at the edge of a slender stream and was made of dark-brown logs intertwined with white ones, giving the appearance of a wooden rail fence from a distance.

Shadows grew shorter as the midday sun rose in the cloudless sky, the hunter-green grass of the hilly yard capturing the brilliant light. Jordan walked toward the cabin and heard what sounded like hammer meeting steel. Walking around the left side, a broad-shouldered man pounded away with an ax on a rock, severing the leg of a black-haired boar from its body.

"Rubin Sawyer?" Jordan called out.

The man continued to chop away at the hog. "That's the name."

"That's a hell of a pig you got there."

"Yep. Just killed her an hour ago. It took three shots to fell her. She rushed me when I checkin' rabbit traps in the brushy thicket in Windy Gap." He straightened and wiped blood off his hands with a dirty rag.

"How did you get it out of the woods?"

"The only way I know. Dragged it."

"Impressive." He extended his hand. "Tom Jordan. I work with TBI. Missing persons in Knoxville."

Sawyer seemed to ignore the handshake offer. "Well, how about you grab this sow's leg so I can get this thing cut and cooked?" Jordan took the boar's bloody leg just above the hoof. Sawyer separated the leg with one blow. "Throw her leg up on the table."

Since Bert had told Jordan Sawyer was somewhere around the age of seventy, Sawyer's appearance surprised him. He looked twenty years younger than he imagined. His hair, trimmed along the temples with gray, was dark brown and wavy. He was Hollywood handsome, with chocolate eyes and a rugged chin with thick stubble.

A piece of stained plywood, hammered between two stumps, waited for the hog. Jordan set the leg on the plywood and Sawyer placed the torso of the animal beside it.

"You ever eaten boar before?" asked Sawyer.

"Once or twice. Never cared that much for it."

"Then it must've been cooked wrong. It's good eatin' when done right."

"I'll take your word for it. Um, Mr. Sawyer…"

"Call me Rubin. Mr. Sawyer makes it sound like I've achieved some sort of educational level that I know I ain't."

"Okay, Rubin. Have you heard about the murders on Iron Mountain?"

"Everybody within three counties has heard about it."

"Well, there are two women still missing and we're trying to find them before they end up floating in the creek like the others."

"I can see why that would be a priority. What's that got to do with me?"

"I heard you grew up on Iron Mountain."

"I did. But, I don't know who's doin' the killin' if that's what you're askin.'"

"Bert, over at the café, says you know more about the mountain than anyone."

"I signed off on that place years ago." Sawyer removed a small silver knife with a white handle from a sheath strapped to the side of his pant leg. He carved the butt away from the bone of the boar.

"I went up to Stoney Creek Holler with Emma Douglas. I guess you know them boys up there. Got run off the road yesterday, most likely by one of them. The clock is winding down for those girls, and I sure could use your help."

"I don't know." He shook his head gently, rubbing his chin as though his mind and heart were at odds.

"If you don't help, who knows how many more women will end up floating in Doe Creek?"

Sawyer continued carving meat. "Like I said, I signed off on that place years ago."

"Well, I'm stayin' at Paul Grayson's place on Iron Mountain if you change your mind."

Jordan turned to walk to the squad car.

"Not so fast," Sawyer said while tossing the pork butt into a white, Styrofoam cooler. "We ain't finished carvin' up this hog."

Jordan took hold of the remaining leg and they scavenged every portion of the sow that qualified as meat, as well as some things that didn't. Jordan watched, certain from the swiftness and accuracy of Sawyer's blade, he'd done this sort of thing for a lifetime.

Twenty One

Jordan looked about the room but only saw the pitch black of night. He dozed off for a few more minutes before a faint roll of thunder roused him. The wind rustled the leaves outside the cabin, and the trees clamored against each other, like waves pounding the shoreline.

Steadily the thunder increased in frequency and sound, and a flash of lightning provided a temporary interruption to the darkness. The storm rolled in from the northeast, building in strength after pushing through the vast Shenandoah Valley. Rain pounded against the house, hammering the tin roof in sheets.

Thunder shook the walls of the old cabin, roaring and rumbling as though it sought to reach the very corners of the world. Storms weren't something that rattled him, and he actually found them quite fascinating. But on this night his palms were sweaty, his breathing labored. His eyes moving about, he stiffened when a bolt of lightning crashed above the cabin, casting a silhouette at the window. He raised up on one elbow, but night swallowed the shadow.

Removing his .38 from the holster on the bedpost, he eased to the window in the darkness, that great equalizer. Another bolt cracked, brightening the room, but the shadow was gone. He looked out into a deep canvas of black in front of him and his heart pounded.

The storm quickly blew past, the thunder fading in sound with each rumble. He returned to bed, his upper body dampened with sweat. In the quiet he wondered—had the storm played tricks on him?

When Jordan's alarm sounded at four-forty-five, he lay on his back staring at the ceiling, frustrated. The storm ended hours before, but he'd gotten little sleep. His walk to the shower was sluggish. The water was slow to warm. He removed his straight razor and shaving cream from his black toiletry bag. He shaved with cold water because he liked the way it slapped away sleepiness. When he stepped into the shower, the slow pulsing of lukewarm water took off the chill. He was coming back to life, ready to head for higher ground.

It was time to hike to the hunter's shack. After Rachel William's husband verified ownership of the bracelet Jordan found on the floor of the shack, he at the least had a location to tie her to. He loaded a backpack with apples, cashews, almonds, and three bottles of water. His plan was to return to the cabin before nightfall. He carried a compass, walkie-talkie, flashlight, a knife in his belt sheath, and his pistol. If the mountain was ready to talk, Jordan was ready to listen—in a prepared sort of way.

His steps were deliberate down the driveway to Shady Valley Road where he turned north. Morning had arrived under a thick blanket of clouds, holding the frost to the ground. He wore thermals under jeans and sweatshirt. A black overcoat. Though he was embarking over unfamiliar territory, there was no sense of panic. He had a job to do. Simple as that.

He stayed on Shady Valley for close to a half mile.

Brown puddles, the remnants of heavy snows, darkened the road like spots on a cheetah. He walked with a slight limp, his leg having regained most of its strength. A quarter mile down the road, a piece of plywood was nailed to a sapling, letting him know he was about to cross the Pete Lowe Memorial Bridge.

The bridge crossed a small stream no more than five feet wide. The surface of the bridge was stone and loose gravel. Two rails of bluish-gray tin, two feet high and twenty feet long, ran alongside the edge of the bridge. The rails were too flimsy to prevent a vehicle from falling off the side of the bridge and into the tiny brook. On his first trip to Stoney Creek, Emma talked about Pete Lowe, saying he was another mountain man like Gaines Logan. According to Emma, Pete was a trapper, a poor man's Daniel Boone. He killed bear, deer, small game, fowl, and even once coaxed a Black Angus away from Hank Burrows' farm in Doe Valley so he could butcher it for a Christmas feast. Lowe died in the late '70's when he got mauled by a mountain cat while on a hunting trip. Emma said the word around Stoney Creek was Lowe strangled the cat with his bare hands as he breathed his last. It was said he was found with the cat's teeth sunk deep in his jugular, the cat expired on his chest.

The sign on the side of the bridge read, "pete lowe—mountin

man."

The slope of the mountain changed to subtle turns as he turned east into the woods, though its northward incline remained steep, preventing him from climbing to the peak. The stillness was smothering

Patches of ferns provided scant color to an otherwise drab floor of brown leaves and rocky earth. Knotty pines hid the treetops of the hardwoods. Small snowflakes trickled through the forest. At the base of an elm was a brown bottle partially covered by moss. Rubbing the gritty soil off the bottom of the bottle, his fingers traced the raised words, Chattanooga Medicine Company 1909. He placed the bottle in his backpack.

The terrain grew steeper and Jordan used the trees for support. Above him, hell's laurels hovered, a menacing wall of green, forcing him to walk a lateral path along an area of pines. No needles were visible on the twisted limbs except at the tops of the trees that stretched a hundred feet high.

The faint sound of music wafted upward from a clearing that bordered a narrow stream. An old man with cotton-white hair played a dulcimer next to a pine box placed beside an open grave. On the other side of the box stood a man, his head bent, eyes closed, and a shovel by his side. Next to him a woman, her hand touching the shoulder of a small child. Their heads were bowed as the old man began to sing.

His brown eyes stared void of emotion. His coarse, tenor-laced voice, combined with the soft sting of the chords, sang a ballad tinted in Celtic harmony.

> *Child of God, jump from the grave*
> *Run from the mountain, run far away,*
> *To streets o' gold and fields o' wheat*
> *Run and bow at the Savior's feet.*
> *Hurry to the heavens, now, hurry to the sky*
> *Run fore the devil knows in the casket you lie*
> *Hurry, hurry from this rugged land*
> *Where evil reigns in the hearts of man.*

His fingers began strumming faster as he sang:

> *The grave is cold, oh sting of death*

165

It steals the soul, steals the body's breath.
But as we lay down our precious kin
He's done flown away to heaven's den.
On past the river Jordan, past the pearly gates
To that place where God almighty waits.

He bowed his head and leaned the dulcimer against the base of an elm.

There were three markers to the left of the casket, odd shaped stones roughly the size of basketballs. Barely legible writings of whitewash were on each. The primitive burial held more truth than any funeral Jordan had witnessed, a ceremony that lay bare before God the very essence of man. A bridging between heaven and earth, proving that the grave was the destination for all men, through thousands of years, the only thing separating them was the marker that would carry into history the verification that they had even existed.

A quick prayer was spoken, but it couldn't overshadow the fact life on the mountain must continue. As they lowered the casket into the grave, the woman quietly sobbed.

After the casket was laid in the ground, the man took the shovel, and looked at the others. "'Nough cryin.' Time to git back to the chores."

The woman and child turned and walked away. Jordan approached the clearing as the man with the shovel returned the dirt to the grave. The white-haired musician eyed Jordan. "You seek the shadder of the trees," the old man said. "God will bring you into the light."

"I mean no harm," Jordan answered. "Just passin' through."

"Leave us be," the man with the shovel said.

"My condolences."

"You's passin' through sacred ground," spoke the musician.

The man with the shovel placed it on the ground and picked up a rifle that leaned against a tree. "Leave us be, mister, or there'll be another grave to dig today."

Jordan stared down the barrel of an old Winchester.

"Git."

Jordan raised his hands, chest high and backed away into the dense backwoods.

The shack was sixty yards in front of him and his pace

quickened. Snow fell harder, the flakes soft and flat, and the limbs of hemlocks gathered them as though they were worth more than gold. The ground had turned white. Lawrence's prediction of the final snow of the spring was off the mark.

He stood in front of the shack, looking out into the woods, hoping to get some feel for where Rachel may have gone. Once inside the cabin the search for clues began.

The pine cabinets were empty. His fingers rubbed along the edge of a small, tin washbasin located near the front window. No cots, no sleeping bags, occupied the cabin. He slid the couch from where it rested against the wall, and rubbed his boot across the crumbs and dust balls that had gathered underneath it. He kicked at the thick gray grime with his right foot, as his left forced a slight, hollow creak.

Hmmm.

Kneeling, he tapped on the floor with his knuckle, detecting a soft spot. He noticed a loose piece of wood and removed it. A panel-like section, a square foot in diameter, came up after Jordan jiggled it. Underneath the floor, it was dark and dank, and it revealed a second panel of wood that held a bundle, a dark clump. Reaching his hand in, he removed a shirt, a gray thermal-style piece with a bloodstained collar. He studied the front, turned, and examined the back. The edges were frayed, and holes were located where bugs had eaten through.

He reached again into the damp opening and grabbed a faded pair of denim overalls and a baseball-style cap. The writing on the hat was faded, the only letters legible a "c" and an "h." Removing his flashlight from his bag, he peered again beneath the floor. The light illuminated thick tracks of cobwebs and the dust-covered panel. Moving the beam of the light about, he spotted something small with a dull shine.

He had trouble reaching it, and had to use the head of the flashlight to tap it close enough to where he could remove it. He dusted it with his glove, squinting his eyes as he examined it closely. It was a black, tight-knit cord that connected at both ends to a porcelain buckle. Jordan rubbed the porcelain against his jacket, revealing two horses silhouetted against the backdrop of a turquoise sky. The detail work on the porcelain was impressive.

Jordan placed the porcelain tie into a plastic bag and then wrapped it inside the overalls. He placed the overalls, the shirt, and cap into his bag, removing the walkie-talkie and apples to allow more room. He bit into one of the apples and placed the walkie-talkie in his coat pocket. Time to have the bloody shirt analyzed, so he took to the woods. The snow was accumulating, now two inches thick below his bootstraps. He moved quickly, retracing his path.

The thick powder made for slow and deliberate travel. The trees again provided leverage for Jordan as he maneuvered across the mountainside. Approaching a slight sunken ravine, Jordan positioned himself to leap a four-foot wide gully that was a watershed when the summer rains became heavy.

He pushed against a locust for support and leapt the ravine. As he landed, his right leg submerged into a snow bank. By the time he heard the sound of the metal jaws clanging shut, his leg was lodged deep in the teeth of the jagged trap.

Jordan's moans echoed through the mountain as he reached for the cold steel. Deep puncture wounds on both sides of his calf soaked his jeans in crimson, and the escaping warmth from his blood evaporated quickly. Each attempt to escape the clutches of the trap tightened the grip of the steel shards piercing his leg. He pushed snow on and around the wounds to slow the flow of blood.

He cried out in pain as he slid the arm straps off to remove his backpack. For minutes he writhed. Pushing his weight upward. He finally dislodged the pack and found the walkie-talkie. His fingers fumbled to push the button, and he called out, "Mayday." Several failed attempts left him disoriented. He was slipping into a state of shock. Minutes trudged agonizingly by, and Jordan drifted in and out of consciousness. He called out one last time then his head fell back into the soft snow.

~ * ~

The warmth from her coarse, yet delicate fingers soothed Jordan's forehead as she brushed away a sweaty clump of hair just above his left eyebrow. His eyes opened temporarily and he caught a glimpse of her timid face. Soft shadows of orange and red flickered about in the darkness from the clouded glass oil lantern she held in her right hand.

His lips parched, Jordan attempted to speak, but she placed two fingers lightly against his mouth. A moist rag touched his left cheek, then his right, somewhat deflecting the sharp pain in his right leg. His eyes finally came into focus and he found himself looking into a pair of pale, blue eyes.

"Where..." he mumbled. "Where am I?" He blinked while waiting for a response. The hay-strewn bed he lay upon had left him achy and stiff. "Who are you?" he whispered.

She dabbed the rag on his forehead. He glanced across the dark room, and again looked into her eyes.

"Who are you?" he repeated.

"I'm Sarah," she sheepishly replied.

"Where am I? How did I get here?"

"We found you in the snow. We thought you was dead."

Jordan's throat ached as he strained to speak. "Who is we?"

"Me and Zeke."

Chills shook his body. Sarah explained how she and her brother stumbled upon him. She had pestered Zeke to let her come with him to check their traps along the ravine. Zeke was responsible for the handful of traps that provided dinners ranging from rabbits and ground squirrels, to pole cats and possums. The trap that snared Jordan was set by Zeke in late winter. He only checked it on occasion as it was several miles from home.

He learned there was an unwritten law on Iron Mountain that traps were to be set around the vicinity of one's home so as not to take game that, by virtue of proximity, belonged to another family. She said Zeke had seen several bear cubs the previous fall in that area, and figured he had as much right as anyone on Iron Mountain to snare one.

Jordan struggled to follow the words pouring from her mouth, his vision blurred, the pain in his leg throbbing and pulsating with each heartbeat.

"How did you get my leg free of the trap?" he softly asked. He winced as he shifted his leg slightly, trying to ease the pain.

"With a crowbar. It took both of us to get it open enough to slide your leg out," Her voice was raspy, and her backwoods accent was heavy. "The snow was all purple-like from all the blood that had oozed from your leg. It had froze together so it looked like you was wearin' one of them things folks wear when they break a bone. It weren't easy gettin' the crowbar in there. Once we got you out, the hard part commenced."

Jordan brushed the sweat from his forehead.

"You was nothin' but dead weight, and after we pulled you loose, Zeke cut your pant leg into strips with his knife and made a tourniquet to slow the flow of blood." Sarah fidgeted with her shoulder length dirty-blonde hair, twirling the oily strands between her index and middle finger. Though her complexion was pale, it contained a certain softness to it.

Jordan began to shake, and Sarah took off her sweater and draped it across his chest. She rubbed her hands along his arms, and then continued on as though she was chatting with a neighbor on the porch.

"So, Zeke cuts these limbs from a maple tree, and bound them with vines from a mountain laurel, making a sled-like contraption. We drugged you up onto it. And then we tied rope to the bound limbs and pulled you across the snow a half-mile up a ravine where our mule was. We lifted you up, and Zeke throwed you over his shoulder and onto the wagon. Sounds crazy, don't it? Like somethin' from one of those Hollywood movies."

"How long have I been asleep?"

"Pert near two days."

"What?" He attempted to pull up on his left elbow, but quickly realized he didn't have the strength to do so. He reached in his pocket underneath a charcoal-gray wool blanket. "Have you seen my walkie-talkie?"

"You mean one of them conversatin' radios? Nope."

"I need that radio." He tried to sit.

"You's too weak fer that. Here, drink this soup. It's squirrel."

She held the wood mug up to his lips, and provided support to the back of his head with her left hand. Jordan gulped the salty brown, lukewarm soup.

"Me and Zeke got you hid good, so you should be okay fer a while. Daddy'll whup us though if he finds out we got you in here. No tellin' what he might do to you."

Those words brought little comfort. Jordan slid the blanket off his right leg, exposing six open wounds caked with dried blood and denim. His attempt to sit caused him to black out. Sarah caught his head and lowered him to his bed of hay.

Within seconds, Jordan opened his eyes and sharp pains ran along his temples.

"Just rest," Sarah said.

Jordan quickly faded out as Sarah spread the blanket across his body.

~ * ~

Lawrence sat at his desk scratching his earlobe with the eraser end of a yellow pencil. His unanswered calls to Jordan's radio had him wondering if he'd met the same fate as Kara Lisle and Patricia Darby. Deputies Myers and Anderson search of the cabin and the surrounding area was fruitless. All hell had broken loose, and Lawrence had no idea where to turn. Johnson County had experienced only one murder in six years, and that occurred when Buck Jacobs, with a belly full of liquor, shot Harold Wilkins for poisoning his coon dog.

Deputy Anderson phoned Lawrence to update him on the hunt for Jordan. Anderson and the other deputies had covered over four miles of backwoods, and even with assistance from bloodhounds, came up empty.

"Bring 'em back in, Deputy. It'll be dark in an hour."

"Yes, sir."

Anderson and the rest of the hunting party called it a day. Lawrence phoned Marty to tell her that her husband was missing.

~ * ~

Jason Lisle walked into Lawrence's office. His face was pale, with bags under his eyes. His hair was unkempt. Dressed in faded blue jeans and a crumpled white T-shirt, Jason stood in front of Lawrence's desk.

"Any news?" Jason asked with faint anticipation.

"None."

Jason rubbed his forehead and shook his head. He was one of the most optimistic people to walk on God's green earth, but his sense of hope was fleeting. Three weeks of not knowing had flattened him.

"Son, maybe you should think about going home. You can't help us here, and you look terrible. When we find Kara, you don't want her seeing you looking like this. Who knows, one look at you, and she might head for the hills again."

Jason attempted a smile but couldn't quite bring himself to crack one. "I can't leave. If I do, I'll be deserting her."

"Son, you're comin' home with me tonight. My missus will cook you dinner, and you can stay the night with us."

"I appreciate that, but I'll just head back to the motel."

"I ain't takin' no for an answer. If you give me any lip, I'll lock you up."

Finally, Jason managed a slight smile.

Twenty Two

Rubin Sawyer pulled his truck in front of Simpson's Hardware store across the street from the McKinley funeral home. A white, ten-gallon bucket rolled to a stop in the back of his truck. After he removed the bucket from the bed, he noticed people standing next to a gray hearse in front of the funeral home. He placed the bucket on the ground.

He recognized Betty Hugeley and her oldest son, J.B. Two American flags were attached to antennas on the hearse. It was the funeral for Arlo Hugeley who fought with Sawyer in Korea. Since Sawyer kept to his business, he seldom knew the day-to-day occurrences of Laurel Springs. Flanked by sadness and guilt, he looked to the sky and shook his head. Instead of attending a fellow veteran's funeral, he stood next to a bucket that would soon be filled with lye. When he caught Arlo's wife's eyes in the hearse window, he saluted. Could he hide the guilt?

Tennessee had a proud military history. In the Army he learned his home state had produced some of the finest soldiers the country had ever known. The hills of East Tennessee were adorned with American flags. More noticeable were the flags that dotted the hillside graveyards of those who had served, and died, for their country. Sawyer was a decorated soldier from the Korean War, certain his pride and valor was passed on by the likes of Davy Crockett and the great frontiersmen of the state.

Sawyer walked into the hardware store.

"Mornin,' Rube," said storeowner Wilbur Simpson.

"How you been, Wilbur?"

Sawyer placed his bucket beside the counter and Wilbur's son Skeeter carried it to the back of the store where he'd fill it with lye.

"Ain't seen you much of late," Wilbur said. "I guess you noticed Arlo's family across the street. Another one gone."

"Ain't that a hell of a note?"

"Where you been? Haven't seen you in a coon's age."

"Lots to do, Wilbur. Lot goin' on. A man cain't spend time wanderin' around the city when there's work to be done."

"I hear you. I was guessin' you'd been on the huntin' trail."

"I have been doin' a lot of that. Spring's comin,' and there's not much of hunting season left. Squirrels, rabbits, turkey. I need to fill my freezer. Got a nice sow up on Windy Gap."

"You know there are things called grocery stores. You ain't gotta kill your dinner anymore."

"That stuff they sell ain't fit for wharf rats. Processed meat. Butcherin' animals that are force fed and kept alive just long enough to fatten 'em up. No thanks."

"Ain't it a damn shame about them gals up on Iron Mountain?"

Sawyer nodded.

"You heard any talk about who might a done it? I figured you mighta."

"How would I know anything?" Sawyer said with agitated curiosity.

"I don't know. Thought since you grew up there…"

"I don't have nothin' to do with that place anymore." He glanced to the back of the store as though he were ready for the chit-chat to end. "Is Skeeter 'bout through fillin' my bucket?"

Skeeter appeared from the back, struggling to carry the bucket without spilling the lye. "Here you are, Mr. Sawyer."

"Much obliged, Skeeter." As Sawyer nodded good day to Simpson, he turned to the door.

"Hope they find them ladies what's missin,'" Simpson said. "That detective feller too."

Sawyer released the knob from his hand and turned toward Wilbur. "What are you talkin' about?"

"Dale Anderson's ma told me this mornin' that the detective from Knoxville went lookin' for the missin' lady folk, and now he's up and disappeared too."

~ * ~

Virgil watched Walter Hicks wander up the narrow path. Hiding in the trees beside him was his best friend Cecil.

Hicks, a traveling preacher from Jonesboro, held a brown bottle in one hand, and a brass money clip in the other. His brown

Fedora was tipped slightly to the left side of his head. Hicks had come to fill his bottle with corn "squeezins." He had a mixture of herbs and spices he called 'bitters' that, when mixed with a taste of homemade liquor, made a strong elixir. Hicks swore the liquor was strictly for medicinal purposes, and therefore never interfered with his ability to preach the Gospel.

Since most everyone knew Hicks in Jonesboro, Johnson County was the place he went when it was time to refill his elixir. And there was no place more convenient than Nate Taylor's. Taylor's property was a short drive off Highway 47, and just a hop, skip, and a creek-crossing jump from Pandora Road.

Not only did moonshine production run deep in Taylor's family bloodline, his product was as smooth a drink that Hicks had ever sampled. Taylor was checking his latest batch when Hicks walked up. Virgil and Cecil hid quietly in the brush.

"How do, Nate?"

"Mornin,' Preacher," Taylor replied. "Haven't seen you in a while. Was worried you may have met a horrible fate. Either that, or Lucille clamped down on your wanderins.'"

"No, nothin' like that. I been spreadin' the Word over in Kingsport. Lotta lost souls up there."

"Amen, brother."

"Well, anyway, my lower back's been givin' me trouble. I figgered your elixir might ease my pain. Mind if I get a refill?"

"Not at all."

Taylor removed a ladle located on a block of wood hammered into a pine. He dipped it into a glass bowl located under a fifty-five gallon thumping keg, filled the twelve-ounce chocolate-brown bottle, and handed it to Hicks. Hicks shook the bottle and watched as the herbs mixed with the alcohol. Taylor drank the remaining liquor from the ladle, before filling it again. Handing it to Hicks, he said, "Have yourself a taste."

"Oh, I'm not a drinkin' man," Hicks said.

"Me neither," Taylor laughed. He placed the ladle in front of Hick's chin.

"Well, maybe one sip won't hurt." Hicks kicked back the entire ladle. "Wish I could find a cow that gave milk that tasted like this."

"Me too. Until then, we'll let my still be the golden cow."

Hicks removed his Fedora, and moved to an oak rocker ten

feet from the still. He placed his hat on a knob on the back of the chair. His tussled, shoulder length hair of silver made him look more like Albert Einstein than a preacher. He wiped his brow and sighed as the alcohol warmed his insides.

Virgil tugged Cecil on his sleeve and they sneaked behind Hicks. Taylor tossed wood on the fire around the boiler, allowing the boys to slip in unnoticed. Quietly Virgil removed the hat and retreated to the hiding spot.

"Gimme your gum," Virgil whispered to Cecil.

Cecil, whose jaws were swelled like a Guernsey cow, spit the gum into Virgil's hand. Virgil spread the gum along the inner rim of Hick's hat. The gooey pink wad clung easily to the felt lining. "I didn't skip school just to waste the day. So, let's see if we can piss off Preacher Hicks."

Virgil returned the hat carefully on the rocker post. He knew the high school principal would report their absences by day's end, and wanted to make sure the day was worth the whipping they'd receive that evening. The pair slipped fifteen feet behind Hick's chair, crouched behind the three-foot stack of wood.

Hicks finally rose, stumbling a bit, placing the hat on his head. He walked beside Taylor and pointed at the keg. "I believe you can cure cancer with this stuff," he said, pointing at the thumping keg. His legs were unsteady and his words were slurred. "'Scuse my rudeness, but I need to be home by sundown. I'm afeared after dark."

Hicks grabbed the right side of the hat in an attempt to bid farewell to Taylor. His wincing told of obvious pain as the gum clung tightly to his hair. He tried removing the left side, and it only seemed to cause more of the same kind of pain.

"What *the* hell?" He grimaced as he pushed with both hands in an attempt to remove his hat.

"His head looks like a parachute," Virgil whispered to Cecil. Cecil's snickers caught Taylor's attention.

"Hey!" Taylor yelled as he looked toward the shed. "What are you little bastards doin' up here?"

The teens took to the woods, laughing as they ran. Taylor retrieved a shotgun from the shed while Hicks remained at the still, trying to remove the cap without ripping his hair from his scalp. A blast of buckshot screamed above the boys' heads, and Virgil tumbled into a patch of ferns. Taylor fired again and the boys descended the mountain in joyful panic.

As they neared the bottom of the hill, Taylor's warning to stay off his land echoed through the trees. Cecil leapt a stream which fed into a spring house and fell into a row of jelly glasses chilling in the cold water. Virgil, who had cleared the stream, turned back to check on his partner. One of the jars had broken under Cecil's ribcage, cutting his skin through his shirt.

"You all right?" Virgil whispered.

Cecil rolled over and looked at small patches of blood coming through his shirt then toward a patch of knee high sassafras two feet away.

"Virgil!"

"Hold it down," Virgil said. "You want your head blown off?"

Cecil reached into the sassafras and slid it to one side. "Look at this."

Virgil knelt beside Cecil. "Oh, shit."

~ * ~

Lawrence had just entered the police station when Adams leaned over the dispatcher's desk.

"Virgil McQueen and the Jackson boy say they found a body beside a spring on Nate Taylor's land."

"It just never ends," Lawrence said as he smacked the desk with his fist.

Lawrence drove along Sanders Farm Highway. The winding road meandered along farmland and dairy barns on its way toward Elizabethton. They found Virgil's white Ford pickup off the side of the road. The boys looked visibly shaken. Virgil sat on the lowered tailgate with his face in his hands. Cecil paced the shoulder beside the road.

Lawrence followed Virgil and Cecil by foot. The boys spoke little, and Lawrence reckoned the discovery of the body was the reason, and understandably so. The climb to the spring was a thirty-minute trip, through scattered grassy hillsides.

"Boys," Lawrence said, approaching the truck. "What in the world were you doin' out here in the first place?"

"Can we talk about that later?" Virgil asked.

Lawrence was surprised that the body wasn't floating in Doe Creek like the others, but as he pushed away the sassafras, he knew it was a male body.

Virgil indicated that the clothes and the cap that lay at an angle on the body's head belonged to Billy. Lawrence called EMS and asked Anderson to summon the Stout family to verify the body was Billy's before it was sent off to the pathologist.

Cecil and Virgil sat stoned face on the trunk of the squad car while they waited on their parents to pick them up. The trauma of finding their friend in the sassafras seemed to overwhelm them.

~ * ~

The first traces of daylight exposed the crevices and corners of the dilapidated barn that had become Jordan's haven. The square structure, no more than twenty feet wide or deep, looked more storage shed than barn. The walls, slender boards of bluish gray, ran vertical from a dirt floor, its bottom chewed away by unknown creatures. The ceiling was a v-shaped tin roof that reverberated when it rained. Along the walls were bags of chicken feed, two fifty-five gallon drums, a pick ax, hoe, and a wooden crate filled with basic tools. Jordan lay hidden behind four bales of hay stacked two-by-two at the back of the barn.

The cool morning air stretched across the earthen floor, and Jordan's face flush with fever. The wounds in his leg were red and tender, and the putrid smell of infection loomed heavy in the air. He struggled to recall the number of days he had lain in his hideaway. Four, he thought. *Or was it five?* Sarah had managed to slip unnoticed to the barn each day with groundhog jerky and boiled rutabagas, as well as a spoonful or two of moonshine in his drinking water for pain.

Sarah was Jordan's Florence Nightingale, and his only hope. The first few times she came to the barn, she appeared jittery, struggling to look him in the eyes when she spoke. But as the time went on, she seemed more relaxed, and perhaps she felt a sense of importance knowing someone from outside her world needed her.

He rose slowly to a sitting position without passing out, bending his right leg Indian style until the heel rested on his left kneecap. Pus seeped from the center of the beet-red wounds. He tugged at the denim patch enveloped by dried blood on the left side of his calf, but the crusty cotton strip was too firmly rooted to remove. He tried to stand on his left leg, but fell hard on the brittle strands of hay beside his mattress.

Sarah's tender hands rubbed his forehead. "You ain't in no shape to stand."

"My leg is infected. You gotta get help. Get your parents."

"No!" She placed her hand to her mouth as if to scold herself for speaking in a loud manner. Quietly, she said, "Pappy'll kill you. For all I know, he might'n kill me too."

"Sarah, I can't hold on much longer."

"You rest. I'm a gonna git help." Sarah rolled him back onto the mattress. "Here, this'll help you sleep." She gave him a wooden cup filled with moonshine and spring water. She covered him with the blanket, again rubbed her fingers through his oily hair, and slipped out the door.

~ * ~

Sarah ran into the thick tree line behind the barn. She knew of only one person who could help. An hour later, she rapped on the creaky door of Hannah Profitt's shack.

"Miss Hannah, I need your help."

"So, child, you come to save the stranger."

"How'd you know?"

"That's not your concern."

"Will you help me?"

"It's not you who needs help." Hannah glanced out into the backdrop of trees over Sarah's shoulders, her beady eyes fixed and unmoving.

"Please."

Hannah turned toward the kitchen, and Sarah followed. The house, musty and dank, was lit only by the glow from a wood stove and a tiny oil lamp. Shards of light sneaked through a cloudy single pane glass window to the left of the stove. In front of the window was a rusty, metal sink hammered into the splintery wall. The sink was littered with wooden utensils and a plastic plate. A metal tub of drinking water sat underneath, a rusty ladle lying on its bottom.

Hannah moved to the right of the sink and slid back a green cloth curtain hiding three tiny shelves. On the bottom shelf were seven mason jars filled with figs and muscadine preserves. The middle shelf contained a burlap sack filled with meal. On the third shelf was a small black bottle that Hannah removed. "Here, child." Hannah placed the bottle in Sarah's hand. Reaching to the shelf again, Hannah's bony fingers lifted a pottery bowl covered by a green hand towel. She pointed to the bottle in Sarah's hand. "Give him a cap full at mornin,' and a'gin at dusk."

"Yes'm. What is it?"

"Bloodroot and ironweed. It will rid him of his fever."

Hannah removed a gray cloth pouch from underneath the sink. She shook it upside down and tobacco resin fell to the dirt floor. Walking to the woodstove, with no regard to the flame, Hannah reached into the fire, filling her hand with soot. She tossed the soot in the pouch and gave it to Sarah. "Shake the soot on his leg. It'll reduce the swellin.'"

After Sarah took the pouch, the hag walked to a corner wall and gently squeezed a black and yellow argiope spider between her thumb and index finger. She crushed the spider against her apron and brushed it to the floor then softly swept her hand across a delicately spun web the size and shape of a widow's shawl. The web collapsed around her hand, and she slowly unrolled it from her skin. "Wrap this web around his leg. It will close his wounds proper."

Sarah hesitantly straightened her right arm, and Hannah wrapped the hair-like strands around Sarah's hand.

"Walk carefully child, but don't tarry. He won't last much longer if you don't get this to him soon."

"Yes'm." Sarah exited the front of the shack. Sarah turned her head, Hannah watching in silence as Sarah entered the woods.

~ * ~

The sweat poured from Jordan's body, soaking his clothes as the hay around him clung to his body. He struggled to keep his wits about him and alternated between a state of sleep and foggy consciousness. The late afternoon light slipped between the boards of the barn, jagged piercings of light skewing his ability to distinguish the shapes leaving him confused, unsure of the difference between the real and the contrived. Nodding off, he quickly slipped into a dream.

In the dream, the walls of the barn pushed inward, forced by the weight of dirt behind them, as though the barn had been lowered into the ground. The hard soil of Iron Mountain was closing in but Jordan had no escape route. His breathing compressed, he tried to call out. He knew it was a dream, but couldn't will his mind to let it end. He struggled to relay to his brain that it wasn't reality. But in that moment, it was only a dream in his mind. Within his soul, it was as true as the earth below him and the towering trees outside the barn.

Twenty Three

The barn door creaked lazily and Jordan opened his eyes. He had dozed off and on throughout the morning. A shadow emerged from the doorway, and Jordan rolled slightly on his side. "Sarah?" he whispered.

Peering through an opening in the stacks of hay, Jordan saw the shadow of a man. He grimaced as he slid his body closer to the bundles. The man, in dingy white long-handle underwear and a gray pair of overalls, rooted around on a shelf hammered to the wall of the dimly lit building. He fumbled around on the shelf until his hand emerged with a claw hammer loosely attached to a slender wooden handle. As he reached to close the door, he glanced at the straw strewn around the hay bales. He stepped back into the barn.

Slowly, he moved around to the side of the four stacks of hay. "What the hell?" he said as Hannah stepped up from behind.

"Pa, what you lookin' fer?"

"Why's the hay stacks out of kilter?"

"I was hidin' in here from Zeke yes'tiday. He was all mad 'cause I took his rabbit gun." She looked nervous as her father studied her face. He scratched the stubble on his chin, his eyes squinting and untrusting. His teeth were sparse and crooked. He had large ears and a sharply bent nose.

"You know you ain't suppose to bein' playin' 'round in here. This barn's for work purposes, not for leisure. And you leave your brother's belongin's be. No time for foolishness." He kicked at the straw on the dirt floor. "Now git this straw up before I take the strap to you."

"Yes, Pa." She reached for the pitchfork. "If you slip on out, I'll get things cleaned up."

He hesitantly walked out of the barn.

Jordan wiped his brow. How much longer could he stay hidden? He rolled on his side to ease the pressure on his injured leg and became pinned between a bale and the barn wall.

"Let me help you," she said.

She placed Hannah's remedies on a nearby bale and eased Jordan back to his make shift bed.

"I been to see Miss Hannah. She done told me what to do." Sarah mixed the bloodroot and ironweed in a cup of spring water. "Drink this."

Jordan choked down the bitter concoction, some trickling down his chin. Sarah reached into the pouch and scooped a handful of soot.

"What are you doing?"

"Shhh. Don't worry your mind about it."

He winced as she pulled his jean pant away from the wound, and she gently tossed the soot on and around the puncture wounds before wrapping the spider web around his leg.

"Miss Hannah said this'll fix you up. Now lie down and rest. I'll bring you somethin' to eat when I can."

Sarah slid the soot pouch and burlap sack underneath a stack of hay and walked out.

~ * ~

The barn door opened, casting light into the dark, dank barn. When Sarah's fingers pressed against his forehead, it was the first time they hadn't felt ice cold. Hannah's mixture had broken the fever.

"Mornin,'" Sarah whispered.

"Mornin,' Sarah."

"You look better. How you feelin'?"

"Much better. I've got to go. So much I've got to do."

"I figgered as much." He detected the disappointment in her eyes.

"I can't thank you enough. You saved my life." Jordan reached to hug her, and his eyes narrowed. "What is that around your neck?"

"It's somethin' I got one day when Zeke and me was a checkin' the traps."

"Can I see it?"

Sarah looked puzzled, but reached behind her neck and untied the article of clothing. She placed it in Jordan's hand. He looked closely at the designs of white in the corner of the blue scarf. "Where did you get this?"

"Near Rocky Branch. Zeke and this feller got mixed up in a ruckus. The boy said something to me Zeke didn't care fer. Said I should come off with him and let him show me how a slut was supposed to be treated."

"Go on."

"I told him to go on about his business. I told him I weren't that type of girl. Between you and me, I don't know what slut really means. Anyways, he then called me a whore. Zeke hit him with the barrel of his rifle. Caught him off guard and he fell into some ferns. I tell you, that boy was big as a grizzly. Lucky thing Zeke cocked his rifle and threatened to shoot his country ass, cause the boy took to runnin.' This here scarf fell off his neck into the fern. I thought it was purdy, and brung it home."

"When was this?"

"I'd say mid-winter."

"I need this bandanna, Sarah."

Sarah handed it to Jordan and he placed it in his coat pocket.

"What in blazes is goin' on in here?" Sarah's father shouted, standing at the barn door. His rifle pointed at Jordan's midsection, his silhouette at the doorway, dark and imposing.

Sarah stepped in front of Jordan. "Pa, don't hurt him. He needed help. He was gonna die."

"Sarah, move away from him."

As Sarah stepped away from Jordan's side, she looked at him with fear in her eyes. When she stood in front of her father, head down, he backhanded her cheek, knocking her into the shelf, scattering tools onto the dusty floor. Jordan stepped to help her, but the rifle pointing at his head stopped him in his tracks.

"Hold it right there."

The man sent Sarah out of the barn. He looked closely at Jordan, using the morning light as a lantern to look at Jordan's face. He studied him. "Mister, I don't know you, and I don't know why you're here. I do know it was the worst mistake of your life." He pointed toward the door with his chin. "Move on outta here. Nice and slow like. I don't want to have to shoot you in my barn."

Jordan slowly picked up the backpack at his feet. The man eyed Jordan closely as he walked to the door.

"Sarah, run git Zeke."

In a matter of minutes Zeke entered the barn.

"D'you bring this here man into our barn?" asked the father.

Zeke looked down at his feet.

"Answer me."

"Yea, Pa."

"You'll get your ass strapped after we're done with him. Git some rope. Two of the little 'uns." The wiry man took hold of a leather strap and draped it across his narrow shoulder, his rifle never leaving the sight of Jordan's midsection.

Zeke grabbed two strips of brown rope, each three feet long, and shut the barn door. Sarah watched from the side of the house as her father and Zeke marched Jordan into the woods. Soon they were on a small trail that moved along fairly flat terrain. Several hundred yards into the dense trees, they came upon a field that faced Snake Mountain to the east. Four spindles of hay sat along the edge of the field filled with goldenrod and sumac. A line of trees behind them rose slightly above the field, making it appear as if nothing separated the trees from Snake Mountain but air.

They came upon a straight, thick poplar and the father commanded Jordan to halt. "Tie him to the tree."

Zeke pressed his hand into Jordan's back, forcing him to the thick tree, and his father knocked the backpack from Jordan's hand. "You ain't gonna be a needin' that where you're goin.'"

Zeke tied Jordan's hands together after he forced him to hug the tree. Zeke made no eye contact with Jordan. Fearing for his own well-being?

As Zeke backed away, his father stuck the barrel of the rifle against Jordan's neck. "Why are you on my land?"

"I'm with the TBI in Knoxville."

"A damn lawman." He pushed Jordan's face against the tree with the gun barrel, the bark scraping against his cheek. He removed the strap and took hold of it by a narrow leather handle. "A big mistake, mister."

The strap popped angrily when it lashed against Jordan's back. Jordan's knees buckled, and he slumped against the tree that bound him. The mountain man delivered another blow, and the sting numbed Jordan briefly before the fire of pain streamed across his shoulders.

The old man dropped the strap, backed away two steps and pointed the rifle at Jordan's head. "I should give you time to make peace with the Good Lord," he said. "But I ain't extendin' you that courtesy."

Zeke looked nervous, and seemed tempted to protest on Jordan's behalf. As the man touched the trigger, a shot rang out, and a bullet struck his hand. He screamed in pain and his rifle fell to the ground. Zeke turned as Rubin Sawyer pointed his rifle at him.

"They'll be no killin' here unless it's you who wants to die," Sawyer said. He looked at Zeke. "Take your pa and leave, son."

Zeke's father squeezed his right hand with his left as blood poured from his fingers.

"I just took off two of your fingers. The next shot will split your throat. Go on. Git."

"Damn you, Rubin Sawyer," the man said as he wrapped his hand in his shirt sleeve. Blood turned his gray shirt crimson in a matter of seconds. "You got no idea what a hornet's nest you're stirrin.'"

"That hornet nest got stirred years ago. And I'm gettin' ready to turn the fury on this whole mountain."

"This ain't over by any means."

"You're right it ain't over," Sawyer said. "The way I see it, it's just beginning. Now, you can take your boy and carry your ass on back home. Otherwise, I'll make it where your family gets to lower you in this cold mountain soil you hold in such reverence."

Both father and son backpedaled. The man, gripping his wounded hand, cut his eyes at Sawyer. When Sawyer cut the rope that bound Jordan's hands with a knife he'd drawn from his belt sheath, Jordan dropped to his knees.

"You ain't got time to waller in your pain and pity. If we don't get a move on, we're gonna face that hick and relatives he never even imagined was related to him. They'll come back with more firepower than we're equipped to handle."

"How'd you find me?" Jordan asked. He removed the cut rope from his wrists, his teeth clenched from the fire coming from the strap wounds on his back.

"The arm of Hannah Profitt stretches a long way. Even so, it wasn't easy."

"How long you been lookin?"

"Two days. Now shut your mouth and move on out of here."

Sawyer carried two sleeping mats and a sack of supplies on his back. He handed Jordan the man's rifle.

As they hurried through the trees, Jordan asked, "What changed your mind?"

"About what?"

"About getting involved with the dealings on Iron Mountain."

"I sensed you weren't going to figure this out on your own. then you went off and disappeared. Besides, it's time to settle the score."

"What score?"

"When we get some distance behind us I'll tell you. Just make sure you keep up."

Sawyer led the way, retreating on a narrow trail that carved a path through dense hardwoods and a constant ebb and flow of peaks and valleys, a continual shift in elevation.

They shadowed the southern side of Iron Mountain, Doe Valley visible in the distance. Jordan sweated and his muscles ached as he fought through pain in his leg and from the strap marks on his back to keep up with Sawyer. For several miles they walked in silence, their breath and the sound of their boots on the ground the only sounds.

The trail dropped under an awning of rocks heavily covered in moss. Sawyer pointed to a fallen tree. "Set and rest. We can't sit long, but get your energy back while you got the chance." Sawyer removed his pack and pulled out a plastic bag of deer jerky. He handed the bag to Jordan. "This will recharge your batteries."

He knelt in the soft ferns, the rocks hovering eight feet above them. "You want to know why I left Iron Mountain?" He looked to the countless row of peaks to the south as though there were answers to mysteries of life. "Plain and simple. Bum Whitfield and his men. They killed my Pap when I was a boy. They executed him right in the middle of the dirt road in the heart of Stoney Creek."

Jordan stared intently at Sawyer.

"When I turned eighteen I swore I would never return," Sawyer continued. "Then you come up here and get yourself in all kinds of trouble. I thought about the reason you were here, and what you're tryin' to do in bringin' all this nonsense to an end. That you're putting your life on the line for a greater cause. And then I stared to think of those young gals that found Doe Creek a means of transportation to their final restin' place, and those unaccounted for who might end with the same fate, and I knew my conscience would never let me live with myself if I didn't help."

"I'm sorry about your father. What happened?"

Sawyer looked at Jordan with somber eyes. "Time to rest the tongue and the body." He lowered both knees to the ground.

They sat in silence for a good ten minutes.

"Time to move," Sawyer said.

As the man rose to his feet, Jordan wondered at his agility. A young man hidden in an old man's body. Sawyer led the way, and they walked single file. In that moment, Jordan was the acolyte and the man he followed more versed than he in the ways of not only Iron Mountain, but surely the world.

They moved east again, where they came upon a dirt road. Along both sides were thick elms and poplars, and the cloudy sky colored the woods a gray that seemed cold and uncaring. Gooseberry vines and briars, long and menacing, lined the edges. On that narrow road, in what seemed to Jordan a place so remote not only in location, but to life itself, Sawyer spoke.

"My pappy was never one to drink, and he refused to play a part with anything havin' to do with moonshine. That went contrary to the way Bum Whitfield ruled, contrary to the ways of operation on the mountain. Bum liked to intimidate, and Pap wasn't into such nonsense. Since he wasn't one of Bum's puppets, Bum took it as a sign of rebellion. In all seriousness, I think Bum was afraid of Pap."

"Why is that?" Jordan asked, almost worried he'd overstepped his bounds in probing further.

"Because he showed backbone with regard to his beliefs. On Iron Mountain, belief is a contradiction in terms. There is no belief, only doubt. Doubt whether life will be anything but hazardful if the law of the land isn't obeyed. Doubt of what good can occur if you're not following orders for the good of the mountain. Up here, all they got is each other, and it's them against the world. And so, Bum decided to send a message, and he sent his boys to get Pap. They dragged him across the holler. Bum said that Pap was workin' with moonshiners from Snake Mountain, and they shot him dead in the road. I was maybe ten years old when it happened."

"Good Lord."

Mountain winds stirred, and the treetops danced above the men, a creaky troupe.

"My ma came runnin,' and tried to send me back to the house. I was screamin' and carryin' on, tellin' Bum what I would do to him one day. All four feet of me. Like I was some warrior. He just held that smart-ass smirk of his. I'll never forget it. I'll never forgive, either."

"How old was Bum when this happened?"

"I'd say early twenties. Old enough to know better. And he's at the top of my list as far as revenge goes."

"Well, you help me catch the one who's strewing bodies across Doe Creek, and I'll help you get your wish."

Sawyer nodded. "Fair enough."

The men slipped along quietly for several hours. When they stopped again to make sure they weren't being followed, Sawyer placed his hand on Jordan's shoulder.

"It's inflamed and red, but it ain't bleedin' too bad," Sawyer said.

Sawyer guided Jordan to a fallen pine, and removed some peroxide from his bag. Jordan lowered his shirt, and when Sawyer poured the liquid on the wounds, Jordan winced.

"While you're at it..." Jordan lifted his pant leg.

"Good Lord, son. You are all kind of tore up." He poured peroxide on the marks left from the trap.

Before they continued on, Jordan removed the bloody shirt and porcelain tie from his bag. "I found this in a hunter's shack where Rachel William's bracelet was found. She disappeared a few days after Kara Lisle was snatched from the cabin." He handed the oval, turquoise tie to Sawyer. "Ever seen one of these?"

"A bolo tie. Cowboys used to wear 'em."

"Know anybody 'round here who wore one?"

"Couple of folks. Preacher Mays wore one on Sunday mornings. His had a picture of Jesus on it. Jenks Crosswhite wore one when he competed in rodeos. I believe Emma Douglas' husband had one. But all them folks are dead."

Jordan showed the bloodied shirt to Sawyer. "You know they never found Emma's boy." Holding the shirt by the sleeves, he stretched the material. "This shirt fit a mighty big man."

"Thomas Douglas was a big ole' youngin,'" said Sawyer.

They entered a narrow hollow, the descent steep, and below them a wide creek rushed eastward.

"Be careful," Sawyer said, "or you'll slide down the mountain and end up in the creek. And it won't be a pleasant event."

They walked a few steps and Sawyer squatted. He waved his hand downward in silence so that Jordan followed suit. His eyes seemed to study the land above them, along the steep mountain incline. Jordan scoured the tree line as well. Two men, different in background, but laced with intensity and desire to survive.

"Get that rifle ready," Sawyer whispered.

Jordan removed the rifle strap from his shoulder.

"We're fixin' to get attacked, Iron Mountain style. Hide beneath that white pine. On your belly. Take everything straight ahead and to your right. Don't flinch when the bullets start. I don't imagine you got many shells left in the clip, so be choosy. And by God, be accurate." A shot rang out from above, and it scraped the bark from a poplar a foot above Sawyer's head.

The mountain came alive in a familiar sacredness where the bullet was judge and jury to settling disputes, claiming stills— claiming land. Jordan pointed his rifle, looking through the sight at nothing; everything.

Sawyer held up five fingers for the ones he'd spotted. He slipped into the ferns, crawling quickly on his stomach to a thick laurel. The limbs tore at his face and shoulders as he wiggled into it. Another shot cracked in the distance, and the bullet ripped through the laurel leaves above his head.

Jordan lay in shooting position, his elbows steadying the aim of his rifle as it pointed forward. The situation was surreal, as though he were playing cowboys and Indians out back of his boyhood home with his brothers. He'd been involved in a couple of shootouts in Knoxville, but those took place on city streets and alleys, not in deep woods on land that despised his presence.

Sawyer aimed his rifle, and Jordan spotted a man crouching in a smattering of ferns sixty yards in front. A shot cracked through the trees, a bullet hitting the wooden stock below the barrel of Sawyer's rifle. The impact knocked the gun from his hands. When he fetched it from the fallen leaves under the laurel, he looked at the split in the stock.

"Ain't that a hell of a note," he said, rubbing the broken stock. His face reddened and his eyes narrowed.

Jordan took two shots in the general direction of where Sawyer had aimed while Sawyer again resumed shooting position. On a boulder forty yards above, a man in a faded baseball-style cap stood taking aim. Sawyer fired, and the man fell off the large rock.

A volley sprayed from the trees, raining down upon Jordan and Sawyer. Jordan joined in, firing toward the source of the rifle blasts, and the mountainside exploded in gunfire.

Sawyer shot at a man running toward the boulder and picked him off in one shot, dropping him into the ferns. The shots poured down from above and Jordan responded.

"This ain't no Western," Sawyer said. "Save your bullets."

As the rain of fire grew, Sawyer turned to Jordan. "We've got one chance to make the outcome turn in our favor." He nodded past Jordan. "See the broken fir?"

Jordan looked down the narrow path from where they'd come. He nodded.

"Run like hell, and slide down the mountain to the creek below."

"No way I can survive that."

"If you go down at the fir, there's one spot deep enough in the creek to hold you. Just stay clear of the rocks." The shots grew louder, the mountain men closing in. "Git. It's your only chance. I'll cover you."

"I'm not leaving you behind."

"When you get to the water, start firing up above me." Two more shots zipped between them. "If you don't survive the fall, my ass is as good as cooked. So make sure you don't splatter yourself on the rocks."

Jordan took to the trail, bent as low as he could while still able to run. Bullets zipped around him and Sawyer returned fire. Behind him the cracks from rifles and the thundering booms of shotguns played a battle's tune. The creek moving fast and hard below him, his gun held high, he slid in the ferns and, lifting his leg like a baseball player sliding into second base, headed down the mountain. He tumbled across small saplings and the limbs of white pines scraped across his body as he dropped from the land toward the creek.

He slid thirty yards then tumbled off a cliff fifteen feet above the water. Jordan slammed into the icy creek, his backside stinging as though it had been hit by a two-by-four. Submerged in five feet of water, his body swirled and turned as he tried to right himself. The gun barrel smashed against rocks along the creek's floor, and yet he managed to hold on. He fought the panic of not being able to breathe, and kicked hard to bring himself to the surface.

He gasped and tried to fill his lungs with air as the water whirled and stirred in jagged waves around him. He exhaled and took in another long breath, and he fought to grab hold of something concrete as he tumbled downstream. Still holding his rifle above the water, he approached a waterfall. He tried to swim to the side, ten feet away, but the current pushed him toward the falls.

He tumbled over the edge, a twelve-foot drop, forcing him into a rumbling pool that bubbled angrily as though it had no desire to receive the water that pushed downward from the creek above. Jagged rocks hugged both sides of the pool, and the force of the water pushed Jordan downward. He still maintained hold of the gun as he bounced along the shallow bottom, and he kicked forward and surfaced, the water lessening in speed and turbulence.

A large rock lay ahead and he moved toward it and took hold. It stopped him from pushing down stream. He gasped for air, water spitting from his mouth and nose as he filled his lungs with air. Soaked and cold, his hair sprayed wildly about, he pulled himself onto the rock. Above the roar of the waters gunfire erupted, faint pops that sounded like firecrackers.

He'd deserted the man who saved him. Looking to the hill behind him, he took aim with his wet rifle. He aimed, but at what, he had no clue. And then he spotted him, rolling downstream, face down. When he came through the falls, Jordan jumped back in the water. He took hold of the lifeless body and steadying himself, lifted Sawyer's torso from the frigid creek. He dropped to his knees and perched Sawyer onto a rock. Blood trickled down Sawyer's forehead, and Jordan's heart seemed to freeze in the moment.

"Rubin," he said, shaking the man. The water raged on around them, as if trying to knock them back in the creek. He took hold of Sawyer's chin, and shook his face. He rolled him over and slammed his forearm into Sawyer's back and water leapt from his lungs and out of the mouth. He began coughing and fighting for air. Slowly Sawyer opened his eyes, though they appeared cloudy.

"I got you," Jordan said.

Sawyer looked about as though his senses had gathered. His clothes clung tightly to his ragged body.

"Are you okay?"

Sawyer coughed and raised up from the rock on his elbows. "In my younger days, I would have glided down the creek like I was on air."

Jordan smiled. "As long as you made it is all that matters. But we need to stop that bleeding."

Sawyer rubbed his sleeve against his forehead. "Ain't got

time to worry about that now." He looked back at the mountain. "Them boys ain't gonna follow the route we took, and if we hurry, I can lead us down a path they won't follow."

~ * ~

Kara's cough worsened with each passing day. Her breathing was labored, and her chest tightened so that the only way her airway opened was when she coughed. She struggled to drink the milk and spring water brought with her meals, and she survived by dipping biscuits in the milk and eating them.

Time seemed to stand still, lying on the cold dirt in the dark, hour upon hour. She tried to cry, but the tears wouldn't come. The previous day she'd dreamed Jason found her, bursting through the door, carrying her away in his arms. How was he holding up? How agonizing it had to be for him. She vowed to cut back on her hours at work, and would change her priorities if she ever got a second chance.

While lying in a fetal position, footsteps echoed outside her door and she began to whimper. The door to her prison cell opened, and she covered her head with her arms, whispering, "No. Please, no." She covered her mouth and coughed deeply.

The tiny silhouette entered the darkness, placing a plastic tray at her feet. Two rutabagas, a cold biscuit, and a jam jar filled with goat's milk would be her meal. The elderly woman rubbed her cold, bony fingers across Kara's forehead. The warmth of her fingers felt good on Kara's skin.

"Please help me," Kara said in strained whisper. "My asthma." The words came in short bursts. "Need medication. Can't make it much longer." Touching the elderly woman's hand only caused the woman to pull away. "Please."

The woman closed the door, the lock clicking shut.

~ * ~

The door opened to Rachel's prison, the slight figure silhouetted in the yellow light from behind her. She slowly crouched and shakily placed the tray in front of her.

Rachel grabbed the shackle that kept her captive. "My ankle is swelling. It's bleeding. Can you open this thing so I can at least move it off my ankle?"

She looked at Rachel's foot, which was positioned in the shadows to equalize both confirmation and suspicion. The woman shook her head.

"Please. I swear I won't do anything. It's just so painful. Please." Rachel searched the woman's eyes for sympathy, but instead sensed burden and apathy, as though a chain bound her heart and mind. When the key opened the shackle, Rachel ripped the metal from her ankle, scrambled to her feet and took off out the door.

Adrenaline rushed through Rachel's tired, unsteady legs, and she ran quickly up the steps. The possibility of freedom fueled her desire to escape. The muted light of day was yet bright enough to force her to shield her eyes with her hand, sliding it above her eyebrows like a visor. The air was cold, but to Rachel, it was warm in its openness, and the feeling of being in a wide expanse not bound by shackles gave her newfound strength.

She wanted to turn and make sure she wasn't being chased, but any motion or thought toward what was behind her would hamper her ability to move to the safety of what laid ahead. Naked as the day she was born, Rachel fled.

She made it through the high weeds and into the thick woods. Soon she came upon the stream and the ravine she crossed when she was captured, retracing her steps out of the hellhole from where she had been placed. Two hundred yards she made it, and she gained speed. She was about to be free, and her adrenaline grew as did the quickness in her weakened legs. Her hair was tussled, the back matted in a greasy ball. Her feet disregarded the cold of the mountain floor. She came upon a steep slope, covered in ferns and she crawled on all fours until she made it to flatter terrain. Dirt filled her once manicured fingernails.

Alex and the girls would be so happy. The look on their faces when she came walking through the front door of their quiet home would make for a perfect homecoming.

The woods were silent except for the heavy breathing pushing rapidly from her lungs. Bursts of breath exited her mouth, flowing in front of her face like steam from a locomotive. She spotted the stream thirty-five yards in front of her, and the rushing sound of the brook was one she thought she'd never hear again. As she stepped into the frigid water, tiptoeing the best she could, the weight of his body crashed down on top of her. She fell hard into the rocks on the other side of the stream.

"No!" she screamed.

He yanked her hair and turned her on her back. She kicked his chest and he slapped her legs away. He squatted to take hold of her waist, and she flailed wildly at his face. A forceful backhand knocked her head into the hard soil. She kicked and hit to keep him off of her. She was weak, but she slammed her fists rapidly against his body.

She backed him toward the water for a moment. When she tried to stand, he lunged forward and landed another blow to her face, knocking the back of her head into a rock partially submerged in the mossy bank. She became limp and her eyes rolled into the back of her head.

Twenty Four

Jason pulled his car off the highway and cut the engine. He leaned back against the headrest and closed his eyes. His face was worn and his six-day beard was scruffy. He hadn't eaten in three days, and he'd driven along the lonely back roads since sunrise.

He got out of his car and leaned his back against the door, looking west across the highway to Iron Mountain, charcoal gray under a pale, gloomy sky. That cursed land. He turned and looked east to a dirt road that ran perpendicular to the highway, and began to walk. A fine mist fell, drifting in the air as if gravity had no control over it. Though it was midday, the dreary skies created a dusk-like appearance.

The road he walked crossed a wide swath of Doe Valley, rolling hills where cattle grazed. Doe Creek twisted through the valley like some angry serpent. In the distance, gray patches of clouds clung to the slants and pockets of Snake Mountain, providing sharp contrast to the dark silhouette the mountain carved in the distance.

The road was full of puddles; rust-colored pools that popped and spit as drops began to fall. He followed the lane to a faded white, two-story house flanked by a pair of tall, Virginia Spruces. Smoke billowed from a crusty fifty-five gallon drum to the side of the house, a small fire popping sparks of wood and metal in the air.

Jason walked through a dilapidated gate lying by the roadside. A man sat beside the drum in a wooden, hardback chair. He was hunched, his spine curved, a look of scoliosis. He wore a black fedora, and a brown sweater frayed at the sleeves, the elbows faded. Dark wool pants. The rain fell about him as he whittled a long stick with a small pocketknife. His face was aged and leathered, and it told a history of hard life.

Jason approached warily. The old man looked at Jason and pointed to a folding chair that leaned against an oak. "Set a while.

You look ragged."

Jason regarded him as one not necessarily wise in his assessment.

"Why do you wander this old road? A road that leads nowhere."

He shrugged his shoulders. "Nowhere. I've become well acquainted with nowhere."

"Me the same. I'm its gatekeeper."

"Maybe it's *somewhere* I need to go."

"What is it that waits fer you somewhere? Or should I say, *who?*"

Jason nodded. "*Who* is right."

"It's always who. Who is it you's a seekin'?"

"My wife," he said with watery eyes. "I've run out of places to look."

"You think it's here she lies?"

Jason looked in the distance. "Here, there, everywhere. What difference does it make? I've about given up hope. She's been gone over a month."

The man continued to whittle, examining his results with one eye closed. He touched the end of the stick with his finger. He looked at Jason, studying him with gray eyes that seemed dulled by time and misfortune. "Hope. A sweet tonic to ease misguided souls."

"Misguided? If not for hope, what is there?"

"Would you reckon that hope plays a part in the outcome you's a wantin'? Does it tip the scale in favor of the results you seek?"

"I don't know." He shrugged. "What do you think?"

"What I believe ain't important." The old man sat back in his chair and looked at the gloomy skies through the tree limbs. He placed the stick across his lap, cleared his throat and ran his finger along his earlobe. "Back in the '20s a family lived in the holler yonder ways." His eyes pointed above Jason's shoulder. "They was two young'uns in the family. Twins they were. One day, while the pap tended to his cattle, and the ma cooked at the stove, the young'uns played in the yard. As the story goes, they spotted a fawn in a nearby field, alone and skittery, and thought it would be a good idea to catch her. They tried to get close, coaxing her their way, but it'd scamper away as soon as they got close. Well, the fawn would stop, and they'd follow. Run a bit and stop. Let 'em get close. Like she was playin' with 'em."

A story unfolding from a peculiar man, and yet Jason listened.

"Now the twins were, best I can recall, the age of six, and they didn't realize that as they chased that little varmint, they was gettin' further from home. By the time they gave up tryin' to catch it, they didn't know where they was. Didn't know how to get back home."

"How long before the parents realized they were gone?"

"Long enough to where them babies was a long ways away from home. Their pap scoured the fields, calling their names. He then took off on horseback, and the ma gathered neighbors who spread the word. Some men in the valley joined in on horseback, and others formed a search party by foot. It was nighttime they fought, and they were in a panic that they would not survive with temperatures fallin.'"

"Did they find them?"

"They searched into the night, lightin' bonfires across the mountain in hopes that it would draw 'em out. Now, the ma and some others waited at home in case the children returned. They held prayer vigils and sang hymns, praisin' God and askin' for unwaverin' hope and the belief that he'd keep the children safe." The old man rubbed the inside of his bottom lip, as if checking for remnants of chewing tobacco. His mouth was missing several teeth. He shook his head and said, "Hope and prayer was all they had."

"So what happened?"

"They searched for two days, snow falling on the last 'un."

"And?"

"One of the men on horseback spotted an old shed near an abandoned field about two miles up the backwoods. He checked inside and found them lyin' agin' the wall."

"Were they alive?"

"Though they was twins, one was a boy, the other'n a girl. The boy was hangin' on for dear life, but his sister was cold and dead there beside him. The man who found 'em wrapped the boy in his coat and got him home before he froze to death."

"Why are you telling me this?"

"It was a life saved. A life lost. Through it all, did hope and prayer play a part in the outcome? Was it responsible for the joy? Weren't it strong enough to prevent the misery?"

"Huh?"

"Did they hope and pray only for the boy? Did they not pray for the girl as much as they did him?"

"Surely it was equal."

"You'd be a fool to think otherwise. And so lies the question—was the hope, were the prayers, beneficial? If so, was only one prayer answered? Did God only have an interest in savin' the boy?

"Either way, don't you think that hope and prayer sustained the parents during the search?"

"Perhaps. But what good came from it? There was still heartache in the end."

"It could have been worse. Both could have died."

"But did hope and prayer play a part in findin' the young'uns? Was it blind luck?"

Jason nodded skyward. "Who knows but God himself."

"So we's left to wonder. We'd a had our answer if both had been found alive. Or, had both been found dead."

"If they had both been found dead, what would that tell us?"

"It would have told everythin.' Nothin.' That it worked. That it didn't."

"In this case, one survived, one didn't."

"In this story comes the true explanation of hope and prayer."

"Which is?"

"That it ain't for us to know whether it makes a spit of difference."

"Guess it's only relevant to the ones seeking hope."

"And the question is—is it relevant at all?"

~ * ~

Jordan followed Sawyer along a narrow path that hugged the mountain range, His knee throbbed with each step and his back felt like he'd been stung by jellyfish. The trail rose and fell as the land became a series of peaks and valleys, the slope to the south dropping downward sharply revealing range upon mountain range until they vanished into the haze at the edge of the distant horizon. Tea olive and honeysuckle in the air. Grassy hillsides far below stood in random shape and fashion, changing and conforming into new shapes.

As they walked Sawyer reasoned the fields below were not

created for planting. They were simply sections where trees didn't grow. Sectioned off by slender rows of hardwoods and underbrush, the fields looked, from a distance, like some giant, rugged atlas laid upon the land.

"Where are we?" asked Jordan.

"Cross Mountain. Connects Iron with Holston Mountain." Sawyer pointed to the northern horizon. "Both peaks run parallel and Cross Mountain pulls them together like Lewis Abbott's bowtie."

The day was moving on toward afternoon and patches of gray clouds rolled in, softening the brightness the sun had cast. Temperatures had warmed to the point all traces of snow had melted. The floor was damp and dark in color.

Cross Mountain was providing a respite from the rough travel, and Jordan was thankful for the easier terrain. As the sun began to drop close to the skyline of Holston Mountain, the land became harder. Meaner.

Talk stayed at a minimum, as Sawyer seemed focused on not only the path but the environment as well. They were entering the heart of Iron Mountain, a place where stills and untrusting eyes hid in the backwoods. Jordan's thoughts were on the bloody shirt, the bolo tie, and the bandanna Sarah wore.

"The sun's gettin' low," said Sawyer. "When night falls, we need to be secured."

"We're not gonna make it back to the cabin tonight?"

"No. We still have a good seven, eight hours of heavy foot travel left."

"We can't afford to wait any longer. Lives are at stake here."

"Hell, you don't think I know that? But we can't move through this kind of terrain in the dark. Besides, this is heavy moonshine area, and these boys don't play around when it comes to someone enterin' their holler." Jordan rubbed his temples. "Hang on, son, I'll get you back tomorrow. You won't do anybody any good if you get killed up here tonight."

Jordan's stomach growled and he wiped the back of his neck with his hand. He was still weak from his ordeal, but he didn't want to let that get in the way of solving the killings and abductions.

"You don't look like you can make it much further," Sawyer said. He unzipped his coat pocket and removed a plastic bag, tossing it to Jordan. "Eat this deer jerky. Make it count because it's the last of it."

"I can keep going. You just worry about yourself."

Sawyer shook his head. "Yep, you look strong as a bull," he said in a sarcastic tone. "If the wind blows hard, it's gonna tip you over."

"Don't you want some of this?" He extended his arm, offering the dried meat to Sawyer, who waved the offer away.

"I ain't got time for that. You just make sure you have enough strength to walk out of here, because I'm too old to carry you. Eat up, city boy."

They walked on, staying away from foot trails. The smell of smoldering sugar and firewood was in the air.

"I'm realizing moonshine is the lifeblood of this mountain," said Jordan as he followed Sawyer.

"The liquor sold in the store is like panther piss compared to moonshine. It's purer than anything the distilleries make. Mountain water, corn from the hillsides and valleys. Can't duplicate it anywhere else. Plus, ain't no money to be made watchin' the trees grow."

There was movement behind a laurel sixty yards to their east, on the down slope. Sawyer signaled Jordan to kneel, and he did the same. Jordan checked the ammunition count of the rifle Sawyer had taken from Sarah's father. "I only have a handful of bullets left," he said softly.

"It ain't the number of bullets that matter," said Sawyer. "It's a matter of seein' them before they see us. We lucked out earlier. Don't expect that to happen again."

A doe stepped out from the laurel, her nose high, sniffing in their direction.

"Time to move," Sawyer said.

The sun quickly faded, an orb that Jordan imagined was disinterested in the world on which it shone. As though there were likely better worlds to brighten. And so the darkness began to reassert itself, creeping in quietly, dimming the land like a silent plague.

Sawyer led on, his head turning from left to right.

"You sure appear to have an appreciation for these mountain men," said Jordan.

"These mountain *men* ain't had no formal education, but they are smart in the ways of the land. They know the sounds of boots foreign to this soil. They know when movement on the mountain is of the hostile kind. They know this land belongs to them, by pedigree if nothing else. And they know that the only law on Iron Mountain is their law. Being one of them, though only through my childhood, I know that any slip up will result in our demise."

Darkness approached, and they came upon a small stream that flowed southeasterly. The water was fast moving, with tea-colored pools hidden in the bends of the creek.

"We'll set up camp here," Sawyer said.

"I still say this is just wasting time. We've got to keep moving."

"Unless you're part coon, and can lead us through the pitch black that's settin' in, we got no choice. Got to keep movin,' huh? Brave talk from somebody who's hungry, bloodied leg, bloodied back. Weak-kneed. You're a sight."

The sharp landscape of the mountain made it impossible to find flat ground. Sawyer retrieved a small ax from a side sleeve of his duffel bag, and chopped away at the base of a slender pine. With ease he felled the tree in less than five minutes. He repeated the process on a tender poplar.

"Try to keep the tree from movin,'" Sawyer said as he cut into the knotty trunk. He chopped away side limbs, leaving four straight sections six feet long. He did the same with the other tree, positioning the sections against a massive rock near the mouth of the spring. The wood angled at forty-five degrees, making a small platform.

"Spread the bed roll across the wood," Sawyer said. "It won't be like home, but it's the best we can do. Best gather wood for a fire. We'll need enough to get us through the night."

Jordan followed Sawyer along the steep-sloped stream, and gathered wood Sawyer cut from fallen trees. He struggled to hold the wood, his knee throbbing and his head feeling light from lack of food.

Sawyer split limbs with apparent, relative ease. He reached up and sliced a six-foot limb from a dying oak. As he did, the limb landed on a large, jagged, bluish-gray rock at the edge of the creek. Sawyer stepped into the water to retrieve it. Jordan stepped in beside him to grab an end of the rotted wood, glancing in the water beside Sawyer's leg. He spotted movement in the darkening water.

"Snake," Jordan warned.

Calmly, Sawyer looked beside his leg, reached down and

snatched the thick creature by its neck. He pulled it from the water as it fought to break Sawyer's grip.

"What the hell is that?" Jordan asked.

"A waterdog." The half iguana, half salamander was almost three feet in length, with skin as dark as coal. It spit through its gills and slashed its tail at Sawyer's arm. In one fell swoop, Sawyer sliced off the creature's head. Blood dripped on his hand as he dipped the lizard into the water. "We got dinner."

They moved back to camp. Jordan started a fire, and gathered four rocks the size of cantaloupes per Sawyer's instructions. He placed the rocks in the fire, positioning them so that they formed a clock with each rock positioned at noon, three, six, and nine. Sawyer skinned the salamander, slicing it in small strips. Inside a zippered pouch of his sleeping bag he removed a bean can with an aluminum foil lid held in place by a rubber band. He removed the rubber band and slid the foil off. With a Swiss Army knife, he scooped a lump of lard from the can. A small, eight-inch skillet tied to the bedroll by a leather lace was unloosened. He tossed the lard in the skillet and set them over the four rocks so it wouldn't fall in the fire. A pungent odor, similar to rotting fish, soon filled the camp.

"You always carry a small kitchen with you?" Jordan asked as he watched the meat bounce in the skillet.

"You prefer starvin'? You would've made a sorry Boy Scout."

"I noticed your fishing rods tied to your backpack. Ultra lights?"

"Yep. Two-piece slim lines."

"Why do you carry two?"

"You'll see in the mornin.'"

Sawyer opened a canteen of water he'd filled at the stream, and they took turns drinking while they ate salamander and dried apricots.

"You fight in World War Two?" Jordan asked.

"Korea."

"As bad as they say?"

"Worse."

"Infantry? Hand to hand kind of thing?"

"Tennesseans always choose Infantry. It's in our blood."

The steep, hard ground underneath Jordan. An expanse of trees and backwoods that seemed endless around him. "I'd guess this place made the adjustment easy."

"Iron Mountain makes you a survivalist. To be anything else is not only dangerous to your well-bein', it's just plain stupid. In the war, my battalion's food supply was cut off for almost thirty days at one point. I taught the soldiers how to scavenge for food. We survived on scorpions and lizards."

Jordan shook his head. "Makes that water dog sound like prime rib."

"There were no rules of war. Ain't proud of what I saw, or what I was ordered to do." Sawyer looked in the distance. "That's all I got to say about it."

Nightfall swallowed the final traces of daylight. Jordan imagined that from the valley below, their campfire's pale light in that dark void of the mountain, resembled a distant galaxy home to a single star. "This is without a doubt the darkest place I've ever seen," Jordan said as the moon, in its last quarter, began rising in the eastern sky.

"You afraid of the dark?"

"No. But I won't lie in saying I'm not fond of this place, this mountain."

"At night, or generally speakin'?"

"Both."

"I don't think that just applies here on Iron Mountain. I think that there's a sort of anxiety, of fear, that is common to man not just on Iron Mountain, but everywhere on this vast world."

"How so?"

Sawyer stoked the fire with a stick. "Some would argue that man is born of purity, a masterpiece of God's work. Others might say that no matter the work of the Good Lord, the Devil waits in the dark, ready to sift that purity like a miner pannin' for gold."

The fire danced about his eyes, stirring them to a shadowy red that looked like some odd combination of solemn evil and restless reverence.

"I'd say everything pure has been sifted from whoever is doing harm to these women."

"You ain't in a position to state one way or the other."

Jordan's gaze followed the sparks rising from the fire into the night air. "No, I suppose not."

"Just know this fear ain't just on this mountain. And it ain't just in the darkness of night. It's everywhere."

The firelight continued to skirt his eyes as he told stories of Iron Mountain that Jordan wondered were truth, legend, or somewhere in between. He described nights where the wind muzzled screams on the mountain. He told of children who disappeared, no one knowing if they'd used the night to escape Iron Mountain.

After they'd eaten, Sawyer tossed three more pieces of wood on the fire. The temperature had dropped into the twenties. Though the moon rose high above Snake Mountain, the towering trees blocked its light, as if to keep Iron Mountain veiled in secrecy. "Zip that coat," he warned. "The cold will cut you to the bone."

As he pulled the brass zipper, Jordan asked, "You got any idea who might be doing all this?"

"Can't rightly say. It ain't the nature of these folks to kill over and over. If they feel threatened, they'll shoot in a heartbeat. But just killin' women folk who mean no harm...that ain't the makin' of these mountain folk."

"You're not convinced the killer is one of Iron Mountain's own?"

"My guess would be he ain't."

Jordan poked at the fire with a stick while his mind searched for answers. The darkness gathered in the distance, closing in around him, like a being feeding off itself, wary of light. The fire cast orange and red shadows against nearby mountain laurels, wavy movements that cast them in some abstract waltz created before man roamed the mountain. Mighty poplars and white pines stood dimly in the firelight like untrusting pillars of the land. "When's the last time you were on this mountain?"

"When I was eighteen."

"That's a long time. Must feel odd."

"Like a thief slippin' in the back door." Sawyer looked off into the distance.

"I guess the townspeople in Laurel City were right."

"About what?"

"How mean and unbearable living up here was. Still is, it appears."

"I think it's the nature of man to magnify tales and legends, whether it's done for effect, or because they're repeating what's been told to them. But in the case of Iron Mountain, the stories pretty much ring true. Life was hell. Dirt floors and no runnin' water. There was no school of any kind. We were taught survival skills instead of

ABC's. What good would readin' and writin' do? You can't plant taters and rutabagas with a book. You can't hunt with a pencil. By the time I was ten I could hunt, fish, trap, and spot federal agents closin' in from the valley."

"Not much of a traditional family setting, I gather."

"Our mothers showed little affection. There wasn't time for it. Too much time and effort spent on daily chores. Now, they watched closely over us. Not in the loving sense, but in the way of protecting an asset, a farm hand. The men hunted, fished, and farmed the rugged countryside with what little they could get to grow. And of course, moonshine was the constant."

Sawyer picked up a handful of dirt and tossed it on the fire. "We better call it a night. Got a lot o' ground to cover tomorrow."

"Don't we want the fire to last through the night? To fight the cold?"

"Not unless you want to take the chance on somebody walkin' into camp and slicin' your throat as you sleep. Your body heat's gonna have to do the job." As Jordan climbed inside his sleeping roll, Sawyer added, "Sleep with your rifle."

Jordan lay on his back, his eyes chasing the shadows cast on the trees by the quickly dimming fire. Sap popped from the embers, cutting the silence. In the distance a bobcat's cry echoed across the high country. An owl screeched. The night stirred as though the cold mountain had just awakened.

~ * ~

"I want you to git," he said, standing behind the dilapidated barn, his warm breath visible in pale puffs evaporating into the cold night air. "Git while you can."

"And go where?"

"Anywhere but here. The detective, the police. They's a closin' in, and it's just a matter of time."

"Shitfire. We never made an escape plan. We got no kin to run to. I ain't got money to find livin' arrangements."

The old man lifted the bill of his cap, ran his fingers across his thinning scalp, and put the cap back on his head. "Look, I don't know where you should go. All I know is, if you stay up on that mountain, you're gonna get caught."

"It's your own hide you're concerned with."

"That ain't so. I'm old. Nothin' left to live for. You're still a young man. You should run for it."

"Even if I do, I cain't never be free. I'll always be on the run. Only thing for me to do is stay hid. Or die tryin.'"

~ * ~

"Wake up."

Jordan rubbed his eyes. Strands of oily hair hugged his forehead.

"We gotta catch our breakfast," Sawyer said.

"We don't have time for breakfast."

"We got a lot of ground to cover, and we need the energy. Besides, you ain't exactly lookin' like the fatted calf. Let's get at it."

"Well, now I know why you're carryin' two fishin' rods."

Sunrise was minutes away and Sawyer stirred the ashes, blowing gently as a few embers sparked. He placed two logs in the fire pit, and quickly brought it to light. He removed a bean can from his sack, much like the one that contained the lard—except for the crusted rust. When he removed the rubber band, and lifted the foil, he said, "Bait's still alive."

The sky had softened and light was returning to the land where the trees didn't smother it as it passed through to the mountain floor. The icy stream was dark, illuminating small bursts of white as water pushed skyward over the cold, gray rocks. Jordan stepped carefully along the water's edge, and felt the steady push of the water against his boots as he tossed his line across the dark creek. The stream was fifteen feet at its widest point.

He turned to Sawyer in that pre-dawn light, silhouetted against the backdrop of the woods like a ghost of an ancient fisherman. "Trout run in these waters?"

"Keep your voice low. Daylight's not far away and bodies are a movin' on the mountain. As far as trout, ain't narry a one. Horny heads run in these waters." Sawyer moved upstream ten feet above Jordan and cast. "They love the fast water, so let your bait hug the rocks."

"Thought horny heads ran only in Doe Creek."

"You're mistaken."

On Jordan's first cast, he felt a sharp tug as his worm-covered hook drifted through the rocks. The pole bent as though a rock had snagged the hook, but the fish surfaced and he pulled hard on the spin reel.

"Ease him back through the rocks," Sawyer said.

He reeled steadily but carefully as the fish fought for

freedom. Sawyer's reel hummed as he reeled in his catch. It was the first time Jordan had fished out of necessity.

The sun soon ascended a red reef of clouds above the ridgeline of Snake Mountain and the swift water sparkled in splashes of white and silver. Sawyer moved about the water as if he were part of it. Within minutes, he caught three fish.

On the bank, Sawyer removed his white-handled knife from the sheath on his belt. Beside the loud water, he gutted and filleted each fish. His knife moved with precision, and he soon had them ready for the pan.

He removed a skillet from a slit pouch of the sleeping bag, tossed lard from the bean can into the pan, and had Jordan set the stones in a circle in the fire. He placed the skillet on the rocks, and soon the lard sizzled. He dropped each filet into the lard, holding them by the tail, and the aroma of fried fish filled the camp. From the moment they made their first cast to the time the fish were cooked was less than twenty minutes.

They removed the fish by stabbing their knives in the tails and placing them on two pieces of foil Sawyer kept in the pouch. The fish were consumed quickly and the campfire extinguished. The skillet was cleaned in the creek.

"Time to move," Sawyer said.

~ * ~

He sat, straddling a fallen elm, and rubbed his Bowie knife against a sand stone. Brittle leaves rattled across the ground around him as the winds of Iron Mountain rolled. His hands were cold, but he worked diligently. Removing the stains of previous deeds. Washing away the sins of the past so new ones could spawn.

He closed his eyes as though trying to leave the world in which he sat. His mind drifted off to a night long ago.

He vividly recalled the lavender and yellow strips mother stitched to make the quilt for the casket. She used a collection of fabric from a dress her mother once wore, strips from a bed sheet donated by Doc Hensley, and the remnants of a child's blanket she found along the bank of Doe Creek one autumn morning. She made it for a special occasion, though surely she was thinking something along the likes of a wedding or child's birth. The colorful blanket was laid across the casket and underneath Elvin's body. The casket was placed by a tiny picture window in the boxy living room for two days for relatives and neighbors to pay their respects.

He slipped into the room late the night before the funeral. Dressed in wool pants and coat, the only skin visible was Elvin's face and fingers. He remembered how the soft glow from a nearby oil lantern gave Elvin's bluish skin a tone of faded orange. The knot on the right side of Elvin's neck where the noose had been knotted showed in the dim light. Compelled, he tugged on Elvin's cream-colored collar, rubbing his fingers along the knot.

The strapping he received on his back that night for "desecratin'" Elvin's corpse was as fierce as any he ever received. The nightmares began soon after, reminders of his pain, internally and externally, at the sight of his dead brother.

His only choice was to stay. There could be no freedom. So, he would live, and die, on Iron Mountain, defending himself, defending the land he claimed as his own.

His oily beard gathered spit from his mouth, and his hat pushed his dark hair downward to his eyebrows. He hadn't showered in days, and his clothes smelled of stale sweat. Pushed over the edge, past the point of no return, he looked at the blade and his strange desires rose.

It was the hunt of the female he wanted. He reasoned they deserved it anyway. They had it coming and were not to be pitied.

On that fallen tree, he occupied a space of his own choosing, though that space was not his at all. He'd created a world set by boundaries within his mind, but his mind was one he could no longer orchestrate. It had no familiarity. It consumed him and the fire burned to set that world to motion once more.

~ * ~

Sawyer and Jordan moved silently through the woods, sticking to a small trail that cut across the southern side of the mountain. The winds were still, and the endless trees, spread across the mountain with no sense of order, appeared lifeless. There were no fields, no breaks in the tree line, and Jordan wondered briefly if they would make it through the claustrophobic setting.

"What's the deal with Bum Whitfield?" Jordan said, his eyes scouring the trees.

"Bum's a direct descendant of Gaines Logan."

"I thought Gaines was a solitary man."

"That he was. It didn't mean he was always alone."

"You tellin' me Gaines sought companionship on occasion?"

"Word was that Jeremiah Shoun's daughter sneaked up the

mountain to pay him a visit. Wanted to know a real mountain man. When Jeremiah found out months later his daughter was pregnant, he went after Gaines. Jeremiah was found hangin' from a holly tree."

"I thought he was killed because he was runnin' around with some gal in Stoney Creek."

"That's what they want people to think. Anyway, Bum is Gaines's grandson. He's royalty. No matter, he's a mean sonofabitch."

"I'll be damned."

The slope had turned downward in that midday light, and Jordan had grown weary. Doe Valley was visible off to the southeast.

"We're less than an hour from the cabin," said Sawyer.

They came upon a dirt road, a rarely traveled stretch that slipped through barren hillsides and empty barns. The temperatures, which had risen to the point where Jordan felt like shedding his coat, began to change. The winds picked up and the powder-blue sky was squeezed out by dark clouds and a slither of fog. Visibility began to drop to the tree lines. Not long after, Sawyer entered the cabin on Iron Mountain, while Jordan grabbed the receiver from inside the squad car.

Twenty Five

Rachel's prayers changed. She had missed her chance to escape. What were the chances it would come again? Hope was gone, only the wish her family would have the strength to continue remained.

Her prison cell was closing in on her. She shook from the dampness; her naked body was calloused with dark sores across her legs, buttocks, and back. Her eyes grew sensitive to the light that slipped in when food was brought to her. She lost all desire to fight.

He had come to her cell two days prior, and she didn't put up the slightest fight when he attacked her, humiliating her, treating her like an animal, satisfying his perverted sexual needs. In some strange way she wanted him to put her out of her misery.

When the doorknob turned, she held her breath. The diminutive figure carried two pieces of batter bread and buttermilk.

"Here," spoke the woman.

"Why do you help him?" Rachel took hold of the woman's bony wrist.

She pulled away from Rachel and retreated through the door. Rachel slapped the plate of food away.

Alone in the darkness again, Rachel was too weak to cry.

~ * ~

Her frail hands scrubbed lye soap on the trays that held Kara and Rachel's food. The sink was filled with brown, soured water. She hardly noticed him walk through the back door.

"Time to eat," he mumbled as she wiped her forehead with the back of her hand.

With a wooden spoon, she scooped lard from a coffee can and tossed it onto a black iron skillet. Chicken gizzards, dripping with blood, dropped into the pan.

"Gettin' low on food," she said. "Ain't nary a piece of meat left 'cept gizzards."

"Damn it, it's your job to make sure we got enough to eat. Shitfire, now you's even lettin' 'em escape. I should just kill you right here and now."

He slapped her face with his open palm. Her body slammed into a wooden crate nailed to the side of the sink. Her cheek crushed a mason jar sitting on the crate, and the crate fell to the floor on top of her. She held her hand to her cheek and blood began to trickle through her fragile knuckles. The attacks were increasing, both in intensity and frequency. Her body couldn't take much more.

"You know I can't leave the mountain with the law snoopin' round," he said. "So you need to git your ass down to the polk fields. Should be some early leaves worth eatin.'"

With tears running down her face, she placed her apron against the cut on her cheek, leaning against the sink. As she steadied herself, he called her attention to the greasy chicken gizzards cooking on the wood stove.

"Just give those whores enough to keep 'em alive." He stormed out of the room.

After dinner, she went into the deep woods. She wore dirty khakis that sagged from her waist and a faded green down jacket with a broken zipper. She had stopped the bleeding on her cheek, though her aching fingers felt the dried blood on the side of her face.

With a brown sack over her shoulder, she followed a path northwest of the shack. She steadied her walk by holding on to limbs of laurels and spruces, walking until she came to a dirt road that opened up into two hilly fields. A carving knife in her hand.

The fields were full of polk plants a foot tall. She began cutting the spindly stalks. The leaves, no bigger than her hands, had not turned as dark a green as they would in summer. She didn't have the luxury of waiting until then. By midsummer black berries would grow on the stalks. The berries were often used to produce rudimentary ink for writing. The stiffness of the leaves meant she would have to spend extra time boiling them to make them edible. She worked quickly, balanced on her arthritic knees. A swirling wind blew, and her bones ached from the chill.

With her bag filled, she tightened it with a cotton cord and tried to lift it. The bag was heavy so she dragged it across the ground.

Ahead, Hannah stood beside a rotting bale of hay. She wore brown corduroys and a black and blue plaid, wool shirt. "Time to free your'sef, Alice," she said, stepping closer to the woman. She touched Alice's face as if to examine the cut on her cheek. "You wear no chains, but you's a livin' in bondage."

The feeble woman looked off into the horizon and shook her head.

"Blood's thicker'n spring water," Hannah said. "But it don't mean you's supposed to be kept in shackles."

Again Alice could only shake her head. "One of them gals is sick," she said. "She cain't stop coughin.' She's a spittin' up blood."

"Come." Hannah turned and began to walk.

They crossed through the polk field to where a line of Norwegian spruces grew. Along the spruces ran a small, slow moving stream edged with clumps of gypsum.

Hannah pulled a clump and placed it in Alice's sack. "Ground the gypsum and blend it with tobac'er. Burn the tobac'er and make her inhale the smoke. It will get her a breathin' right."

"Thank you, kindly."

Hannah looked at her as though one might regarding a circus sideshow freak.

Alice gazed at her feet.

"You'll be meetin' your maker soon." She placed her fingers to Alice's chin and stared at her weathered face. "Lessin' you do somethin' about it first."

She touched the cut, and Alice winced, but she allowed Hannah to trace her fingers along the wound. She removed a pouch of snuff from the pocket of her pants, took a pinch of it, spit on the small sliver, and rubbed it along the wound. "You're cursed if you stay. Death howls in the wind." She looked high into the treetops. "It cain't be silenced much longer."

Alice dragged her sack along the ground and headed back to her shack. Hannah was right. She was a prisoner, only with wider boundaries, and moving walls. Many times, she'd pledged she was going to run, but every time she made her mind up, she couldn't. He had complete hold of her and held the trump card that made it clear she could never leave. When she stopped at the back door, Hannah's words played in her head.

~ * ~

Shelby Stanley lowered the tailgate of her late model Chevy truck and removed a pitchfork that lay in between two stacks of hay. Spring was on its way, and the planting season was upon her. The inventory of hay was starting to thin in her barn, and the fields needed to produce new growth so the three hundred head of cattle she owned could eat for free.

Shelby's father had acquired the largest spread in Johnson County, and when he died eleven years ago, he left Shelby in solid shape, financially. She had worked hard to make sure her father's wealth grew, so his legacy could continue.

She had married her high school sweetheart in '95, and when he left her for the local veterinarian six years later, she swore independence with regard to any need of men. She lost her mother to cancer when she was eight, and developed a strong-willed approach toward survival. So she ran the farm alone after her father passed away. In her mid-forties, gray streaks becoming more prominent in her hair, with a face that still seemed youthful in the bathroom mirror.

Shelby removed six bales of hay from the truck and placed them in a nearby field. Wiping the dust from her stone-washed jeans, she felt sweat building under the rim of her brown cowboy hat.

~ * ~

He watched from the darkness of the trees. He bit his lower lip, incensed by situation and circumstance. The truck cranked and rolled along the dirt road, in between two fence lines. His yearning to overpower grew, his hatred again taking control.

She removed the last three bales of hay from the truck and placed them over the fence. The Black Angus cows walked from the field, at a steady pace as though they were ready to eat. She leaned her elbows across the top of the red, wooden fence, and talked to the cows. She called some by name, and they seemed to respond in some sort of bovine glee when she called them. As they began to eat, she stepped up a notch on the fence and reached outward to pet a calf that followed her mama.

He slipped up from behind, took hold of her legs and flipped her over the fence onto the hard ground. The startled cows moved away from where she lay on the ground. The calf cried and ran under her mother's belly.

She rolled on her back, her eyes looking steely into his. He punched her jaw, and pulled the hat off her head. She kicked at him, and he hit her with his fist in the cheek. She cried out, and when she saw the knife, she recoiled.

"What the hell are you doin'?" She kicked at the knife. "Get your ass off my farm."

He smirked, amused she thought she might have any say so to the outcome of the situation. "Git up." He kicked her boot.

She backpedaled on her elbows several feet.

"I said git up."

"I'm tellin' you one last time. Get the hell off my property."

"Well." He grabbed at her pant leg, and she kicked his hand. He smiled when she did it again; he wanted the fight. He wanted her to put everything into keeping him at bay. For saving herself.

He walked beside her, snatching a hold of her jacket. She slugged his arms as he lifted her from the ground. When she was on her feet, standing in front of him, he towered over her. Her brown eyes stared hard at him, as though she could intimidate him.

She broke his grip on her and slapped his face. He winced for a second, and blood formed on the corner of his mouth. He touched the back of his hand to his lip while holding the knife with his other hand. He looked at the blood on his hand and smiled. In her eyes, he sensed rebellion, a hatred toward him, and it gave him a sense of justification.

He noticed a small shed forty yards away, and he pulled her toward it. "Time to pay fer the sins of those who come before you."

She dragged her feet, and scrabbled at the ground, and so he lifted her, carrying her with one arm, her boots slipping across mud and cow manure. She flung her fists at him but it didn't slow him down. He held the knife skyward, careful not to let it cut her arms when she flailed at him. He wanted her clean, prim, and proper, so he could feel like he was squashing a rose into the thorns underneath it.

The shed was eight-by-six, with a tin roof. A three-sided shed, it housed a cart, three bags of fertilizer, and several small tools. She looked toward the road. Maybe she should have chosen a farm not so desolate.

"Take off the boots, and them jeans." He let go of her arm.

"Kiss my ass, hillbilly." She slapped him again. "You want them off, you're going to have to take them off with those filthy paws of yours. I won't bow down like some trembling puppy just because you have that knife. Big man. Big asshole is more like it."

"I like a feisty gal. And you ain't gettin' off that easy. This requires participation on your part. Now, get 'em off."

"Go to hell." She spit in his face.

She kicked his chin and tried to run, but he took hold of her long hair and dragged her back into the shed, tossing her on the bags of fertilizer. He drove the knife into a side pole of the shed. "Have it your way, then." He slapped her face and shook her by the jacket.

She looked at him and smiled. "Best you got? I know preschoolers who slap harder than you."

His anger charged through his veins, and he rained blows upon her. And she became the embodiment of every woman's contrariness with regard to man; of their mean-spirited desire to be in control, no matter the situation. He pummeled her over and again until her body was lifeless.

Then he removed those ostrich boots and those tight, fancy jeans. He sought to humiliate her in the afterlife, picturing her above them, having to watch as he raped her limp body.

Twenty Six

Deputy Anderson was filling out an arrest warrant when Jordan radioed the Laurel City police department. Helen Jackson stood at Anderson's desk, pointing to scratches and bruises on her teenage son's face, who'd been roughed up by the Hollister brothers at a party the night before. Though Mrs. Jackson looked highly upset and animated, she took a back seat in importance when Jordan's voice crackled over the two-way radio.

"What's your status?" Anderson asked while signaling silence with his index finger to Mrs. Jackson.

"I'm on my way to the station," answered Jordan. "Where's Lawrence?"

"Givin' County Council a progress report on the investigation."

"Progress is on its way. Call forensics. Think I got the missing link. Be there in twenty. Got Rubin Sawyer with me."

"Ten-four."

Anderson assured Helen Jackson the Hollister boys would be dealt with and ushered her out the door. After alerting forensics at East Tennessee State's medical center in Elizabethton, he headed across the street to the county offices. Walking in the one-story, red brick building, he spotted Abigail Truesdale, Town Treasurer and part-time secretary, sitting behind the Tax Assessor's counter.

"Seen Buford?" he asked.

"Just left a few minutes ago," she replied. "Went out the back door with Luke Wilson." Wilson was the senior member of County Council and the anointed grandfather of Laurel City.

"Much obliged," Anderson said as he hurried to the glass door that led a small gravel parking lot.

"How's your ma?" Abigail asked.

"No time to talk," he said as the back door closed.

~ * ~

"Afternoon, Bert," Lawrence said as he plopped on his favorite stool at the counter of Bert's Cafe. Wilson sat next to Lawrence.

"How you boys a doin'?" asked Bert.

"Not worth a flyin' flip," answered Lawrence.

"Got a fresh pot of coffee brewin,'" Bert said.

"Pour us a couple o' strong ones," Lawrence said while grabbing the sugar canister on the counter. The lunch counter was empty except for Ed Tabor and his ninety-year-old father. The father-son duo came every day to Bert's, and had done so for almost twenty years.

"This killin' has the whole town on edge," Wilson said.

"Sure has," answered Bert. "Ain't had no business in a week or more."

Wilson looked about the room. "It's like this every place in town. None of the menfolk want to leave their wives and daughters home alone." Bert poured coffee into a red, checkered mug adorned with Conway Twitty's face, circa 1965.

"Can't rightly blame 'em though," Lawrence said.

"Can't blame 'em one bit," Wilson added.

As Wilson and Lawrence quietly talked, Anderson walked through the door. "Sheriff, just got a call from Jordan. He's on his way."

"On his way from where?"

"Didn't say. But he says he's got somethin' that could crack the case."

"Hold that coffee, Bert."

Lawrence was out the door.

The entire police department waited for Jordan and Sawyer to arrive. Myers and Anderson did inventory on the files of the case, placing them neatly on Lawrence's desk. He examined pictures of Becky Shoun, Patricia Darby and Barbara Thomas, trying to freshen his mind about the women who'd had the misfortune to cross paths with the killer.

By the time Jordan walked through the door, Adams had almost chewed through his pencil.

"Where the hell have you been?" Lawrence asked as he leaned back in his chair.

"Had a couple of detours," answered Jordan. "But they were well worth it." Jordan removed the bloody shirt from a paper bag.

"Need this analyzed immediately."

Lawrence touched the sleeve of the shirt. "What's this?"

"I found it underneath the floor of the hunter's shack the dogs led us to. Found this too." He held up the bolo tie.

"Hell, I seen that before," said Myers. "It's uh, um…"

"Thomas Douglas'?" Jordan asked.

"Yep. That's the one. It was his daddy's. Gave it to Thomas on his birthday. Seventeenth birthday, I believe it was."

"Forensics will match the blood of this shirt to that of Thomas Douglas," Jordan said. Momentum had changed in the game.

"If it does, what does that tell us?" Anderson asked. "You think he was a victim just like these other ladies?"

"I believe he was, but for a different reason."

"What reason is that?"

"You just get the match verified, and I'll show you."

~ * ~

Alice stirred. The cut on her cheek had made her face swell, and it hurt to blink her eyes. She ground up the gypsum in a wooden bowl. She stood to the side of the house, out of window view, behind a crepe myrtle. After she ground the crystals, she poured them on top of four tobacco leaves that overlapped each other. Carefully she rolled the leaves together and gently placed it in her sweater pocket.

The north wind brushed against her face and neck as she walked onto the porch. She had prepared polk salad on two plates, and added a pair of parsnips she had found in the cellar. Her hands trembled as she walked in silence down the weed-laced path to the cellar.

Alice heard Kara's hacking cough when she started down the cellar steps. They were becoming harsher and more frequent. When she entered the room, Kara was delirious. Alice removed the gypsum-laced tobacco and placed it on the floor beside Kara. Shakily striking a match, she lit the tobacco.

"Sit up, child," Alice said as she bent on one knee. Kara slowly began to rise. Alice held on to Kara's arms until she was on her hands and knees over the burning tobacco. "Breathe it in." Kara coughed several times and Alice steadied her over the smoke. Kara struggled to inhale, to fill her failing lungs. She shook her head and tried to push the old woman's hands away.

"Leave me alone," she said. "Just let me die."

"This ain't the time to give up, young'un. Do as I tell you. You got too much to live for. A whole life ahead of you."

Kara coughed so deeply her stomach became rigid, making her ribs ache. "I'm never getting out. Just let me die and end the misery."

Alice pushed her head downward, over the fire. "Breathe it in, child."

She tried to fight, but Alice kept her frail hand to the back of Kara's head. As though too tired to resist, Kara inhaled. She coughed.

"That's good. Do it again."

Kara inhaled again, deeper than the first time. After letting go of the smoke from her lungs, she inhaled once again, wiping blood from the corner of her mouth. Her coughing began to subside and she continued breathing in the smoky tobacco. She raised her head and breathed deeply the damp air in her prison cell.

She leaned into Alice's arms and cried. Alice ran her hands along Kara's matted hair. Alice fought back her own tears, and for a moment, she hugged the young stranger's trembling body.

She slid the plate of food beside Kara. "I have to go. Eat, child. You have to gain your strength."

She locked the door behind her.

Alice picked up the plate she'd left in the hallway and entered Rachel's door. The light from the hallway revealed the wound on Alice's face. Rising up, Rachel touched her chin, but Alice turned away into the darkness. Rachel again turned Alice's face back to the light.

"He did that to you," Rachel whispered.

Alice could only lower her eyes where a tear fell. Rachel traced two scars on Alice's face with her middle and index fingers. The scars began at her left cheek, crossed her nose, her right eyelid, and ended at her hairline. "You're a prisoner just like we are."

Alice nodded in silence, stooped, placing a slender object on Rachel's tray. Making slight eye contact with Rachel, she locked the door behind her. Rachel crouched, holding the phone beside the tray. Beside the leafy dinner was a rusty ice pick.

~ * ~

Cotton Monroe moved hurriedly into the sheriff's office. The limp in his left knee caused him to move awkwardly through the doorway. A manila folder was squeezed tightly between his elbow and his hip.

"Hey, Sheriff," Cotton said, his wavy white hair giving him the appearance of a giant cotton swab. "I got the results you was lookin' fer." Cotton handed the folder to Lawrence, who sipped a cola at his desk. "These papers important? Think it'll tell you who the killer is?"

Cotton was a twenty-one-year-old man-child who ran errands for the police department and members of the health department. Barely surviving childbirth, his umbilical cord wrapped around his left leg, he was left to live his days walking with a heavy limp. Though he struggled to walk, he drove a county truck with automatic drive. He had been sent to ETSU for the forensics results.

"Don't know Cotton," Lawrence answered. "Let's have a look."

Lawrence glanced over the lab results. The blood on the shirt indeed matched blood taken from Thomas Douglas' tractor the day he disappeared. It also matched the blood type listed in a file in Doc Jacob's office eight years prior when Thomas Douglas unwillingly had a physical.

"Cotton, you done good."

Cotton smiled, nodded and slipped out the front door.

~ * ~

Jordan pulled into the parking lot of Hank's Zippy Mart, an abandoned tractor parts shop converted into a small diner and convenience store. Lawrence had told Jordan that Hank's hot dogs were famous because of some secret recipe chili supposedly concocted after a local cock fight. Cars lined the building, almost hiding the glass booth pay phone that stood at the left edge of the building.

Jordan hurried to the phone and dialed collect.

"Hey, sugar," he said.

He heard Marty cry.

"Oh, my sweet Lord. Thought I'd never hear your voice again. I'm going to beat you senseless when you get home. Are you okay?"

"I'm fine. And I'll be happy to let you smack me around when I get home. Anyways, this is all about to end. How are you? How's Jessica?"

"She'll be doing fine after she finds out you are okay. Mom took her to the store just to occupy some time."

"Give her a big kiss for me, and tell her I'm coming home soon."

"I'm holding you to that promise. Be careful Tom. I love you."

"You bet. I love you too."

Jordan re-dressed his leg wound in the cabin after taking a much-needed shower. The radio scratchily relayed the message from Lawrence. "The results match."

"All right, we're gettin' somewhere. Here's what we gotta do now."

"I'm listenin.'"

"We have to exhume Burley Greer's body."

"I'm not followin' you."

"My hunch says Thomas Douglas' body is inside that casket, not Burley Greer."

"I'll be damn."

"Get the proper permission. Can you have it by the morning?"

"I'll do my best."

Twenty Seven

It took several cranks for Early Waters, caretaker of the Laurel City Memorial Gardens, to fire up the backhoe. Roby Greer had buried Burley on a hillside on his property, next to Elvin. Early eased the backhoe off the trailer, and started up a steep hill toward Burley's gravesite. The small cemetery stood along the edge of cow pastures connected by barbed wire fences that cut the field like giant sutures. Lawrence and Jordan followed behind the backhoe on foot, alongside a fence intertwined with briars and weeds. The rusty wire dropped in spots from where cattle had leaned in to snatch grass growing near the gravesite.

The gravesite was waist deep in chickweed and blackberry vines, a sight that seemed more suited for Iron Mountain than the rolling meadows of Doe Valley. The small headstones were barely visible through the green leaves and tan vines. The morning sun warmed Jordan's shoulders, and the churn of the backhoe interrupted a silent peacefulness along the meadow.

"So, what happened up in them woods?" asked Lawrence while pointing out Burley's stone to Early.

"If the mountain was talking to me like old Hannah said it would, it was saying, 'get the hell off my mountain.'" Jordan shook his head and pulled a slender blade of yellow grass from the tender soil. "In all seriousness, it did seem like Iron Mountain herself was lookin' out for me. If it weren't for the young gal and her brother who pulled me from the trap, I'd have never made it. And that scarf around her neck was the clincher. It was just like the one I found where the Darby girl had been placed in Doe Creek. Thanks to Hannah's crazy remedies, I bounced back pretty quick. And thank God for Rubin Sawyer. I didn't care to die huggin' a locust tree."

"Rubin Sawyer is a man's man."

"He's got my vote."

Early's backhoe struggled as the tall weeds and topsoil

twisted and turned underneath the steel claws. When the bucket finally penetrated the ground, it began lifting the earth above the casket with relative ease. The pine casket had turned gray, and it almost matched the color of the dirt above and around it. Early's son, Cale, followed behind with a red contraption that looked like a giant Venice Fly Trap. The steel device twisted and turned, removing the casket like a dentist pulling an achy molar. As the casket lifted, roots and mounds of dirt from the pit came with it.

Cale placed the casket on a flat spot in the cow pasture. The men gathered round, as did Jesse Long, Denny Cagle, and Bud Lambert. Cagle was with forensics at ETSU and had come for the hair and tissue sample that would be used for a DNA match with Thomas Douglas' blood. Bud Lambert was an Environmental Health Officer from Elizabethton who worked the eastern part of the state. He supplied the men with masks and gloves, and would disinfect the area after Cagle was done.

The tattered white dress shirt on the body had come apart along the arms and the buttons. A hat which lay across the chest was black as soot, the cardinal feather in the band still showing a slight hint of red. The skin was completely gone, and teeth and hair remains were scattered about along the jawbone and the sunken skull.

"Did you see the body when it was lyin' beside the lake?" asked Jordan.

"Yep," answered Lawrence. "His face was cut so bad it was impossible to recognize him. It looked like his head had been run through a meat grinder."

"The entire facial structure is shattered," Cagle said. "What a hell of a way to go."

"Here we are disturbin' his final restin' place," said Lawrence.

"We have no choice," Jordan said.

Cagle went to work.

~ * ~

Roby Greer sat across from Bum at an oak table in Bum's kitchen. Bum placed his foot on an oak butter churn cornered by a plywood kitchen counter and the wall. The house was cold and damp, an absence of warmth or emotion. An absence born of despair and a focus on survival. The pale white smoke from smoldering embers in the wood stove clouded the room into a thin haze.

Daylight slipped through the dingy kitchen window, caught in the smoke like some obscure web that refused to let the light escape.

"Did you see 'em do it?" Bum asked. He lifted the handle of a black tobacco cutter and sliced off a grainy chew. He ripped a chunk with his teeth, and small bits of the brown leaf dotted his lower lip and his chin. He placed the remaining chew in the chest pocket of his overalls.

"Saw it with my very own eyes," Roby answered. "They tore the ground up with a backhoe. When they hoisted that casket out the ground, I damn near passed out. It won't take long for them to know it ain't Burley in that box. And I figger it won't take long for them to come after me. I got so scared I just turned and run." He removed his sweat-laced brown hat and rubbed his forehead. "I thought we had created the perfect plan."

"This situation has turned out like somethin' conjured up by the devil himself," Bum said, shaking his head.

"Don't give the devil credit."

"Well, I might not give him credit, but it appears he made damn sure God was occupied with somethin' else." Bum shook his head and sucked his teeth as though some strange meat was stuck between them.

"You don't think God knows the score?"

"He sure don't seem to be aware of the situation."

"Ah, you don't know nothin.'"

They rose from the table, men troubled by the current state of affairs. They walked to the porch, looking out into that great expanse of trees, the winds roaring high above.

"I'm gonna need your help," Roby said. "It's just a matter of time before the police come after me. And I ain't got Iron Mountain to hide behind."

"That I cannot do."

"Well, you backed this whole thing. Burley was just a puppet of your'n."

"Hell, you're the one what started it all, stagin' your boy's death. Besides, I didn't tell him to start killin' ever'thin in sight. He was supposed to just do away with that first gal in the cabin. The one from up north."

"It's a little late to divvy up blame. I need you to hide me."

Bum plopped down in a hickory rocker near the door, looking as though the weight removed from sitting could do nothing to lift the weight that pressed on his mind. Beside the rocker was a small table made from the trunk of a sycamore. Bum grabbed a jar of moonshine that sat on the table and twisted off the metal top, taking a long draw that caused him to cough. Tobacco rolled from his mouth into the jar, circling and turning the moonshine to brown. He wiped his mouth with his sleeve. "Cain't do nothin' fer you."

"Just like that, you're gonna turn your back on me? Thought we was in this together."

Bum's jaw tightened so that his stained teeth were barely visible. "You come to me, remember? You asked *me* for help."

"I helped you too. Gave you freedom to run your stills. To keep the law and everybody else away from your mountain."

"Wouldn't a mattered no way. We defend ourselves. Somebody come on our land, we'll provide justice the way we see fit. Our people survived years before you and I came along. They'll survive long after we're gone."

"Don't turn your back on me."

"I can't help you. Now git the hell off my porch."

"But…"

"Lessin' you want me to blow a hole through your gut, you'll slip on outta here."

~ * ~

It was another restless night in the cabin. Jordan lay in bed, his eyes fixated on a ceiling void of light. Was his hunch right? Were Kara and Rachel still alive? Doe Creek had not produced their bodies, so there still was a thin ray of hope. Apprehending the killer seemed a real possibility now.

Cicadas filled the night air with their chaotic rhythm of song. Is this how it sounded when God unleashed the locusts on the Egyptians? Sleep was the furthest thing from his mind. The hunt was nearly over. He yearned to hold Marty, to tell bedtime stories to Jessie again. The sacrifice they made to carry on without him was unfair. Maybe this would be the last time they'd have to do it.

He rose and walked to the bedroom window and peered into the darkness at something more than a just a cabin window. Rather, a porthole where a madman's hatred for women led to torture, rape, and murder. Jordan rubbed the window frame where the killer had most likely stood, and surely not just when Patricia Darby and Kara Lisle were inside the bedroom.

He slipped on a pair of jeans and boots, grabbed his jacket

and walked outside the porch. The winds were gentle, of quiet demeanor, as if to show him there was a side of beauty and reverence to Iron Mountain. A tranquil presence of goodness, a message the people of Iron Mountain were all God's children, and the oppression shown by a certain group of mountain men were not a reflection of the hearts and souls of a simple people who lived in a place where survival was foremost.

He walked through the woods, the moon illuminating enough of the night to distinguish the trees from the darkness, the predawn chill clinging to the mountain floor. He followed a trail that led him skyward for a quarter mile, to a peak that opened up another world behind Iron Mountain. The skies to the east were turning to shades of violet and soft orange and the moon brightened the western sky, several days past its full stage. As he breathed in the pure air, the valleys lay in their stillness below, soft and stoic. The faint lights of Damascus danced in the distance as though they were restless entities entirely, seeking escape from the bricks and boards that held them hostage.

For the first time, the mountain revealed herself as she was a million years ago, before man brought evil to the land. When it was God's masterpiece and God had reveled in the majesty at His creation. There was serenity in that darkness, in that isolation. It was a freedom of some sort where having someone else in his presence might dilute the power of it all.

The morning sun lightened the cabin as Jordan compared files of the victims at the kitchen table. When Lawrence's voice came across the walkie-talkie, Jordan placed the files on the table and looked out the kitchen window into the vast expanse of woods.

"Got the results back," Lawrence said. "Thomas Douglas was surer than shit the body found in Burley Greer's casket."

Jordan popped his fist on the table and nodded. Hannah's comments finally made sense. Burley Greer was foreign to the mountain, an outsider who settled on Iron Mountain hoping to become immersed there as though he was given acceptance to be considered one of her own. Burley was the outsider Hannah talked about.

Jordan walked outside to the squad car. Rubin Sawyer waited, leaning against the passenger door.

"Ready to get your man?" Sawyer asked.

"I'm waitin' on you."

"Huntin' him down ain't gonna be easy, but we know who we're after. He may know the mountain well, but he doesn't know it like I do."

"The question is, is he acting alone?"

"Not sure if any others are in on this thing. Like I said, killin' for a reason, whether it bein' to protect life, protect a still, that's understandable. But killin' just for the perverted enjoyment of it, well that don't sound right. Especially if it means bein' in cahoots with someone not born and bred on this mountain."

"Regardless, it's time to go after him."

Sawyer sat at the kitchen table as Jordan put on a black Gore-Tex jacket. TBI was written across the back of the jacket in yellow. He placed a black .38 in his holster and snapped it in place. He placed six clips of shells in a leather case inside the jacket. He snapped a .380 pistol into a holder above his ankle.

"Fancy pistols," Sawyer said. "Think I'll just stick to my Springfield."

Jordan followed Sawyer to his truck where he removed a long, silver case from behind the seat. He unlatched the metal snaps and took hold of his rifle. After placing the case back in the truck, he snatched a green hunting jacket from the front seat. The jacket had two rows of bullets that ran across the midsection, lining the jacket in bronze. He placed the gun on his shoulder and tightened the strap.

"Lawrence and his men are meeting us at seven thirty." Jordan placed a county map on the hood of the squad car and looked at his watch. "That gives us about ten minutes."

The edges of the map were torn, the center split in three places. There were markings in red to identify the hunter's cabin where Rachel's bracelet and Thomas Douglas' shirt were found. He had marked the location of the Iron Mountain cabin, Roby Greer's house and the spots on Doe Creek where the three women were found.

"Here's where Sarah and her brother got into the skirmish with Burley." Jordan pointed with his index finger.

"Rocky Branch. That's about a half mile north of that hunter's cabin," Sawyer said. "There's an old logging road that splits it like a wishbone, near Noah Timbs' old house. His place has been abandoned for somewhere near fifty years."

"Think that might be where our boy's holed up?"

"I'd reckon that place would be held together only by weeds

and cobwebs by now, but it is the only shack in that part of the woods as best I know. That's not to say others ain't been built since I left the place."

"I think we use the hunter's cabin as a starting point," said Jordan. He tapped the red circle with his index finger.

"Good idea. If the Greer boy is up there, we need to pen him in. Otherwise, he'll surely head back further in the mountain."

"We best circle from above, don't you think?"

"I think that's smart. He ain't gonna hunker down and fight. He's gonna run deeper into the hills."

~ * ~

Roby Greer pulled up in front of the run down shack. He ran to the door in a panic and banged on the splintery wood, turning the knob when he got no response. From the side of the house, Jakob said, "What the hell you doin'?"

Roby stepped off the porch. "They know it was Burley. By now they prob'ly know I was in on it too."

Jakob spit and wiped and his lip with his sleeve. "You're just worried about savin' your own hide. Your boy could face the electric chair, and you're skeered you might get implicated."

"They'll most likely come after you too."

Jakob scratched his neck, and spit tobacco juice. "Tell 'em to come on. Let 'em step foot on my land."

"It ain't so much me I'm worried about. It's Burley. He cain't go to prison."

"We'll be ready."

"I need to stay here. Got nowhere else to go."

"No," Jakob said simply.

Willie walked up from behind the house with two brown jugs filled with moonshine. "We best deliver this load to Hank in Bluff City."

"The law's comin' after Burley," Jakob said. Willie placed the jugs in his truck. "Won't be long afore they come 'round here."

"They do, and we'll blow 'em straight to hell," Willie said. "Git the rifles and all the ammo you can find."

"What about me?" Roby asked.

"What about you?" Willie stated more of a comment than a question.

"What do you need me to do?"

"We need you to screw yourself." He nudged Roby with his

arm as he headed past him toward the house. "And git off my land before I shoot you."

~ * ~

Lawrence called the deputies together and they emptied the gun case in the storage room. There was a nervous energy, and adrenaline was building. He tried to project a calmness though his stomach was in knots, nauseous to a degree. As far as the deputies, they were eager to end the terror that had gripped the county, but would the prospect of gunfire dim the eagerness? The deputies, weapons in hand, jogged to their vehicles as Lawrence walked behind them.

"Want the sirens on, Cap'n?" Anderson asked on his car radio.

"No," Lawrence replied from the lead car. "Let's not make the town any more wound up than it already is. Just turn your flashers on. We should slip through relatively unnoticed that way."

The mini-caravan moved westward and within minutes was on Highway 47. Doe Valley, like always, oozed peacefulness and serenity. The morning sun was slowly burning away the haze in the valley, and the southern ridge of Snake Mountain stood tall, an azure wall. The highway was empty except Elridge Jenkin's green tractor. The tractor, better known as the Green Hornet, looked to be idling in neutral when passed by the police cars.

The Brushy Fork van joined the hunt at the turnoff on Shady Valley. Six hounds looked anxiously out the windows. Jordan and Sawyer waited at the edge of the driveway outside the cabin in the squad car. Lawrence rolled to a halt and lowered his window.

"Hunter's cabin?" he asked.

"You got it," Jordan replied.

Jordan and Sawyer fell in line behind the van to make the two mile drive along Shady Valley.

The men pulled to the side of the road, and the hounds jumped out, leaping about as the officers held onto their leashes. Myers opened the back door of his squad car and Sam came barreling out. He looked strong, his tail wagging and his head high.

"Here he is," Myers said.

Jordan rubbed beneath Sam's chin. "Today's the day, old boy," said Jordan. "Let's go find her."

Twenty Eight

Jordan walked in front of the posse with Sawyer, occasionally pointing when he wanted to make directional changes. The three guards from Brushy Fork walked the dogs in pairs, firmly holding the leashes, rifles strapped to their shoulders. Myers and Adams flanked the right side of the guards. Lawrence and Anderson manned the left. Sam walked alongside Jordan, his nose to the ground, testing the land in front of him.

Deep in that mountain land, the sky disappeared behind a veil of dull clouds. The winds had turned from the north, with bitter gusts that howled down the steep slope toward the valley. The clouds were not the rainy or snowy kind, but a smooth, ashy blanket. The deepness of the forest deflected most of the graying sky, giving the woods the look of an indoor rain forest.

The hounds howled erratically with no sense of unity. Like coyotes circling wounded prey, the dogs seemed as if they knew they weren't searching for clues rather the killer himself. The group retraced their steps to the cabin, seventy yards apart. As they did, the remote forest came to life in sound and motion.

They entered the down slope and their travel eased. When they reached the stream at the low point of the ravine, Jordan looked at Sawyer. "Where's the hunter's cabin?"

As he waded across the creek, Sawyer said, "Turn northeast."

The dogs stepped high into the water as though they were untrusting of its depth. They hopped and splashed across the rocks as they crossed. The stream was high, the result of the melting snow. The frigid water splashed against the legs of the men, their boots repelling most of it. A great horned owl awakened on a limb of a tall locust, and his mighty wings whooshed above the posse as he took off in search for quieter woods. Myers ducked his head at the sound, as the tension seemed to build in all shape and form.

They climbed northeastward for close to an hour, but their steps and movements were as steady as when they first began. Spread in equidistance, Jordan and Sawyer in the middle. The dogs sounded a bit restless. One of the hounds nipped at its partner's leg.

~ * ~

Alice walked timidly into the kitchen. "Food's all gone," she said. "Polk salad. Flour, corn meal, gone."

"Damn you, woman," Burley said. "I told you to feed 'em enough just to keep 'em alive." Burley grabbed his rifle and walked to the back door. "Time to cut back on the number of mouths to feed."

Alice followed him to the door. "Enough o' this," she cried. "This killin' cain't go on."

He brushed off her comments. Burley walked the path to the cellar. The mountain was tightening around him, and he knew it. Was he the only one who understood that what he did to his captives was exactly what they deserved?

He hadn't intended to kill Patricia Darby, initially. He wanted to humiliate her, degrade her. He wanted her to suffer, the way he wanted Pauline Hickson to suffer. But Pauline never came on Iron Mountain, and he wasn't crazy enough to think he could snatch her from the valley without someone seeing, someone knowing.

Besides, the Darby girl made it almost too easy. She shouldn't have walked alone on Shady Valley Road that day. In skintight jeans, a white sweater with no bra—he could see the outline of her nipples through the thin material from where he watched her from the trees. *Whores, everyone of 'em.*

When she bent to pick wildflowers alongside the road, sticking her shapely tail out, she was doing it just to tease him. *She know'd I was a watchin.'*

He followed her back to the cabin. He watched her through the bedroom window as she placed a flower behind her ear, becoming a slut for her husband, or boyfriend, whichever he was. She was a bad girl, no different from Pauline. Where Pauline teased, Patricia Darby was not going to get off that easy.

Burley watched the things she did to her man that day, and it disgusted him. It was so easy to slip into the cabin when the guy took a shower. Good thing the kitchen door was hard to lock. When she opened the refrigerator for something to drink, he'd already slipped in through the door, pressing the knife against her back, his hands covering her mouth, muffling her screams.

It wasn't until Burley bragged to Willie about kidnapping Patricia Darby that killing her was brought up. Bum, who soon found out, convinced Burley if he didn't kill her, the law would soon come. It would be just a matter of time before they would find him, and figure out Thomas Douglas lay in the pine casket under the chickweeds at the meadow.

Bum said killing her would scare the tourists away that Johnson County was trying to bring onto the mountain, and the folks on Iron Mountain would accept Burley. It was a deadly initiation to become one of Iron Mountain's own.

Only those born of the mountain were truly part of the mountain.

When Burley killed Patricia Darby, he wasn't prepared for the fight she put up. It was supposed to end quickly, strangling her with a rope. But she struggled, kicking, hitting, making it hard to keep his grip tight enough to stop her screaming. It wasn't until he used the knife that he finally silenced her.

Watching her finish her last breath fueled something evil within him, and his desire to punish the women who came upon the mountain grew. It birthed a fascination seeing them struggle, to see them look at him in their final breath, pleading, hoping, he would save them. They're final look of desperation made him feel alive, as if he had taken their soul and it became part of his.

The day he spotted Barbara Thomas walking along the Appalachian Trail alone, he couldn't resist the chance. *Dumbass girl shouldn't walk Iron Mountain by herself.* He acted as if he couldn't start a campfire when she walked up the trail, asking her for assistance. His only mistake was scaring her to the point she ran, and he should have silenced her quicker. He didn't pay attention to the backpack she dropped on the trail.

He kept Barbara Thomas alive longer than Patricia Darby, raping her, beating her. The dirtier her body, the more bruised—it only increased his desire. He searched the mountains for new victims. His plan was to keep them as long as possible, humiliating them into submission.

Burley stepped into the cellar. With the investigation tightening his boundaries, he had no choice but to kill the girls. Shelby's body would soon be found, if it hadn't already. Besides, they had too many mouths to feed, and he was only concerned with feeding his own.

It stood to reason Kara, so close to death, should be the one to finish off first. But Burley was in the mood for a fight, and wanted someone who would fight back. He leaned his rifle against the cold earth wall outside Rachel's door, removed his knife from his sheath and entered. Rachel cowered in the shadows, the whites of her eyes bright against her grimy face.

Burley pulled on the chain that held the shackle locked around her ankle, dragging her toward him. The hard floor scraped her thighs as he bounced her across the dirt. He grabbed her by her wrist and slid her in front of him. She said nothing, her eyes locked in on his. His large body cast a massive silhouette upon her.

He took her by the hair and squeezed it so she'd wince in pain. Placing the knife to her face, he whispered, "It's Judgment Day." Burley hit her across the face with the handle of the knife. "Afore I kill you, I'm a gonna have my way with you one more time."

He stared at the shape of her buttocks as he pulled her to her hands and knees. The bruises on her body, the filth that covered her, the stench in the air from living like an animal, only increased his desire. He unlocked the shackle that held her ankle, and set his knife on a shelf above her. He pulled her by the waist with both arms.

Since she looked like an animal, he was going to force himself upon her like one. Was she was too tired to fight, or had she just given up? He reached with his other hand to unbuckle his overalls at the shoulder.

He couldn't see much more than the silhouette of her on hands and knees, and his mind focused on the task at hand. He closed his eyes, lost in the physicality of it all, as he once again dominated her.

When he was done, he fumbled for the buckle of his overalls, now in a groggy state of mind. He hardly noticed her slip away on the cold floor. When she turned and lunged upward, driving the ice pick deep into his shoulder, at the base of his neck, he fell back into the shelves. He cried out as jars crashed down upon him, trying to grab hold of the pick handle pressed against his neck. Rachel bolted for the door in a panic. She struggled to make it up the cellar steps.

Burley let out a loud moan as he removed the ice pick. Blood squirted from the entry wound. He stumbled to the door and grabbed his gun. As he made it to the top of the stairs, the echoes of the hounds froze him in his tracks. His shoulder bleeding profusely, he watched Rachel run southward. The dogs yelped and barked, the sound quickly growing in intensity. He took off northward into the woods.

~ * ~

The louder the dogs became, the faster Rachel seemed to run. She tried to yell but her chest was heavy with exhaustion. She made it out of the weed strewn clearing and stumbled into the underbrush. Her calloused feet left a trail of blood on the cold ground. Sam pulled away from the posse in a dead sprint.

"Weapons ready," Lawrence yelled.

The men began to jog, Rachel now seventy yards in front of them. The dogs pulled hard on their leashes as they followed the unbridled Sam. Rachel collapsed over a fallen limb, crying and panting. With her face down and tears flowing, she struggled to stand. A familiar lick on her face by Sam caused her to cry out, a sound of painful joy. She rolled on her back, pulling him to her, squeezing him as he licked her. Tears poured down her face as she tried to hold onto her squirming dog.

Jordan was the first to reach her. "Rachel Williams?" he asked, his gun pointed skyward. A nod was all she could manage. "Lawrence," Jordan yelled. "Radio EMS. Get 'em up here. Now!" Jordan dropped to one knee. "It's okay, ma'am. You're safe now."

Rachel, still clinging tightly to Sam, cried out, "He's wounded. I stab the bastard's neck." She pointed toward the cabin. "He's up that way."

"We'll get him. You let these men tend to you and we'll take it from here."

"There's another girl in the cellar. I think she's in bad shape."

"I'm on my way." He waved Anderson in. "The deputy is going to take care of you now. You're going to be just fine."

Anderson placed his jacket around her and Jordan said, "Let's move."

Guns drawn, the search party approached the clearing. Jordan led the way, with Sawyer and Lawrence close behind. As they waded through the weeds to the steps of the cellar, a shot rang out from the woods and Myers fell in the weeds. Jordan saw Jakob standing at the edge of a hickory tree sixty yards to the left of the shack, setting his sights for another shot. Willie, on one knee, ten feet to Jakob's left, fired off a shot that caught Lawrence in the arm. The posse scattered, returning fire. The clearing, a kidney-shaped area barely twenty yards wide, provided little cover. Willie and Jakob looked to have them hemmed in, and when they stepped closer, Jordan yelled, "Take cover!"

One of the guards tried to make it to the cellar entrance, and Willie's shot shattered his spine. The posse returned random shots in rapid fire to slow the movement of the brothers. Myer's lifeless body lay next to the cellar steps, and the dogs circled his body, barking wildly.

A shot rang out and Anderson fell to the ground. Spotting Willie behind a poplar, his rifle pointing at Anderson, Jordan took a shot. Willie flinched, looked at Jordan, and fired. The bullet thumped the ground two feet from where Jordan knelt. Jakob and Willie moved closer, steady, aggressively, using the trees as shields. The posse scattered to the weeds and Jordan and Sawyer, who crouched behind an elm, aimed and fired. Bullets splintered the trees that protected the brothers.

The barrage of bullets by the posse allowed Sawyer to look at the ground around him. Crouched, he pointed to a trail of blood and said to Jordan, "He's headed deeper in the mountain. Probably on his way to Stoney Creek." Jordan nodded as shots buzzed around them. "Gotta get to the trees."

Jordan's eyes scanned the landscape, doing a quick tally on his posse. "Pepper their asses," he commanded. The guard who was uninjured, Adams, and the wounded Lawrence returned fire, forcing the brothers to stay hidden behind the trees. Jordan scurried to his right into the woods, Sawyer following behind.

Now protected by the dense forest, Sawyer again looked to the ground. "He's losin' blood, and he's runnin' scared. Stay close to him, but let him wear out."

"What about you?" Jordan asked.

"This fox is all yours. I'm going to exact a little vengeance on the Parker boys. Their grandpappy was one of the men who dragged my daddy across the holler the day he was shot. Time to even up the score."

~ * ~

Sawyer blended into thick hardwoods, easing his way to where Jakob and Willie crouched. Shots rang out in a furious volley.

The brothers' sole purpose was to defend or die, as was the way of Iron Mountain. Lawrence, though wounded, continued to shoot, furiously attempting to prevent the brothers from picking them off in the weeds. Jakob shot at the guard as he made a dash for the tree line. The guard dropped into the weeds, and the dogs' leashes became tangled underneath his body. The body count grew.

Sawyer inched closer to the brothers, slipping within fifty yards. He set up on one knee beside a plump laurel, setting his sights on Willie. As Willie moved to his left, his eyes burning like coals, aiming his rifle at Lawrence, Sawyer's shot pierced Willie's ear. Jakob watched his brother fall.

"Willie!" He fired two shots in Sawyer's direction, and scrambled to Willie's side.

The side of Willie's head was split open, and Sawyer watched Jakob clinch his teeth and let go a piercing yell. Jakob fired again at Sawyer and backpedaled up the slope.

Sawyer pursued Jakob, and the hunt was on. Twice Sawyer had a clear shot at Jakob's back. Thoughts of his father dying on that dusty road on Stoney Creek flashed through his head, and he refused to take down Jakob from behind. He'd earned the right to see the man who would retaliate for the killing of his father.

~ * ~

The day was getting late and the clouds thickened. The winds began to howl, a bitter gale that cut through Burley under the rattling treetops. Who pursued him? Sawyer? Indeed, Burley was headed to Stoney Creek as though he had earned the right to protection from the folks of Iron Mountain.

Though he moved hurriedly, he grimaced with each step. Blood ran down the underside of his thermal shirt, which had adhered to his wound. He stopped and knelt in the ferns, looking behind him for movement, pointing his rifle at every tree as though there were thousands of men aiming their guns back at him. After a moment, he turned and stood, heading northward again. Soon he spotted the shacks of Stoney Creek in the distance and picked up his gait.

He came upon two women who knelt beside a stream washing clothes. They wore scarves about their head and faded dresses pulled up to their knees. One wore brown boots, untied. The other had black boots, hardened looking, with no laces at all. One motioned to a small child to stand behind her after she spotted

Burley. He looked at them with a hopeless fear. His footsteps were unsteady as he ran past.

When he burst through Bum's front door, Bum's wife sat spinning yarn on a wooden wheel.

"Where is he?" Burley shouted.

She spoke no words, looked at him briefly and resumed her work. Though he carried a gun, she looked as though she felt no fear. "Checkin' his stills, I reckon," she finally offered. She looked at him with tired eyes.

"I'm wounded. I need help."

She continued with her work, her head looking down at the spinning wheel.

"Did you hear me, old woman?"

"My hearin' works fine. Your world may be fallin' like a paper house, but that don't make a spit of difference to me. I got enough to concern myself with than worryin' about your misguided soul. Outsider."

"Damn you, woman."

He went to a bedroom, rummaging through a small cabinet where he removed a cloth towel. Wincing, he pulled his shirt away from where it pasted to his shoulder and placed the towel over the wound.

~ * ~

Skirting behind a smothering line of laurels, Jordan spotted Bum's shack. He worked his way around a group of red spruces with low reaching limbs. The thick needles offered protected movement. Squatting behind a fallen oak with withered brown leaves, he knelt twenty yards away.

A shadow moved inside the kitchen window.

Jordan was again on Stoney Creek Holler. Before, he came in search of clues; this time he came for the killer. A rifle shot split a limb above his head as he looked in the tiny window. He took to the ground as three men took shots at him from the ridge thirty yards above. He returned fire and scooted through the trees toward the shack.

The shots surrounding Jordan were warning shots. These men had no direct dispute with him. Otherwise, they could have felled him with the first shot. He dodged a few more errant bullets as he made his way around Bum's shack. He ran to the front of the house and burst in the door, gun pointed and ready to fire.

Bum's wife, without raising her head, said, "Leave me be, revenuer."

Jordan stood, his eyes in constant movement, gun pointed to the ceiling. He stepped carefully toward the bedroom, glancing back at the elderly woman for signs that might signal Burley was hiding. He checked both bedrooms, ran outside, and again took to climbing the mountain.

~ * ~

Jakob headed to a cave where moonshiners once hid supplies in the days of Prohibition. The damp cave was used to store meat and goat's milk, holding them for days when federal agents roamed the area. The mountain's slope was steep, though Jakob traveled through the trees with little effort.

The cave's entrance rose to a height of sixteen feet, with roots and vines dangling from above like a crown of disorder. The width of the cave was ten feet at best, its left side turned inward like cartilage that covers a sow's ear. Thick strands of ivy intertwined along rusted barrels outside the entrance. He knelt beside one of the barrels to reload his rifle. Reaching inside his coat pocket, he winced. Only three shells remained. The click of the shells pushing into the cartridge was sharp and quick.

The winds howled, and shadows moved about amongst the endless backdrop of trees. The temperature had dropped to freezing, and Jakob's breath blew hard, puffs of white disappearing into the air above him. The backwoods of the mountain had always provided comfort, yet now he felt the shadows closing in on him.

As Jakob approached the entrance of the cavern, a twig snapped near a balsam fir thirty-five feet away. He raised his rifle, head still, eyes moving about. The clouds were skirting across the mountain in thick waves of gray, making it hard to distinguish the trees from the shadows. For an instant, he saw the silhouette of someone slipping behind a white pine. He raised his rifle and tried to set his sights. The fog rolled and faded the shadows to gray.

Despite the bitter wind that howled into the cavern, his hands began to sweat. Sounds of the mountain crept upon and around him, sounds that suddenly seemed foreign and dangerous. A whistle in the wind. A strange rattle in the treetops. Shrill calls from strange birds that seemed to offer foreshadowing of darkness to come. The sudden unfamiliarity of the trees had him nervously looking about. Had the mountain turned against him?

A rock bounced off a weed-riddled barrel to Jakob's right, and he fired a shot in despair. He crouched to his knees, but saw only vague forms and shapes. He backed into the cave's entrance, standing at the doorway. As he prepared to enter, a rock skipped against the ceiling above his head. In a panic, he shot skyward, scattering chunks of the black rock upon him. One bullet remained. He tried to slip back into the cave but found it blocked by a recent landslide.

Iron Mountain had closed her doors.

"It's over, son," Sawyer called out from the shadows.

He saw movement in a nearby spruce and fired into the thick needles. The movement ceased and he stepped away from the cave, moving slowly to the tree, just twenty feet away. He stepped slowly, and carefully parted the limbs with the barrel of his gun while he looked about. As he did, he heard the lever load a shell in Sawyer's Springfield. To his left, Sawyer stood pointing the rifle at Jakob's head.

"End of the line," Sawyer said.

Jakob stepped back. "You turned your back on this mountain, on us, years ago. So you got no right to be concerned in these here matters." He dropped to a knee, his empty rifle lying across his thigh.

"I've got all the right in the world. And I'm about to change how business is done on this mountain."

"From what we was told, Bum ended your business a long time ago. Way I hear it, your daddy screamed like a little girl when they dragged him 'cross the holler."

"Too bad Willie never got the chance to scream. I would have loved to have heard it."

Jakob seethed. The barks of the hounds carried up the mountain and he turned his head, his eyes glancing toward the source of the barks.

"They're comin' for you," Sawyer said. "But you and me both know this is gonna be settled here and now."

Jakob lowered his hand slowly and gathered soil from the cold ground. He looked again briefly toward the yelps of the dogs, as if he were determining in his mind the distance between them and where he sat. Quickly he tossed the dirt at Sawyer's face then charged ahead with his rifle raised high. Sawyer rubbed his eyes with the back of his left hand, his right still holding his rifle.

Jakob raised his gun, prepared to swing the butt of it like a baseball bat. As the barrel approached Sawyer's head, Sawyer pulled his trigger. He stumbled to his knees, clutching his chest as he fell backwards into the underbrush. He breathed hard twice, clutching his chest and looked at Sawyer, whose eyes showed no mercy.

He tried to run, but stumbled, collapsing hard to the cold ground. Blood poured from his mouth, and he tried to stop it with his hand. He was coughing, gagging, and his chest began to heave in short bursts. Crawling, as though he could survive if he could just keep moving, he cried out, "Help me."

~ * ~

Sawyer watched each and every painful breath until he grew quiet. He knelt beside Jakob's body and placed his rifle on the ground. He looked out into the mist, as though oblivious to the approaching deputy and the cries of the hounds.

He had seen more than his share of the dead, mostly from the war. Many had been at the hands of his doing. It was his job; it was what he was trained to do. He was a necessary evil. The uniform carried the military's endorsement of his right to kill, and on the battlefield, he had to kill to survive.

For Sawyer, the killing wasn't what bothered him as much as the reason God created a world that allowed it to happen. But God created both the lion and the lamb.

It was easy to know which role Iron Mountain played, and it played the role well. But was he any less a predator?

Twenty Nine

Lawrence ripped his sleeve off and tied it tight above his wound to slow the bleeding. He radioed for more assistance from the county EMS units and from the Medical Center in Elizabethton. Adams tended to Anderson, who seemed alert though lying on the ground. Sawyer returned with the remaining guard and the dogs.

With one arm, Lawrence flipped Myer's body, which lay beside the cellar. Myer's eyes were fixed, blood trickling from his nose. As Lawrence closed the young man's eyes, he heard the faint sound of coughing from the cellar.

"Police," Lawrence shouted outside Kara's prison cell. "Move away from the door."

Lawrence popped the lock with one shot. When he entered the dark room, he found Kara curled on the floor, shaking violently. He removed his coat and placed it around her. She cried in his arms, her body blackened by dirt and bruises.

Adams came in the room with a hatchet and split Kara's shackles. He lifted her in his arms and carried her up the steps. Outside the cellar, Rachel, Sam tagging at her heels, stood shakily. Her body shivered. She led them up the path to Burley's house. Inside the house, Anderson placed Kara on Burley's bed, wrapping her tightly in wool blankets. Lawrence removed Kara's inhaler from his coat pocket and went to the kitchen. Rachel was wrapped in a blanket at the kitchen table.

"You okay, ma'am?"

Rachel nodded, eyes red, tears streaming down her cheeks.

"EMS is on the way." He placed his hand on her shoulder. What else could he say or do to comfort?

He walked outside to where Anderson lay. The wind blew and Anderson shook. He knelt and slid Anderson's jacket at the waist to check the wound. His right hip was bloody. He removed his jacket and placed it over Anderson's upper body.

"You holdin' up okay?" Anderson looked worried but nodded. "Hell of a day, huh, son?"

"Yes, sir," Anderson said softly as Lawrence put one knee to the ground.

An ambulance siren wailed in the distance.

"Florence Nightingale has arrived." He looked to the trees and turned his head. Anderson flashed a slight smile. "You're gonna be just fine, son."

"Any word from Jordan?" Sawyer asked as he approached Lawrence.

"None."

"Let's get a move on then. How's your arm?"

"Just a nuisance is all." He nodded toward the woods. "Lead the way."

The men disappeared into the woods.

~ * ~

Burley stepped quietly through the backwoods. Fog moved in separated bunches across the mountain, like weary souls in search of their final resting place. The dark skies made it impossible to distinguish whether it was the break of dawn or high noon. Raindrops began to fall, slowly at first, but gathering in speed so that the mountain hummed in constant sound and movement. Small patches of snow were still visible across Carson's Hill, its barren bald carved angrily from the backside of Iron Mountain, domed in white.

The sharp rise in elevation dropped the temperature dramatically, the cold wind slapping Burley's face as he grabbed hold of tree limbs and underbrush for support. When he finally ascended the top, clouds of slate lowered, swallowing the hazy fog. The treetops disappeared into a purplish mist, the sounds of their chaotic swaying a haunting melody. Iron Mountain seemed to be in no hurry to give way to spring, fighting with bitter reluctance.

His heart was filled with the unlikely bed partners of fear and rage. Under his breath, he swore vengeance against Sawyer, in part for turning his back on a place Burley wished for a lifetime he'd been born to.

He came across a trail that turned northwest and led him through land of a flatter nature, a soft dip in the mountain like the crevice in a fedora hat. The land was more favorable for crossing, and with him weakening from the loss of blood, it was his only chance to escape. He soon came upon terrain that rose and fell in gentle waves.

The path Burley walked was an unfamiliar one, and the lowering clouds moved quickly to the east. What was this claustrophobic state within him, within his psyche? There was no sky, no mountaintop, to validate that the heavens were above him. Rather, it was a ceiling that seemed to tighten his ever-shrinking world.

He passed a small field of dead corn stalks that bordered a gravesite. He sidestepped the small, unmarked tombstones and pushed on until he came upon a long meadow, the grass low and sprinkled in clover. Blood dripped, purple drops that seemed large and self-contained. The adrenaline surge was running low as the loss of blood slowed Burley's ability to flee; the anger of being chased drove him forward.

Would he be remembered? Would he be talked about with the same regard as Gaines Logan? Each body tossed in the creek was to honor Iron Mountain. Had he sacrificed enough to achieve legendary status? He could go to his grave with comfort if that were the case.

He ducked behind a bale of hay, trying to gather enough strength for a final dash to the woods. He spotted Jordan entering the field nearly two hundred yards back. His shirt darkened by blood, the smell in the air, he was like a wounded animal.

He looked behind, only sixty yards of sweet grass and clover now separated him from Jordan. He had to make it to the deep woods west of the meadow. On one knee, slipping around the bale, Burley fired off a shot that grazed Jordan's thigh. Jordan returned fire with his .38, penning Burley behind the bale. Grimacing, he watched Jordan scramble to a bale thirty yards away.

"Give it up Burley," Jordan yelled. "You got nowhere to run."

Damn lawman. Burley spotted another bale twenty-five yards away. *Gotta make it to the woods. Disappear into the trees.* He fired off another shot and bolted for the bale. *Gettin' closer.*

Burley turned to gauge his distance, and saw Jordan's gun jam. He tossed it on the ground and removed a pistol hugging his ankle. Burley fired another shot and continued on. The drizzle turned into a steady rain.

When Burley looked again, he'd lost sight of Jordan. There

were two bales close by Jordan could be hiding behind. One bale was forty feet or so away, the other closer to thirty. The loss of blood made it hard to think. He took off to another bale. *Almost to the woods.*

The rain poured, and the winds whipped and blew it sideways. The drops stung Burley's face as he searched for Jordan. He gasped when Jordan jumped from behind the bale, kicking the rifle from his hands. He sprang toward Jordan, slamming his shoulder into his midsection, causing his gun to drop as Burley drove him to the wet ground. Jordan hit Burley with a quick series of punches to the face, and rolled him to his side.

Jordan's momentum forced Burley on his back, and Jordan slugged him again, landing a hard fist to the jaw. Burley pulled his knees toward his chest, and rammed his hand to Jordan's face. Jordan's grip now loosened, Burley pushed the detective in the midsection with both feet, sending him into the hardened roll of hay. He stood, removing his Bowie knife from his sheath.

"Time fer you to die like the other'ns," Burley said. "I'm gonna gut you like the pig you are. You bastard, thinkin' you can come after me on my mountain." His blade was dimmed by the pouring rain. He charged Jordan, trying to drive the knife into his chest. Jordan jumped to his left and the knife met only air.

"Your mountain? You're a foreigner just like me." Jordan backpedaled two steps. Lightning laced the skies and the ground shook underneath their feet. "To these people, you're a Gaines Logan wannabe."

He leaped forward and took a swipe at Jordan's face.

Jordan circled him like a cat toying with a mouse. "Tell me Burley. Why'd your father help? Did he help you kill Thomas Douglas? Did he help you kidnap the women?"

Burley slipped to one knee on the wet ground as he tried to maneuver closer, but was able to regain his footing. The rain poured off the bill of his hat, forcing him to squint. Jordan's hair lay flat against his face from the flow of water and he wiped his eyes with the back of his hand.

"Who was the guy in the cave?" asked Jordan.

"You mean Earl? That girl was a gift to him and the Parker boys. A down payment on my right for acceptance."

"That's a hell of an initiation fee."

He took a half-hearted swipe at Jordan again, which Jordan

easily dodged.

"Why the Douglas boy?"

"He caught me stealin' his prize game rooster. Pulled a rifle on me. I told him I'd be back, and he'd pay fer it. I came back the next day with my knife. Caught him off guard while he was a plowin.' I didn't mean to kill him. Just to cut him and make sure he knew I meant business. But when I cut him, he tried to kill me. I swear he did. I had no choice. I had to finish him off. I showed him who the real man was."

Jordan moved to his right.

"Pa and me tore his face up after I kil't him. Was Pa's idea to conjure up the boat accident. Nobody questioned Pa when he told 'em it were me layin' on the bank of the lake. I took to the mountain. Took hold of the Timbs' cabin. Only a few people knew."

"Bum being one of those people."

"He knew. Had no problem with it."

Rain poured across the field in rolling fashion and the trees along the edge of the field rattled like bones.

"Give it up, Burley."

Burley again lunged at Jordan, knife extended. Jordan slipped to his right and punched him in the face, knocking him to the ground. Jordan jumped on Burley's back and grabbed his wrist, fighting for control of the knife. Burley attempted to fling Jordan from his back, his size advantage negated by his loss of blood.

He lowered one shoulder and they tumbled to the wet ground, Burley on his back and Jordan on his side. He hadn't shaken Jordan's grip on his wrist, the knife pointing skyward. He elbowed Jordan, and turned the steel blade toward Jordan's chest. He felt Jordan's grip tighten and the point of the knife now turned toward Jordan's neck.

Weakening, searching for adrenaline, Burley couldn't stop Jordan from rolling, the grip on his hand feeling stronger. Momentum rolled them twice. With Burley again on his back, Jordan took hold of Burley's wrist with his other hand, and the knife began turning, so that it pointed at Burley's chest. The knife that killed Patricia Darby, Barbara Thomas and Becky Shoun, inched toward Burley's torso.

Jordan stared into his eyes and pushed forward with his body. Burley's strength was fading, panic overtaking him. He cried out and began kicking. The knife pierced his skin, and Jordan's steely eyes staring at him as in some crazed trance. He felt the knife entering him, ripping his flesh. Jordan climbed on top and with a final push, plunged the knife deep into Burley's chest. His body shook violently as he clawed at Jordan's face. Blood, mixed with spit, came out of his mouth as he struggled to breathe. He gasped as Jordan pushed down on the handle of the knife.

His eyes locked onto Jordan's as he breathed his final breath.

Thirty

The rain had eased into a mist when Alice stood to the side of the woodpile underneath a locust tree thirty yards from the shack. Her wet hands trembled as they touched the smooth tree trunk. She quietly walked to the back door and watched EMS technicians tend to Rachel in the kitchen. Deputy Anderson was receiving assistance from two medical personnel in the ferns, preparing to load him on the stretcher that would eventually transport him out of the woods. She watched as Lawrence had his wound cleaned and bandaged and heard the faint sounds of other emergency personnel making their way up the mountain. Two EMS techs, one speaking via radio, disappeared behind the back of the cabin.

Alice cried as she watched Rachel, wrapped tightly in her blanket, talk with Deputy Adams. Kara was carried out by stretcher through the porch door. Rachel motioned to the two men carrying her, and she knelt and hugged Kara. No words were spoken. They seemed unwilling to release their embrace.

The fog lifted, the rain stopped and night was coming on quickly. Jesse Long was busy taking photographs of Deputy Myers, the fallen prison guard, and finally, Willie. The dead were bagged. Jordan walked into the clearing with Sawyer and Lawrence. Behind him, the two techs carried Burley's body on a gurney.

Alice listened, silent as the maple she stood behind.

"Hell of a day, huh Cap'n?" Lawrence asked.

"It's been a hell of a month," Jordan replied.

"This our man?" Lawrence asked, pointing to the bag that held Burley.

"Yep."

Alice walked from the woods and quietly moved up beside Burley's body. With tears in her eyes, she touched the zipper on the bag.

Lawrence turned. "Alice?"

She spoke no words, but simply patted the bag that held Burley.

Jordan looked at the old woman. "Who?"

When Rachel placed her hand on Alice's shoulder, she sobbed. "He's your son?"

The woman, tears streaming down her face, only nodded.

~ * ~

In front of the Sheriff's Department news trucks had gathered from towns like Boone, Damascus and Elizabethton. Lawrence watched them from the window in his office. Reporters waited outside the front door. News would spread quickly now. Lawrence was too tired to grant an interview. He was simply thankful the terror was over.

~ * ~

It was nearing dusk. Jordan rode in the passenger seat while Lawrence drove to Roby Greer's farmhouse. He spotted Roby on the porch, his dogs on either side of him. Roby looked tired and worn and from a distance, relieved when the car pulled to a stop in front of his house.

Though Jordan was anxious to arrest Roby Greer, there was no joy in it. It saddened him somewhat to know Roby had lost his sons, and his wife was held prisoner by her own boy. Roby spoke not a word, just rose from his chair with a small carrying bag. His dogs began to bark, but he signaled their silence. Lawrence cuffed him and placed him in the back of the squad car.

Though he'd worked many murder cases, nothing had affected him like this one—emotionally or physically. It would have been easy to toss a smirk at Roby for bringing him to justice after the calloused treatment Roby had given him during the investigation.

In the end, Jordan got his man. He won the game. That was all that mattered.

Thirty One

Rubin Sawyer kicked the door open, knocking the black, skeleton-key lock to the floor. The kitchen was in disarray, and various articles of clothing littered the floor. By the looks of it, Bum Whitfield was on the run. Sawyer turned to the porch, looking at the other shacks around the holler. He walked to the trail in front of Bum's house, and stared into the cracked doors and windows that held watching eyes.

Raising his rifle toward the sky, he yelled, "You tell Bum Whitfield it's only a matter of time."

Sawyer lowered his rifle and then pointed it toward Bum's shack. "Tell him not to rest. Tell him to sleep with a gun on his chest. Tell him to look over his shoulder when he walks the mountain. Tell him I will be back, and I'm gonna send him straight to hell."

~ * ~

Jordan stopped his car and looked for a street sign. There was nothing to indicate the name of the earthen road, but based on instructions from Bert, it had to be the right one. He reversed the car, and turned onto the lane. The road sloped downward with rolling hills to the right where cattle grazed. On the left were patches of hemlocks and spruces that sheltered a smattering of goats. Flimsy barbed wire fences, held loosely by sapling trunks, somehow managed to keep the goats from wandering onto the road.

After a couple of twisting turns, Jordan pulled up to a small, gray A-frame house. Though the siding of the tiny home was virtually void of color, patches of crimson Bee Balm and orange Turk's Cap Lily grew in the soft hunter-green grass in the front yard. On a tiny porch, next to what looked like a GE Frigidaire from the fifties, lay The General and Dan'l Boone. They barked and ran toward Jordan's vehicle.

Beside the house, Emma plowed a tiny field for her spring

planting of sweet corn and tomatoes, squash and cucumbers. She turned at the commotion of the dogs circling Jordan's vehicle, and killed the tractor's engine.

Jordan walked across the treeless yard and the pups sniffed his khaki pants and trotted behind.

"Well, well," she said with her hands on her hips. "If it ain't Dick Tracy makin' a house call."

"Hello, Emma," he replied, forcing a smile. "How are you?"

"Hangin' on like a hair in a biscuit. What brings you up to the exciting metropolis of Cracker's Neck? Somebody steal your gun?"

"No." He laughed.

"Well, I know it ain't hikin' lessons you's a come to offer. You couldn't find your way through the fun house at the Fair." As Jordan moved closer, he noticed her looking at the bruise on his cheek, and the bandage above his right eye. "Good Lord. What kinda wildcat d'you fight?"

"Emma, the search for Thomas is over."

Emma slowly stepped off the tractor, inhaled deeply and stared Jordan in the eyes. She wore the same hat as she did at their first meeting, pushing it upward in the manner she did then. Her faded dungarees looked two sizes too big and her down jacket had tears on both sleeves. Her boots were covered in clay. The smell of sweat drifted from her body, but not in a smothering way.

"You found my boy?"

"Yes'm."

"Is he dead?" she hesitantly asked.

"Yes, Emma. Yes, he is."

Emma glanced at the soft dirt at her feet, and shuffled it with her left boot. "Where'd you find 'im?"

"He was buried in the casket that was supposed to contain Burley Greer's body."

"I don't understand."

"Burley killed Thomas. Then he and Roby staged Burley's death."

"Where the hell is Burley?"

"He's dead too. Now. He was the killer we'd been searching for."

"Good Goshamighty."

"I wish I was bringing you good news Emma. I really do."

Emma looked away, her gaze seemingly following the slope of the valley toward Iron Mountain in the distance. In that moment her wall came down. He saw it in her eyes, in her face. Her spirit of tomfoolery and child-like innocence was gone, and the mother within her seemed to resurrect itself.

"You found my boy." She rubbed her hands together as though she was trying to shine a pebble with her palms. "He was a good boy. Didn't deserve that kinda endin' to his life. And at such a young age."

"I know." He nodded.

She took a deep breath. "Now I can bring him home. Lay him next to his pappy on top of Carter Gap." Tears filled the edges of her baby blue eyes.

Jordan moved forward and wrapped his arms around her. Her tough exterior had washed away like the last snow of spring. "Sometimes life flattens the human spirit."

"But the Lord picks us up, helps us dust off our britches, and stand tall again."

"That He does." He took her by the hands. "Thank you for all your help. We couldn't have done this without you."

"Well, I just did what anybody else woulda done 'round here."

He hugged her quietly as though his heart was saying goodbye to hers. He smiled at her and turned to walk to his car. It was time to go hold Marty and Jessie.

~ * ~

Jason held Kara's hand tightly as they walked to the car from the Medical Center in Elizabethton. The sun was sinking low between two ridges of Roan Mountain, much as it had when they approached Doe Valley what seemed a lifetime ago. The beautiful setting went unnoticed to him, and talk was virtually nonexistent. The sooner they returned to the everyday world in Charlotte, the quicker the trip to Iron Mountain would fade. But could it ever fade completely?

He placed his hand on hers on the center dash. She seemed to force a light smile, and he glanced out her window at a group of horses eating on a grassy hillside. He pointed them out to her in hopes of soothing her mind. As he started to turn his eyes back to the road, he looked again at the horses. Underneath a giant holly standing alone on the hillside, he saw movement in the shadows.

Surely, it was simply motion from the breeze.

An Exciting New Mystery Coming Soon
From Chuck Walsh

When Rubin Sawyer, a former resident of Iron Mountain, partnered with Knoxville detective Thomas Jordan to find who abducted women along trails and cabins of the mountain, he was deemed a traitor. As an act of revenge, his granddaughter is snatched from the banks of Doe Creek and taken to the bowels of the mountain. Soon after, hikers along the Appalachian Trail become sacrificial lambs, part of a bloody, cunning game of maneuvers designed to lead Sawyer to the mountain's infamous Hanging Tree.

READ THE PREVIEW

Backwoods Justice

Chapter One

MONDAY

His footprints measured his life; a life marked only by the tracks from his worn leather boots. Few would acknowledge his existence. Yet there he stood, a shadow in the soft morning light. evil veiled by lazy streams and wildflowers. His breath was foul and dry, his palms sweaty. Sent by the creator of law where no sense of accountability existed.

He'd come to deliver backwoods justice in the guise of revenge, the great equalizer. Down from that land of ten thousand hills, into the valley, below the doorstep of the place that time had forgotten. A plague sent from a Godless land.

~*~

The sun rose above Snake Mountain, carving shapes from the shadows that blanketed the hillsides. An easy breeze slipped along the valley, casting a shimmer on Doe Creek, distorting the mirror image of Iron Mountain in the distance. Carter Valley had sprung to life, her pulse running through the winding veins of the creek, her breath the wind that rustled the wheat and cornfields. A mix of Shorthorns and Angus cows were scattered about the valley like a disinterested audience. In the distance, a tractor rumbled. Peace blanketed the land.

Christina chased a butterfly along the edge of the grassy bank of Doe Creek as Rubin Sawyer slid a worm onto a silver hook, his brown eyes squinting slightly as he maneuvered the hook. The creek was running fast and flat, thirty-feet wide. What seemed like an endless array of rocks battled the rushing water, generating a constant hum of motion and white turbulence.

"If this doesn't work, "Sawyer said, "I'm wading into the creek and grabbing the fish by its eyeballs." He rinsed his hand in the creek, the icy water stinging his fingers. And yet it was a sting that warmed him like a hearth round a winter's fire. With a hook in one hand, the rod in the other, he pulled gently on the metal prong just to watch the rod concave as it would when the next fish snatched the bait.

"Patience, Daddy," said Jolene. "You know this is the first time she's so much as held a fishing pole."

"I know that. But it shouldn't take so long to catch on. I've already shown her a dozen times how to reel in a fish. It took no more than twice for you to figure it out. And *you* were younger than her."

"That's because I'm the daughter of the great Rubin Sawyer." Command rose in her voice when she spoke his name. "I had no choice. I had to be a fisherman and a hunter. You should have named me Annie Oakley Sawyer."

"I never forced you into it." Sawyer waved his hand into the air as if shooing away all notions in the world contrary to his. "You were born with the desire."

She glanced at Christina. "That's true, I guess. But she's more suited for chasing that butterfly than catching a fish in Doe Creek."

"Well, butterfly or bull horn. It's all the same. She just needs to pay closer attention to the details of it all."

"She's only five, Daddy."

Sawyer kept a watchful eye on Christina as she chased the

butterfly. "That's old enough."

"Just because she hasn't taken to reeling trout from the creek, doesn't mean she's destined to hate the outdoors. Have you heard her do the wood thrush lately? She practices every day. Her tiny throat just a-flutters when she makes that call. And you know why? Because of you. She wants to do it just like you."

"I'll give her that. She's not bad."

"Not bad at all."

"It's good for her to learn the ways of the mountains. Pride in her surroundings."

"Bird calls, she likes. Fishing, not so much. Not yet, anyways." With pouty eyes, she said, "Go ahead, Daddy. Do the call and watch her reaction."

Sawyer shook his head in contempt of his daughter's ability to snuff out his cantankerous moods. Turning his disposition from ornery to one where life couldn't be any better.

"Come on," she encouraged. "Just once. That call always let me know you were close by, watching over me."

"Hold the pole," he said.

After she took the rod, he turned toward Christina, flapped his hand across his mouth, his throat emitting a series of quick, high-pitched sounds. As if on cue, Christina, in hot pursuit of the butterfly, stopped and placed her hand to her mouth, responding to his call.

Jolene smiled. "Love that sound." She carefully handed the fishing pole to her father.

Christina slipped further along the winding bank, nearing a thick patch of yellow grass, tall and rangy. Sawyer cast his bait into the water and glanced at her crouching by the water's edge as the butterfly lit on a rock. "Go fetch her and we'll try this again. I'm going to toss the bait over by that pool yonder, where the fish are schoolin'. All she'll have to do is reel him in."

Jolene called out to Christina, who ran along the creek with the black-and-gold creature that seemed bored with the world in which it flew. Carefree, Christina skipped along the bank, her pace not far behind the butterfly. The creek turned northward, an elbow-shaped bend. As Christina followed the path of the insect, she fell out of Sawyer's view.

Jolene quickened her pace, making it to the bend in the creek. She took hold of a tree branch while his hand monitored the pulse of the rod. She stepped on a massive boulder that rose from the water's edge, as if strategically placed by God to keep floodwaters from rising on the western bank. "Christina? Baby?"

"You see her?"

"No," she said with a sense of urgency.

"What do you mean, no?" Sawyer shouted. He reeled in the line, backpedaling, no longer concerned for what swam in the shallows of the creek.

"I mean, I don't see her." Jolene placed a hand above her eyes like a shield from the sun. "Christina!" Frantic, she screamed the name again.

Dropping the pole on the bank, Sawyer sprinted toward Jolene. *How can she not see her?*

The creek bank stood motionless as the waters of Doe Creek surged over the rocky bottom. Despite the continual shifting of the water, the creek seemed eerily void of movement. Fifty feet away, on the eastern bank a cornfield, brown remnants of the previous growing season, rustled, though the winds were still.

Jolene jumped from the rock and for a moment seemed frozen beside the bank. Ten feet in front of her, the butterfly lit on a small branch of a poplar whose branches hung above the creek and she again screamed, "Christina!"

The panic in her voice quickened his pace, his boots pounding the dirt and pebbles.

Sawyer honed in beyond the creek to the cornfield, but a stretch of birch trees that hugged the far side of the stream hindered his view. "Christina!" he called out, sweat building in his hands. Any sign of stoic calmness was quickly fading. For sixty yards he ran, at times splashing into the creek to get around rocks that dotted the bank. He struggled to keep from falling in the water. His gut tightened. Where the hell did she go?

When he made it past the birch trees, his sight line opened. A hundred yards to his right, where the dormant field sloped up to the base of Iron Mountain, there was movement near the massive hardwoods, sentinels to that dark and dense world. Sawyer leaped into the icy water, wading and sidestepping the rocks, before running into the field. A distressed whimper carried on the breeze tightened his gut. Behind him, he heard Jolene crossing the stream, calling out Christina's name.

On into the woods the shadows went, Iron Mountain now a

protective border. Sawyer ran into the forest, thick in underbrush. A trespasser on an evil land where he'd long stood witness to rugged soil and ragged hearts. He stopped, the silence suffocating both spirit and hope like some mammoth candle snuffer.

About The Author

Chuck Walsh developed a passion for writing in 2004 after his mother was diagnosed with breast cancer. He wanted to write something to show how much she meant to him. And it was a chance to test the question, "Wouldn't it be great to go back in time, knowing then what you know now?"

From there the writing bug had him firmly in its grasp, and he haven't slowed down. He loves fiction, and loves to write stories that are deep in prose and storyline. He truly wants the reader to know intimately each and every character in my books, and wants each word, sentence, paragraph, and chapter to have meaning and purpose.

Chuck Walsh is a native of Columbia, SC. Chuck is a graduate of the University of South Carolina. He and his wife, Sandy, have three children: Stephanie, Brent, and Jessica.

Visit our website for our growing catalogue of quality books.
www.champagnebooks.com